"*Alight*, the prequel to the *Ariboslia* series, tells the story of Cataleen and her brother Aodan, identical twins born with extraordinary powers who find themselves facing a terrible trial that threatens to tear them apart. *Alight* is an enchanting fantasy tale for all ages, filled with magic, mystery, scary monsters, a touch of romance, and most of all, the love and provision of God. It reminds us that no matter what storm we are facing, we can trust God to see us through. It's a must-read if you've read the *Ariboslia* series—or even if you haven't!"

— GINA DETWILER, AUTHOR OF THE FORLORN SERIES

"*Alight* is a wonderful story set in a beautiful and fantastical world with an undercurrent of danger. I was hooked from page one, invested in the characters' journeys, how they grew and adapted in the face of life-changing events. The theme of the importance of trusting God's will carries through just as strongly in this prequel as it did in *Astray*, *Adrift*, and *Aloft*. Would highly recommend to readers of all ages."

— A R GRIMES, AUTHOR OF WYLDLING SNARE

"*Alight* is a wonderful prequel and introduction to the Ariboslia trilogy, which I read last year and loved! Filled with interesting characters, alternate worlds, exciting and terrifying adventures, and a variety of good and bad creatures, *Alight* grabbed my attention from its first page and held my focus from beginning to end. I highly recommend this book and its series to fantasy fiction lovers, especially those who have enjoyed books like C.S. Lewis' *Narnia* series and J.R.R. Tolkien's *Lord of the Rings* series!"

— MONIQUE SUMMERS, THE GINGER LIBRARIAN

"Another wonderful book by a favorite author. *Alight* helps answer questions about what happened before *Aloft* and makes me want to go back and read the whole series in order. I love the look into Notirr culture." ~ SHARON SELIG

"This was a great story, and I can't wait for the next one!" ~ VICKIE GRIDER

"If only it were a perfect world. But it's not... hence... a lifetime spent around bullies can be tiring, draining and leave a mass of destruction in their wake. The aftermath can be so devastating that we find ourselves wondering how can we ever move forward again. This story hits so close to home that it took me extra long to read b/c I spent a great deal of time crying. A gripping read from start to finish." ~ANGEL CROSS

"A great story and easy to read of how Cataleen, Aodan and Faolan have a bond like brothers and sister. The bonding between all of them was amazing and how they had each other's back no matter the situation. With the different creatures that they will encounter will take you on an intense adventure.... I enjoyed the book tremendously. Lots of intense situations and will keep you reading to the end. Was very hard to put down. It will take you on an intense adventure where anything could happen." ~ DEBBIE HARRIS

"Cataleen and Aodan are twins who are able to know what the other is thinking and/or seeing. Aodan has the stronger ability. Faolan has a common birthday with them and is as close as a brother. After their fifteenth birthday, their species can shape-shift. This story begins around their fifteenth birthday. But there's more to Cataleen and Aodan. In some way, they're connected to the fasgadair. Tormentors, banishment, Morrigan, consequences of decisions made... How and where is God in all this?" ~ AMBER

ALIGHT

ARIBOSLIA PREQUEL

J. F. ROGERS

NOBLEBRIGHT
PUBLISHING
www.noblebrightpublishing.com

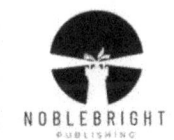

Alight - Ariboslia prequel

Copyright © 2023 by J F Rogers
All rights reserved. No portion of this book may be reproduced except by permission from the author.

This book is a work of fiction. Any resemblance to existing people or places is purely coincidental.

Edited by Brilliant Cut Editing
Cover design by 100 Covers

ISBN: 978-1-955169-12-7

Published by Noblebright Publishing
Sanford, Maine
www.noblebrightpublishing.com

The heart of man plans his way, but the Lord establishes his steps.
~Proverbs 16:9

ARIBOSLLA

PRONUNCIATION GUIDE

PEOPLE
Achaius \ ah-KEY-us
Aodan Tuama \ AY-dən Too-AH-ma
Brayan Tuama \ BRAY-ən Too-AH-ma
Be'Norr* \ beh-NORR
Cahal Fidhne \ kah-HAHL Feen
Cataleen Tuama \ Cat-ah-LEEN Too-AH-ma
Declan Cael II \ DECK-lən Kale
Evander Fidhne \ ee-VAN-dər Feen
Faolan Màrr \ FWAY-lahn Mahr
Fiona \ fee-O-nə
Gi'Wrann \ Jee-RAHN
Joshua Webb \ JAWSH-oo-ah Wehb
Lorcan Grear \ LOR-kan
Mirna Tuama \ MEER-nah Too-AH-ma
Morrigan \ MORE-ih-gən
Nathaniel Urchardan \ nay-THAN-yəl OOR-dahr-hahr-stahn
Pepin \ PEP-in
Sully \ SUHL-ee
Tevin Grear \ TEH-vin

CLANS
Ain-Dìleas \ ahn DILL-ay-ahs \ from Bandia
Arlen \ AHR-luhn \ from Kylemore
Cael \ KALE \ from Notirr
Treasach \ TRAY-zack \ from Gnuatthara

RACES
Fasgadair \ faz-geh-deer
Gachen \ GAH-chen
Pech \ peck

PLACES
    Ariboslia \ air-eh-BOHS-lee-ah
    Bandia \ ban-DEE-ah
    Bàthadh Sea \ BAH-həg
    Ceas Croi* \ kase kree
    Cnatan Mountains \ crah-dan
    Diabalta \ DEE-ah-BAHL-tah
    Gnuatthara \ new-TAH-rah
    Kylemore \ KY-əl-more
    Notirr* \ no-tear
    Somalta Caverns \ SOH-mahl-tah

THINGS
    Aotrom* \ OO-truhm \ color
    Bian \ bee-ahn \ gachen coming of age
    Beò feur \ bee-OH FEE-ahrd \ animals that look like grass
    Buille cridhe \ bool-yah kree \ a potion
    Co-Cheangail \ koh-kang-gale \ a committee of United Clans
    Drochaid* \ DROH-hach \ the amulet Pepin created
    Leanabh \ YEHN-əp \ baby
    Measach \ MEH-sahk \ fruit
    Neas \ nees \ weasel
    Seilcheag \ SHILL-ay-hehg \ snail
    Toradh \ TAHR-əg \ fruit

Uinnseann \ OON-shang \ tree

*trill the r

PROLOGUE

ALMOST FIFTEEN YEARS AGO

Brayan's heart raced the ever-darkening sky while he, his boss, and Oskari lugged the last log to the cart. As his imagination went wild, he tried to squelch the icy claw chilling the back of his neck. He felt *something*—like the sizzle of water in a frying pan, only cold.

Images flashed across his mind. Animal carcasses with twin pinpricks at the base of their necks, bloodless. The latest victim an elk. Rumors chased the images with a crazed traveler's claims of *fasgadair*—half-dead men who drank blood. Brayan shuddered.

He scanned the woods, certain something was there, watching.

Crash!

In his distraction, he'd pushed his end of the log into another log rather than on top. The cart pitched forward, and the horses complained.

"Watch it!" his boss growled. Brayan shrank, throwing his boss an apologetic smile, and righted the log.

Once they loaded the cart, his boss sat up front and gathered the reins. Oskari took his place beside him on the bench, and Brayan arranged the leather mat to protect his skin from the bark, then nestled among the logs. His boss clicked his tongue, signaling for the horses to move. Brayan braced himself, bouncing as they gained momentum along the bumpy trail.

He sighed and rested against a log. The scent of fresh-cut *uinnseann* trees calmed his mind. But the dark sky stole his comfort. If only he could snap his fingers and appear by his wife's side.

He breathed in the woodsy scent again and caught a whiff of something else. Something unfamiliar—like the air following a lightning storm. Every hair on his body reacted as if tugged upright by an unseen force.

The cart lurched.

Brayan slid along the logs and banged his head against the back rail. He bit back a curse.

The horses' whinnies and the men's screams shot through the air and straight into his heart.

He sprang into a crouch, every sense on full alert. "What—"

The men's wails cut short. One, then the other.

The abrupt quiet shocked him like a dousing of icy water. He fought to catch his breath, to capture his thoughts before they ran away without him.

The horses reared, fighting their constraints, sending the cart rocking. He had to get the reins. He scrambled over the logs and slipped. Pain shot up his right arm and hip as he slammed against the jostling logs.

The horses bolted. The wagon mad-dashing along the rutted trail, he clutched the rail. Fighting to climb into the seat, he peered over the edge and confirmed his fears—the seat was empty.

He had to get to the reins. Scraping his skin and nearly catching his feet in the churning timber, he had almost lowered himself onto the seat when the lightning scent intensified, intermingled with coppery blood. Wind blasted his ears, and something grasped his arm, yanking him from the cart.

Time seemed to slow. The inhuman thing laughed and dropped

him into the mud. The cart clattered away. Sound dulled as if the horses' thundering hooves and the crashing wagon were with him underwater, then diminished to a haunting echo.

Before him, yellow eyes within a cloaked shadow reflected the moon's light. The demon seemed to siphon the air from the sky. Brayan's blood froze. He tried to run, but some force emanating from the creature held him firm.

God, help!

Sharp canines pierced his neck, and he cried out. Blood gushed from the wound, rushing like water pumped from a well as the beast sucked. His consciousness threatened to slip away, along with the precious life force the demon stole.

Mirna. Oh, Mirna. I'm so sorry, my love.

"Do ye wish to live?"

The demon's voice made Brayan convulse as if to prevent the sound from contaminating his ears. He blinked. With each blink, ghoulish eyes came into focus. Of course, he wanted to live. If only to return to Mirna's side, stilling her fears. He had a life to live with her. A beautiful life. He tried speaking, but his throat burned. "A–aye." He coughed, angering the wound in his neck.

Brayan licked his dry lips as thick liquid dripped onto them, coating them with the coppery stuff. He gagged. Was that blood? He rolled and spat the foul swill.

"Nay? Don't care to live?" The demon sounded confused, offended. "Then don't."

The blood drinker departed along with his suffocating presence. Brayan's senses returned to him, and he breathed easier. He needed to stop the bleeding. He tore his shirt and wiped his tongue free of the demonic elixir. Had he ingested any? He pressed the rag to his wound.

God, let me live. Don't let me leave Mirna this way.

He applied pressure. How much blood had the fasgadair drained? He pushed himself to stand, but the trees spun. Nausea soured his gut. He staggered and collapsed. On the ground, he strained to lift his head, then fell back. His vision blurred. Then blackness overtook him.

CHAPTER ONE

CATALEEN

Would I become a bird tomorrow? I stifled a squeal and fought to keep from sending my brother another image of a bird, but everything within me wanted to burst like an under-milked udder. I'd waited for this day my entire life. Our birthday. The day we'd change into our animal forms at last. I breathed in the salty air and tilted my face toward the gulls and terns flitting about, dotting the skies, beaches, and ocean, calling out to one another in an endless song. A multitude of tiny starlings flocked together, forming a sizable bubble in the sky, darting one way, then changing course as if they were of one mind. "If I were a starling, would I fall into line with the others? Or would I be an awkward outsider?"

"Awkward outsider." Aodan spoke like a true brother.

"Oh, what do ye know?" I snarled at him.

"Cataleen, ye know we don't have the answer, so why ask?" He shook his head, damp yellow hair falling over his forehead.

Faolan laughed. "Ye don't hear of clan members shifting into wolves and joining a pack or an elephant joining a herd or a lion joining a pride."

I scoffed. Whilst I appreciated his humoring me, unlike my brother, I hated his telling me the most obvious things. "When was the last time you've seen a wolf pack, elephant herd, or lion pride to join?"

"None who shift into a bear hibernate for the winter." Faolan continued as if I'd never replied. "Whatever it will be like when we change, we'll never be completely animal."

"I know that." I slumped back against the dock, my damp hair wetting the wood.

What would it be like to be a bird? The sky for a playground. Soaring above troubles. The wind brushing your feathers. I raised my arms, spreading my fingers to catch the wind, my mind already aloft. Nothing would bring me greater pleasure. "Do ye think we'll reach our bian tomorrow?"

"How many times can ye ask the same question?" Aodan growled. "And would ye *please* stop filling my mind with birds? I can see them for myself."

Rocking my head, I snagged my hair on the wood and tried to close the connection with him as I gazed upon a gull preening its feathers. "I'm too excited. 'Tis hard to control the mind-link when I'm excited."

"Ye don't say."

His sarcasm grated, but his negativity wouldn't sidetrack me.

"Regardless of my shortcomings"—I glared at my twin and sent him an image of a diving tern to spite him—"many change on their fifteenth year, to the day. 'Tis not uncommon." I shielded my eyes from the sun peeking through the moving cloud. "I wonder what I'll be."

"A rat." He kicked my leg.

I peeled myself off the dock and pinched him.

"Ow!" He grasped his arm. "Really, Cataleen. Ye know how anxious I am." His face softened, allowing a rare glimpse of vulnerability in his purple eyes. "What if the change doesn't happen on the morrow? Some have waited months. Years even."

"I refuse to believe that will happen to us." I quirked my lips. "But I suppose we're all eager for our animal totems."

Faolan pushed his wet locks away from his face. His black hair was darker still with dampness. "Perhaps not as sick with it as Aodan."

"That may be true." I basked in the glow of Faolan's smile. "I love that we all share the same day of birth, if not the same ma and da."

Faolan released a puff of air and waved as if dismissing the subject. "Family is more than blood and lineage. Our shared day is further proof of what we've always known—yer triplets, not twins. And I'm the third."

"Aye," Aodan cut in, "'tis a matter of fact established long ago. Must we revisit it so often?"

"If we had it yer way, we'd never speak of anything again!" I glowered. "'Tis fun to discuss. Must *ye* be such an ostrich, spoiling our joy?"

He crossed his arms and gave a solemn nod as if he saw it as his duty. "I must."

An image of Eimear in her ostrich form looking grumpier than usual filled my mind. I laughed and pushed his shoulder.

His scowl cracked, and he grinned.

"Sake! I'm right here." Faolan crossed his arms.

"Apologies, Faolan. Aodan sent me a picture of Eimear as an ostrich. We'll try not to use the mind-link in yer presence." I threw Aodan a warning look, then chuckled to change the subject. "Remember when we tried convincing our ma to marry yer da so we could be siblings?"

"My da was angrier than a wasp protecting a disturbed nest." Faolan's shoulders quaked with silent laughter. "Lesson learned. Just because two people are widowed does *not* mean they have any interest in marrying one another."

"At least we tried." I squeezed the dripping water from my hair. "So tell me, brother. What do ye wish to be?"

"Ye already know." Aodan flashed several images of lions and tigers. All midroar. Then, as if remembering our promise to Faolan, he added, "Something fierce. Preferably a big cat. With sharp fangs."

I rolled my eyes. His answer never changed. "What about ye, Faolan?" If only he could send me mental pictures like Aodan. I eagerly awaited his ever-changing response. What would it be today?

He shrugged, his shoulders reaching the tips of his wet hair, sending fresh drips down his chest. "Maybe a platypus."

My nose wrinkled. "What, in God's creation, is a platypus?"

"It's like a beaver with a duck's bill."

I flicked drying hair away from my shoulders. "Now you're making things up."

Faolan's jaw dropped in mock hurt. He wagged a finger toward Aodan. "Tell her."

"'Tis true. Remember old man Brolach? His totem was a platypus."

"What? I never saw him."

"That's because he was a platypus." Aodan held his arms up as if holding up evidence that spoke for itself.

"What about—" Faolan was about to ask me what I'd like to be, but Aodan pressed a finger to his lips.

"Don't ask her."

Why couldn't Aodan humor me as Faolan did? "Our bian is tomorrow. Tomorrow! Can I help it if I'm excited?"

"No, our *birthday* is tomorrow," Aodan corrected. "Our bian is whenever we shift into our totem forms—which may or may not fall on our birthday."

"Sake! Yer such a crab. Would it kill ye to indulge yer sister?"

"It very well might." He lowered himself to lie on his back.

"Let's test that theory, shall we?" Faolan grinned at me. "What do ye want to be, Catty?"

I beamed. Unlike my brother, Faolan had infinite patience with my obsession for dreaming about my future totem. "There are so *many* things I'd love to be." As Faolan's grin deepened, I returned my attention to the birds flitting about without a care as if the sky belonged to them alone. "But if I had a choice, I'd choose—"

"A bird." Aodan and Faolan spoke in unison.

I braced myself and kicked each of them.

"Is it our fault we know ye too well? Ye do overshare." Aodan grew somber. "I hope we reach our bian tomorrow if for no other reason than to avoid Tevin's taunting." He slipped to the edge of the pier and dangled his feet in the water. "He'll only get worse."

I hadn't considered Tevin. My good mood deflated like a sail in a dying wind. That boy's sole purpose in life was to torment others, particularly those who failed to reach their bian. I groaned. "Sake! It makes no sense—he's fifteen and hasn't reached his bian yet."

"Since when has Tevin ever had sense?" Aodan asked.

Faolan shrugged. "Miserable people like to make others miserable. Look at his da. Wouldn't ye be a wee bit nasty if yer da was Notirr's self-appointed dictator? He seems to forget that our elders make and enforce the rules. Vinegar flows through that man's veins. He has nothing to offer his boy but a taste of his own sourness."

I took a deep breath, refusing to allow the crabbit man to dampen my spirits.

"Never mind Tevin. This is us. Our day. Our totems. He's no part in it." Faolan stood and shook his shaggy black head like a dog, sending water droplets raining. "We'll find out tomorrow if we'll reach our bian or not. Either way, life will go on. We'll survive."

"Hmph." If only I could be so confident.

Dusk drew near. We dried as much as possible, but there was no drying the length of my dress before retiring to our dwellings for our evening meals. Its damp fabric weighed heavy and wrapped around my legs, threatening to trip me.

Tomorrow was our birthday. My light mood added an occasional skip to my step as we strolled along the path, weaving through our clan's homes in the grassy mounds. When I passed through the shadow of one house, the lowering sun met me on the other side in a warm orange glow. Peepers from the nearby pond sang their evening summer tune. The promise of the morn flitted its wings, then settled upon a perch in my heart.

Shouts sounded through the hills, jerking me from my reverie. "What's that?"

We pivoted toward the uproar. Cries of excitement? Fear? I couldn't tell. Aodan sprinted toward the sound.

"Aodan!" I called to his departing backside. "Ma's expecting us!"

Faolan watched me with a frown, but his feet moved to follow Aodan.

Two clansmen brushed past us toward the main gate.

"What's the commotion?" Faolan asked.

"Giants!"

CHAPTER TWO

FAOLAN

Giants? I turned to my friend rushing headlong into trouble, then back to Catty. I had to stand by Aodan. But I must keep Catty safe. Somehow, I had to get them both in one place—away from the giants. Nothing was safe from the gargantuan creatures of lore. The beasts would squash our homes as if they were mere anthills. But to where could we flee? Their home was probably the safest place. "Go to yer mum. I'll fetch Aodan."

Catty's hands found their place on her hips. The stance she took when she was ready to hold her ground.

We didn't have time for her stubbornness. I clutched her hand, leaning forward to meet her eyes, hoping she'd read the urgency within. "If they are giants, 'tis not safe. Go home. Watch over yer mum. I'll fetch Aodan and return."

A crowd filtered through, breaking us apart. Two carried pitchforks. Others brandished shovels and axes. Just what were their intentions? To poke the beasts' calves, provoking them further? "Go home!" I called over the incoming tide of people and allowed the horde to sweep me away.

I kept looking back. She disappeared and reappeared as the sea of people parted. The fright in her wide eyes tore at my soul. Then she ran against the current. Now, a new dread churned in my gut as I headed toward the gate with the bloodthirsty mob.

Villagers obscured my view. Beyond them, just outside the gate, stood two men and a woman. Although taller than anyone I'd ever seen—head and shoulders above the tallest man in the crowd, they were no giants.

I shouldn't have to look for giants. Gachen barely reached the knees of such beings. Was this what all the fuss was about? Unusually tall people?

The strangers looked like gachen, more rugged, with angular features—and in need of a bed and a bath, not an uncontrollable mob.

Strange markings ran down the side of the older man's bald head, disappeared under his scraggly salt-and-pepper beard, then reemerged, ran down the side of his neck toward his chest, and hid beneath his torn tunic. The woman contained her wild mane in multiple braided rows along the front of her scalp, then released into a mass of blonde snarls dangling past her shoulders. She stood a head shorter than the older man and clutched a bundle to her chest. A babe? A head shorter than she was, the younger man on her opposite side gave the three the appearance of a staircase. Even the shorter man towered over everyone in attendance. Tangled black hair fell into his eyes. He had no facial hair and no visible markings.

Were these giants? Had their stature been exaggerated like the fish in fisher's tales?

Something about their weary, solemn faces tugged at my heart.

Tevin's father, Lorcan, stood before the older man, red-faced, shouting something to someone. Quin, perhaps? With his height and mass of red hair, it could be. But then, many redheaded clansmen lived in Notirr. Hopefully, it was Quin. From the look of this clutter, elders were in desperate need.

I strained to hear what they were shouting. But the overall clamor rendered all words unintelligible. My chest tightened for the weary travelers. They'd survived who knew what, only to deal with Lorcan in their faces now. That man didn't have a charitable bone in his body. Worse, he was probably responsible for riling up the villagers.

Should I do something?

Could I do something?

I was still a child. Tomorrow I would be a man. But even then, I wouldn't be an elder. Only the guards and the elders should be here now. The clan entrusted them for such times as this. Everyone else was just in the way, adding to the mayhem.

That reminded me, where was Aodan? There. Far too close to the gate. I took a deep breath as if preparing to dive underwater, then pressed my way through the warm, overly ripe bodies. Once he was within reach, I grabbed his tunic and yanked.

Aodan grasped my hand and peeled my fingers from his shirt. But when he came close to success, I switched hands. Despite his efforts, I pulled him free from the crowd, then released my grip.

He smoothed his wrinkled shirt, then cuffed the back of my head. "What were ye doing?"

"Come. Yer mum and sister are waiting. Get home to dinner."

Aodan tucked his chin and stood taller, deepening his scowl. "Yer not my da."

"Nay, but someone has to look out for ye. Yer mum and sister are probably off their heads with worry. And, truly"—I motioned toward the crowd—"the elders could benefit from everyone else going home. Let's leave them to get this sorted."

"Nay. I want to find out what happens." Aodan gazed at the chaos with longing. "They're no giants, ye know. 'Tis just a family from Gnuatthara. They're Treasach."

I'd never seen anyone from Gnuatthara. The Treasach clan had seceded from the Co-Cheangail during the clan wars centuries ago. The Treasach and Cael clans have had nothing to do with each other since. That some would show up now piqued my interest more than their size. Cautious hope soothed the tightness from my chest. Could this be the beginning of a reconciliation between the clans? "Why are they here?"

"From what I can gather, they're seeking refuge."

As I suspected. "Then why is everyone so riled up? Why *wouldn't* we help?"

Aodan tipped his head and threw me the most obnoxious are-you-daft look I'd seen on my mate yet. "They're Treasach, excommunicated from the Co-Cheangail for turning their backs on the One True God."

"So, isn't it a good sign that some have sought refuge? Might this be an opportunity to bring them back to God's grace? It's been hundreds of years!"

Aodan shrugged as if it didn't matter to him in the slightest. He was just here to satisfy his curiosity. "There are those in the village who oppose. Tevin's father for one. And look at their size! Do ye think the elders will open up our village without questions?"

"So you support Lorcan now, do ye?"

"Of course not!"

Lorcan shouted at a guard. Who did he think he was? No one had elected him an elder. Nor would they. Ever. No wonder his son was such a dobber.

Rage billowed, twisting within. I huffed it out like an angry bull. "Now that I'm right scunnered, let's go." I tugged on Aodan's sleeve. "Before *I* do something stupid."

He jerked himself free. "I told ye—I'm staying."

Sake! I clenched my jaw. "And what do ye expect to accomplish by being part of this muddle? Yer only making it worse. 'Tis growing dark, and the elders need to get rid of all these rabble-rousers so they can get these people inside the gates and undercover before attracting the real monsters. So, let's leave and let the elders and guards do their jobs."

Shoulders slumped, Aodan scuffed his boots in the dirt, keeping his eager gaze on the turmoil. Sometimes—nay, often—I didn't understand my friend. Why, in God's creation, would he want to take part in that muddle? No good would come of it. Those poor people came to Notirr for a reason. If only those who existed just to cause problems would follow my advice and leave too. I threw Lorcan a long, hard stare as if he might sense my thoughts and realize the error of his ways. Then I turned to my friend who could be reasoned with, wrapped an arm over his shoulder, and walked him home.

CHAPTER THREE

CATALEEN

I paced in our sitting room, circling the low table in the center. The faint low-tide scent of our fish dinner hit me anew with each return trip toward the kitchen. Every time I walked toward the window, I ducked to peer out at the path toward the gate, pausing and grumbling each time someone other than Aodan or Faolan passed by. At least the clan was returning to their homes without panic. That was a good omen. But *something* was happening, else the boys would have returned by now.

"Would ye please sit?" Ma shuffled about the kitchen, plating food. "Yer making me fret."

I threw my arm toward the door. "There are giants out there, Ma. *Giants!*"

"Pish." Ma dismissed my concern with a wave. "Giants don't exist."

"Then what is the clan so worked up about?"

"This is a sleepy village, Cataleen. They want a good stirring."

Was I like that, too? Needing something to distract me, I sat as Ma shuffled about the small space. "How can ye be so calm? Even if there aren't giants, there are fasgadair out there. Animal carcasses drained of their blood meet us outside the gates daily. Why don't the blood drinkers just come inside and kill us all?"

Ma placed a plate before me, then sat across the table. Crow's-feet deepened around her eyes. "'Tis likely only one passing through. But that matters not. God's hand of protection is on this place."

"You always say that." How oft had I wondered if I'd look like Ma when I was older? We're both fair-haired with the same purple eyes, oblong faces, and petite noses. But now I wondered if I could ever be like Ma *inside*. Unruffled by the possibility of giants and the reality of fasgadair.

"'Tis the truth."

"It wasn't true for Shea MacClune." Aodan and I had tried and failed to pull the story of Shea from her and several other older villagers. But everyone remained tight-lipped. So many versions of stories about the fasgadair that attacked the boy ran rampant. Perhaps now, whilst she attempted to distract me, I could pry the information loose.

She scoffed and reached for the pitcher on the table to fill her glass. "'Tis an old story. Why rehash it?"

"To *re*hash something, it would need to be hashed in the first place. Why won't anyone speak of it?"

She folded her hands over her plate. "You'll be an adult tomorrow. I suppose yer old enough." Then she threw me her stern no-nonsense look and jabbed a finger in my face. "I trust you'll use the information to make smart decisions without losing sleep at night."

That was the reason for withholding the story? So we wouldn't lose sleep? "Isn't that the purpose of all the tales the older folk love to tell? To scare wee ones into fearing every shadow and never sleeping again? Giants? The Bogle? Ogres. What other purpose do stories of such unholy creatures serve?"

Ma chuckled. "Don't act as if yer somehow holier. I've heard ye tell the wee ones about the Bogle to scare them into obedience."

"Well, that was the example I was given, wasn't it?"

"Those stories, as ye know firsthand, were meant to inspire obedience. They weren't real." She took a long drink of water. Then eyed me as if having second thoughts.

Ugh! How could I be so careless as to distract her? "Tell me." I leaned forward on my elbows, then shifted, straightening in my chair. This was the closest I'd come to getting her to open up. If only Aodan were here.

She steepled her fingers. "The villagers learned what they needed to know from the fasgadair who attacked wee Shea, bless his soul. They share what they've learned, so villagers will know how to protect themselves. But clan members have left Notirr because of it. So, I'll share what I know, but be wise with the information. Do not unnecessarily scare anyone. Understood?"

I wanted to know who left. But that wasn't the most pressing issue. "What happened?"

"One villager, Niles, happened upon the fasgadair with the lad in his arms. While the demon was distracted, Niles used his pitchfork to spear the unholy thing." She wrinkled her nose as if she'd witnessed the gruesome event. "Some villagers heard the thing scream before falling to its death and came running. Unfortunately, the boy was dead. But the fasgadair came back to life. Niles stabbed it again and again. But the beast kept healing itself. And it regenerated fast. When he struck its heart, the thing seemed to die, but not for long. He killed it repeatedly before chaining it up."

"The shack?" An image of the rickety building on the village outskirts popped into my mind. "Near the cornfields?"

She cocked her head. "Ye know of this?"

"Do ye jest?" Seriously? Parents were too clueless. "There are *so* many rumors about that place. They say it's haunted by the spirit of a fasgadair who died there. We used to dare kids to spend a night in there. None lasted long. They'd swear the building started shaking or a blood smear appeared on the floor or the chains that held the fasgadair rattled or they'd seen its ghost."

She raised her eyebrows and rubbed her cheeks. "I never knew that.

Of course, there's no such thing as ghosts." Her look seemed to require a response.

"I know, Ma." I groaned, then rocked on my elbows, pressing into my folded hands. "Then what happened?"

She shrugged. "All we know of fasgadair came from that one. That's how we know the sun weakens them, so they shift into their animal totems when sunlight is unavoidable. If they're killed in their totem form, they'll still regenerate, but not until the sun goes down. Lack of blood also weakens them. Although they get hungry, they don't seem to die of starvation. The only way to kill the demons for good—"

"Cut off their head." Every child in the village knew all this.

After a nod, she took a long drink.

"Is that all?" How disappointing.

"What do you want me to say, Cataleen? Once they killed the beast for good, there wasn't much left to learn. Other than it turns to dust once it's truly dead."

"But that doesn't explain why the fasgadair don't attack our village." Ouch, that sounded so whiny.

"The captive claimed that some fasgadair resist what they are and feed on animals. Any fasgadair who embraced what they became would be a fool to venture so far from more populated areas."

"But it killed Shea!"

A frown masked Ma's face. "Apparently, the temptation became too—"

The door burst open, and Aodan slammed it behind him. "They're not giants." He tromped to the table, jostling everything upon it as he sat.

"What was it?" I ogled him as if he'd just returned from the moon.

"Yer supper is cold." Ma filled his mug.

"A Treasach family. From Gnuatthara." He accepted the cup and gulped his water.

"Treasach!" So many exciting things were happening and on the eve of our fifteenth birthday. I propped myself up on my elbows. "Tell me all about it."

CHAPTER FOUR

FAOLAN

I woke feeling as if I'd never slept, still thinking about the Treasach. Our elders had better welcome them, despite Lorcan's objections. As an urge to ensure they'd taken in the strangers overcame me, I hopped from my bed and dragged my covers onto the floor. I had no basis for comparison, but I was proud of my clan, aside from Lorcan, Tevin, and the few who followed them. The Cael always came around to help one another, to mourn losses, to celebrate marriages, birth—

Birthdays? Today's our birthday.

What time was it? I wasn't late for breakfast, was I? This blasted bedroom had no window. No way to tell the time. I yanked my tunic from the drawer and flung it over my head, eager to spend my favorite day of the year with Aodan and Catty. We'd celebrated together for as long as I could remember. Mirna always prepared my favorite breakfast —haggis, neeps, and tatties, followed up with her famous black bun. Best in the village. My mouth watered, and my stomach grumbled as I tugged on my loosest trousers. My waist would need room to expand.

The Treasach could wait until after breakfast.

I hopped from my room, yanking a stocking onto my foot. My father stood in the kitchen at the counter eating porridge. I hurried past him into the sitting room to our dwelling's only window. Dim light peered through. The sun wasn't up yet.

Da poked his head out from the kitchen. "No need to hurry. Yer not late."

I grabbed my shoes, then dropped into the cushioned seat by the window to put them on.

He shook his head at me and left the entryway. His voice wafted through the opening. "There's a nip in the air this morn. Grab a cloak."

I plucked my tattered coat from its hook by the door and slipped it on.

"Enjoy the festivities, lad."

"Thanks, Da." When I opened the door, a chilly wind swept through. I shoved my hands in my pockets and walked the path through the hill homes to Aodan and Catty's dwelling.

When I raised a fist to knock, the door burst open. Catty poked her head through the gap, a grin spreading out her cheeks. Any tension taking residence in my shoulders slipped away. She threw the door wide and stepped back to allow me inside where the peppery scent of haggis and the warmth from a log on the hearth met me. *Ahh.*

"Have ye felt anything yet?" She cocked her head as if she could see the animal within and coax it from me.

"Like what?" I removed my coat and hung it on the hook.

"Oh, I don't know. Do ye feel... *different?*"

"Just hungry for yer mum's cooking." I cut through to the kitchen where Mirna plated deliciousness.

Mirna kissed my head as I sat. "Enjoy your birthday breakfast, lad."

"My hand was tingling earlier. I think something is happening." Catty sang the last words and danced to the table.

Aodan appeared from his bedchamber, tying his tunic. "Her hand fell asleep, and now she thinks she's transitioning. Talk some reason into her."

Hands braced on her hips, Catty pouted. "'Tis not the same feeling."

"Maybe it *is* yer bian." I drank in her look of adoration. As much as her actual brother enjoyed extinguishing her hopes, I loved to ignite them. It was worth every expression she threw my way.

She slid her hands from her hips and pressed her lips tight, growing serious. "Have ye heard word of the Treasach?"

"Nay. I came straight here." I inhaled the aroma and smiled at Mirna. "Let's enjoy yer ma's meal. When we meet to harvest the apples, we'll get an earful."

I STEPPED out of my mate's dwelling and rubbed my stomach. As expected, I'd overeaten. The main meal had more than satisfied me, but the black bun... One loaf could satisfy the entire village for a week. One bite would've put me over the edge, and yet I put down an entire slice. Way too much. My stomach gurgled in rebellion. But I didn't regret it.

Now, off to the orchard to help pick apples. I left the path for the shortcut through the woods, imagining what the rest of our day would hold. Our clan would prepare an evening meal, and we would all eat under the pavilion together. Then we'd dance around a bonfire whilst musicians played. Hands in the air, I danced a few steps and tripped.

What had caused me to stumble? I was usually sure-footed. As I glanced back in search of the offending object, I pitched forward with a ripping sound and caught my fall with my hands.

Wait—What?

Padded feet with claws peeked out from my coat sleeves in muted colors. The trees, shrubs, wildflowers—every colorful thing was now a dull version of what they'd been moments before. What happened to orange? The blossoms on the shrubs now looked green, blending in with the leaves.

Had I done it? Had I reached my bian? What was I? Canine? Feline? Some kind of bear?

I stepped out of my shoes and kicked off my stockings, but wriggling out of my clothes was tricky work. Once free of my pants, I found a large tear, despite their looseness. That explained the ripping sound. Rolling on my back, I freed myself from my coat. My tunic was another matter. There was no freeing myself from it.

Da would not be happy about my destroyed clothes, but it was a common occurrence with the first change. He'd understand.

How long would the change last? If what others said was true, I should be able to control it now. I ensured I was alone, then ducked behind a tree and turned back to my human form.

How I did it, I did not know. Was it simply because I wanted to change? Whatever it was, it came naturally. No wonder those who'd gone before couldn't explain it.

I removed my tunic and shifted back to my animal form to study what I could see of myself. Not a bear. I was much too skinny. I felt a weight on my rump. A tail? I wiggled my rear, and a fuzzy thing appeared. I swiveled for a better look. Gray, black, and white fur. Must be some kind of dog. If only I had a looking glass. Or still water. I spun in a circle to get a better look, then stopped.

Was I seriously just chasing my tail?

My groan came out as a growl. Definitely a dog. Good thing dogs couldn't blush. And good thing there were no witnesses. I sniffed the air, just to be sure.

Colors weren't as vibrant in my totem form, and orange seemed to be missing. But I could smell. And hear. Everything. Focusing on it overwhelmed me. I detected the slightest movements from a wider range than I had before. Between my nose and my ears, I could "see" better than ever. But it would take some training to get used to this, to differentiate all the scents I'd never smelled.

My heart hammered with the thrill, and I pranced about on all fours. So much to learn, to explore. A scent caught my attention, and I pressed my nose to the ground, snuffling.

Animals had passed through this spot recently. I could see them, but not by sight. In a new way. As if attached to strings. I followed one of the "strings" jagged paths along the ground, then circling up a tree. Sure enough, a chipmunk perched on a branch overhead. Treed, it screamed in a series of shrill chirps, piercing my dog ears. I rubbed a paw against a sore ear, wishing I could block both as the critter skittered further up the tree.

So, superhearing had a downside.

Although I wanted test my new form further, I wasn't prepared to come across any villagers. If they thought I was a wolf, they'd kill me to protect their livestock. And I didn't want to change into a human without clothes on hand. So, keeping to the trees, I headed toward the cornfields where I could run freely without being spotted. I gathered my clothes in my mouth and dragged them along.

On my way, scents and sounds bombarded me. Salt air invaded from the Bàthadh Sea. Crashing waves thrummed, even from this distance. Smoke wafted in, billowing from chimneys in homes where their occupants cooked blood sausages or porridge with cinnamon for breakfast. I sniffed the ground. Aromas I couldn't identify trailed off in every direction. A gachen's sense of smell was shameful compared to a canine's. It would take years to isolate each of these scents and learn to what they belonged.

I wandered further from the homes and closer to the cornstalks. Their leaves whistled in the breeze. New scents hit me. Something of a warning raised my hackles, and I slowed.

The shack.

I shuddered as I eyed the dilapidated building. What were those strange scents? And why did it make me want to cower and flee? It was as if an evil cloud surrounded the place. Could dogs smell ghosts?

Nay. Ghosts weren't real.

But demons were.

I dared another step toward the building, then changed my mind. Keeping a wary eye on the place as if a demon might jump out at any moment, I skulked away. Once the smell dissipated, I ran to the cornfield.

The moment the cornstalks swallowed me, I allowed my animal self to take over and bounded through them. How good it felt to run! My heart maintained a steady beat despite my speed. Air and leaves rushed through my fur. My feet skimmed the ground.

My transition wasn't anything like I'd expected, yet exactly as everyone before me had said, despite the vagueness of their stories. Perhaps I'd built it up into something else. The reality was a conundrum—somehow much less, and yet so much more.

Finally, I understood the challenge of sharing such an experience with someone who'd never transitioned. But I'd try to share what I'd learned so far with Aodan and Catty. I'd tell them at the orchard after I changed my clothes. But they had chores to finish first. Hopefully, Aodan wouldn't slack off again and delay their arrival. I itched to share.

But what if they hadn't reached their totems yet? Should I tell them? They would be so happy for me, but even more disappointed if they hadn't transitioned, too. We all wanted to do this together. Nay, I wouldn't tell them. Not yet. Not until they had news to share, too.

CHAPTER FIVE

CATALEEN

Aodan and I finished our errands and ran to meet Faolan in the orchard. We were later than usual. I'd had such a hard time focusing on my tasks. My thoughts twisted like vines, choking each other out, making it impossible to trace one through to its completion. While I walked, I scanned the area for the Treasach, itched to see the shack by the cornfield one more time, and wondered about the tingling in my hand.

So much was happening all at once. Nothing *ever* happened in our quiet village.

Why were the Treasach here? Why were they so tall?

Would we reach our bians today? What would it feel like?

I had to tell Aodan and Faolan about my talk with Ma about Shea MacClune. Not that she'd told me anything new.

Faolan stood at the orchard's entrance, arms crossed, head down with Achaius and the MacLaughlin brothers in the midst of a heavy conversation. Faolan raked a hand through his hair and blew out a breath as if exhaling foul air. Achaius kept shaking his head. They spotted us, and with solemn shrugs to Faolan and a slight wave our way, Achaius and the MacLaughlin brothers moped toward the barn. I quickened my pace and ran to meet Faolan. "What was that all about?"

He looked different, aside from whatever weighed down his shoulders and pulled his face into a frown.

What was he doing in those snug brown pants and that blue tunic? Hadn't he been wearing his loose trousers with a white tunic at breakfast? "Why'd ye change yer clothes?"

His mouth twitched, and he tugged at his collar as he did when he was nervous. "I, uh, spilled—"

"Any word of the giants?" Aodan called from across the distance, taking his time.

Faolan glanced about as if concerned the Treasach might overhear. "Stop calling them giants. 'Tis rude. They're just people seeking refuge."

"Aye. *Giant* people."

I aimed my pinched fingers at him.

Aodan recoiled, rubbing his arm as if I'd stung him. "What?"

Faolan and I shared a knowing, unimpressed look and rolled our eyes. We fell in step together and went to fetch buckets.

"Did ye know what's been happening in Gnuatthara?" Faolan asked.

"Of course. Doesn't everyone know what's happening in a city centuries removed from the Co-Cheangail and an entire lunar cycle's journey away beyond fasgadair-infested lands?"

I elbowed my brother. "Must ye always be so biting?"

He clutched his chest, feigning hurt. "Do ye not know me at all?"

"Well." I bowed to Faolan, gesturing for him to go on. "Those of us who are slightly less aware of worldly events would like to know. What news have ye?"

"I don't know if I should share, I mean... 'tis gossip from the MacLaughlin brothers. Who knows how accurate—"

"Consider us duly warned." Aodan wagged his fingers. "Out with it."

"Apparently, the Treasach are paranoid about the fasgadair—"

"Everyone is." Aodan flicked back his unruly yellow hair. "That's not news."

"I can understand why they would be." I threw him a warning look, which he failed to catch, so I projected the look to his mind. "They're not believers, and they're much closer to Diabalta."

"But did ye know they've been purposefully increasing their size over the generations?" Faolan asked.

"What? How?" I imagined people pulling someone's neck in one direction and their legs in another. I shuddered, shutting off the image in my mind.

The image must've leaked to Aodan, unless something else caught him as funny. He snickered.

"They've been—" Faolan coughed.

Were those tears in his eyes? I'd never seen him like this, other than when his ma passed. I placed a hand on his shoulder.

Aodan edged closer. Even he appeared concerned. "What is it, Faolan? What happened?"

He huffed out a breath and turned as if he couldn't meet our eye. His temple pulsed from grinding his teeth. He scowled. "They've been killing babies."

"What?" My voice came out in a disbelieving breath. I must've misheard him. Or misunderstood.

Faolan rubbed his face, then held his hand over his mouth as if to keep more words from escaping.

My chest squeezed. "What are ye saying? They don't kill babies on purpose. Right?"

He wrinkled his nose. "They do. They give some herbal mix to pregnant women to bulk up the baby. Then, if the child doesn't meet a certain height and weight at birth, they…"

"Kill them?" Aodan's ears reddened as they always did when he was outraged.

Faolan nodded. His mouth twisted as if preparing to spit out something foul. "They abandon them on a rock as a sacrifice to the fasgadair."

My stomach clenched, threatening to make my birthday breakfast reappear. I wanted to cry and throw up at the same time to rid myself of all the churning emotions.

"So, they're protecting themselves from the fasgadair by offering their runts and breeding themselves to be larger in the process?" A green hue sallowed my brother's skin. "That's the vilest thing I've ever heard."

"What of those people?" I pointed toward the main gate as if the Treasach family were still there. "Why have they come here?"

"To save their baby. They escaped before the guards took their infant. There are refugee camps, but they're overrun and not fortified. The west would bring them closer to the fasgadair. Given the shoreline on the east and the mountains squeezing them in, they had no place to go but north, to us."

"But it's such a long journey! I'm surprised they survived, especially with fasgadair nests all over the place." I couldn't imagine being driven to make such a quest. But then, how much of this was true? "How did the MacLaughlin brothers learn this?"

"Eavesdropping outside the elders' meetinghouse."

"But it makes no sense." Everything within me twitched, ready to brandish weapons to fight the evildoers. "They kill babies because they aren't a certain size? How can they know how big a baby will grow to be?"

Faolan shrugged, then grabbed the back of his neck. "They're afraid. Scared people do stupid things."

I imagined myself as a baby—abandoned, scared, alone, crying out for those meant to protect me. How many children had died so needlessly? I wrung my hands together, fuming. "They would've been stronger with greater numbers."

"And what good is being larger?" Fists clenching, Aodan spoke through gritted teeth. "More blood for the fasgadair."

"I'm just telling you what I heard." Faolan held up his hands as if to defend himself. "The visitors want our help to save the babies. It may be a bit late, but at least they want to do something."

"How can we help?" Part of me wanted to pack up, charge to Gnuatthara, and steal all their babies. But then reality hit me. My righteous indignation deflated, and my shoulders slumped. "It's too far away. Too dangerous."

"Apparently, others had fled north before them." Faolan grimaced. "The family was hoping to find they'd arrived safely."

I groaned, wanting to do *something* but helpless to do anything. "If these large-bred gachen can't survive the journey up here, a one-way trip, what could we do to help?"

"I don't know." Faolan's grimace dissolved. "The elders still need to deal with the villagers who don't want Evander and his family here."

"Lorcan and his bootlickers." Aodan scoffed, running a hand through his yellow hair.

How had the world gone so wrong in such a short time? If only we could return to yesterday before the Treasach appeared. When our only concern was reaching our bains and discovering our totems. But after what we'd learned, it all seemed trivial. Something had to be done about these babies.

✡

I TRIED to shut everything else and enjoy my day as I prepared for our birthday celebration with the clan. I threw on my best dress. The deep purple matched my eyes, making them pop in the dull looking glass. The soft material hugged my torso and swished around my legs like a warm summer breeze. Hopefully, if I reached my bian today, I'd turn into something small, like a bird. I'd hate to ruin my beautiful dress.

I pranced from my room. "Are you ready, brother?"

He sat on the chair before the window, his chin resting on his hand, his eyes boredom-glazed. "Aye. So I have been for quite some time now."

"Now, now." Our ma pulled a shawl from the back of the rocker and threw it over her shoulders. "Let's not bicker on yer special day."

We followed her along the path through the hill homes to the village tent.

"Why haven't we changed into our totems yet?" My voice bordered on whiny. I thrust my forearm across Aodan's chest, stopping him. "Ye haven't yet, right?"

He pushed my arm away and scowled. "Nay. Ye think I wouldn't tell ye?"

No, he'd have no trouble flaunting the news. Faolan might hold back.

"Ma, what was it like for ye? Ye know. When ye first changed?"

"'Twas a long time ago." She slid the shawl off her shoulders, apparently realizing it was still summer and the afternoons didn't carry the chill the mornings sometimes did. "But 'tis as those before ye have always said, ye just... change. One moment yer in yer gachen form, the next... yer totem." She threw me an apologetic look. "I wish I had more to share."

"I don't get that." I had drilled many people only to hear exactly that. Why I should now expect another answer? I didn't know. But there *had* to be more to it than that. "The first time is the only time you can't control it? After that, it's only when ye want to?"

"Aye." She sighed despite her infinite patience.

Aodan smacked my arm. "Why do ye keep annoying Ma? Ye know all this."

Ma gave my shoulder a reassuring squeeze.

I walked the rest of the way in silence, willing my mind to still... as if that were possible. The hill homes subsided, but the trail carried on, winding through the trees. When the woods opened, a sizable crowd already gathered about the pavilion. The sweet smell of roasting meats turning on spits wafted our way. Several people stepped forward to congratulate us on becoming men and a woman and to inquire as to our bian.

How infuriating.

By the third explanation that no, we had not reached our bian yet and the third sad smile accompanied by weak words of encouragement, I was done. Somehow, it all made me feel like a wingless bird.

How many people had I done this to? Never again. I'd never ask another person if they'd reached their bian without knowing for certain that they had.

Please, God, let them stop asking.

Why would I make such a request to God? This was the purpose of such a celebration. Something the clan did for every villager on the day of their bian. And everyone wanted to know the totem.

Quin approached with the Treasach family. The elder carried himself as if he were in the presence of old friends, disarming the villager's sidelong and upward glances as they passed. With the sun behind them, a long shadow preceded them, covering my family and me with shade.

"Mirna." His smile warm, Quin grasped Ma's hand. "Please allow me to introduce Evander, Neilina, and their children, Cahal and Duana."

My gaze rose and rose to impossible heights to meet their eyes.

"This is Mirna, her children, Aodan and Cataleen, and their friend, Faolan. 'Tis their bian today, thus the celebration."

"Ah." Neilina's face brightened. Her dark eyes shone like obsidian. A stark contrast to her blonde hair, fashioned in an unusual way. Rows of tight braids gave way to an unruly mane. The effect was startling, yet beautiful. I imagined how my hair might look that way. Nope, it would fall flat. Mine didn't have the thickness to give the bulk I'd need to have the same effect.

The woman gazed at each of us as she bounced the large bundle in her arms. "Whose bian?"

"All of us." I motioned to the three of us. "Aodan is my twin. But Faolan is our unofficial triplet."

"Well, that's quite the coincidence, is it not? All the more reason to celebrate." The woman's glowing smile set me at ease. "Congratulations on reaching adulthood. Thank you for allowing us to share this day with you."

Surprised by the woman's unexpected kindness, I wasn't sure what to think of these people. Although large and imposing, they seemed genuine. And they didn't ask about our bians. "I'm glad you made it here to celebrate with us."

The woman's smile faltered, and her gaze flew to her husband.

I cringed, realizing my error too late. I hadn't intended to remind them of their difficult journey. Or of the others who hadn't survived. Who knew what horrors they met along the way?

The giant man, Evander's face morphed from remorse to joy. "We are grateful to have made it as well. God blessed our journey for a reason, I've no doubt."

"Yer–yer believers?" I stammered.

"Cataleen!" Ma laughed and seized my hand, throwing the visitors an apologetic look.

"Not to worry." Neilina waved as if dismissing the issue. "I understand her confusion. Most Gnuattharans are not believers. But there are a few."

"And what are the believers doing to help the babies?"

"Cataleen!" Ma squeezed my hand. Tight. "My apologies."

Wincing, I tried wrenching my hand from her unnatural grip. When she released me, I gave my hand a shake, testing for broken fingers.

Evander cleared his throat. "There's no need sidestepping the issue. This is why we are here... to see what we might do to save lives together. We're only sorry it took the threat to Duana's life to motivate us to obey God's call. But He has led us here, to you, and we look forward to discovering what He plans."

I kept wiggling my fingers. While not broken, they still hurt. Sully was a Seer and spoke for God, but I'd never met anyone on a quest for God before. Somehow, they seemed even bigger than they had a moment before. Why had God sent them here, of all places, to our quiet village set so far away from anything? What could we do to help?

Better yet, what did God have planned?

CHAPTER SIX

FAOLAN

I cocked my head back to view the son, Cahal, while the others spoke. With dark coloring like his parents, his smooth skin and ebony eyes held a youthful glow. His thick neck rivaled my waist, even after my generous breakfast, and his muscles bulged beneath his tunic, threatening to tear the material if he flexed. But, despite his height and girth, he didn't appear much older than the twins and I. "Cahal, care to sit with us?"

He glanced at his parents, who nodded.

I led him to our usual spot at the longest table under the canopy, viewing the new boy askance. He had yet to say a word. If he couldn't speak, this would be an awkward evening.

Catty chewed her cheek, something she typically only did when taking a test. "So, Cahal, how old are ye?"

"Sixteen summers." The wood groaned beneath him, complaining under his bulk.

Catty met us on the other side of the table. "Ah, so yer only a little older than us."

"Have ye reached yer bian?" Aodan pushed me back to see Cahal.

"Aye."

Getting him to talk was like nailing porridge to a tree.

"What is your totem?" Catty twisted her mouth to get a better bite on her cheek.

"Polar bear."

"Polar bear!" She gave me a light smack on the arm with the back of her hand. "I've never met a polar bear before. Perhaps when we finally reach our bians, we can all run together."

I itched to shift into a wolf again. How wonderful to run in totem form with my mates at my side.

Aodan huffed and rapped his knuckles on the table. "Assuming we can run."

Catty heaved a heavy sigh. She seemed to grow more and more discouraged as the day wore on. And our strange, all-too-quiet companion wasn't helping.

Although everything within me screamed to share my news, I couldn't do that to her. So I stifled the shouts tearing through my lungs, fighting for release. "When did ye reach yer totem?"

"Two moons after my fifteenth summer."

"So, ye were late too." I raised my eyebrows at Catty. "See? 'Tis not uncommon."

Aodan slapped the table. "We're not late yet. The day isn't over."

The secret raged in my gut. I'd never lied to them before. Or withheld anything that mattered. But Aodan cared more than he let on, and he'd likely harbor resentment. Catty would be happy for me, but she'd think something was wrong with her.

Nay, I couldn't do that to them. I could wait. Hopefully, I wouldn't have to wait long.

✡

THE ENTIRE VILLAGE crowded the tables under the tent. Lamb, neeps, and tatties filled our stomachs beyond capacity. Nothing but crumbs remained on our plates as we prattled away, digesting our meal. We needed to lean in to hear anyone speak over the raucous chatter and laughter. Lanterns encased in bubbly glass dangled from above, making everything sparkle in the darkening sky.

Claang! Claaang! Claaaang!

Conversations hushed as gazes drifted toward Sully in the center of the crowd ringing a cowbell. When had his beard whitened? His hair still looked mostly blond from this distance. He seemed to scan the crowd despite his blindness. Once everyone was quiet, he lowered the bell. "With great honor, today I introduce the newest men and woman in our clan in order of birth on this very day fifteen summers ago— Faolan Màrr, son of Boyd Màrr; Aodan Tuama, son of Brayan Tuama; Cataleen Tuama, daughter of Mirna Tuama."

Cheers erupted. I caught Catty's gaze, then Aodan's. We all beamed.

Another sound came from the ranks. Was that a boo?

Uncertainty flickered when we scanned the crowd for the source. There, at the southernmost table, sat Lorcan and Tevin. With hands cupped around his mouth, Lorcan booed us while Tevin smirked in his shadow.

My nails clawed the table as I fought to remain seated. My gaze flicked to Catty. The hurt in her eyes fueled me further, as did Aodan's scowl and clenched fists. His temper was worse than mine. If I struggled not to shove my way through the crowd and punch Lorcan's nasty face, a civil war must have been raging within Aodan. His eye twitched, and his temple pulsed above his clenched his teeth.

Several elders shot up from their seats, and Sully seemed to look for the rabble-rouser.

Quin's face flamed as red as his hair. "This is a special occasion for the clan. Those who don't offer well wishes for these fully-fledged clan members are not welcome here."

Rumbles ran through the clan.

Lorcan rose from his seat. His shaggy reddish-blond hair and beard resembling his lion totem. "If this is a special occasion for the clan, why have we traitors in our midst?"

"And just who might these traitors be?" Quin's arms shook.

Sully squeezed Quin's shoulder and ushered him to sit. "This is not the time nor the place for dispute. Lorcan, I invite you to meet with the elders in the morn to discuss your concerns. You're welcome to remain and celebrate our newest clan members. But if you're unable to refrain from poisoning this joyous occasion, we welcome you to retire for the evening."

Lorcan grumbled something to those at his table, setting off a wave of nervous chuckles. "I'll see you in the morn."

I expected him to leave, but he sat back down. No doubt ignoring Sully's request and spouting off to any who would listen.

Sully raised his mug. "To Faolan, Aodan, and Cataleen. May God fill you with His peace and prosper as He wills."

Everyone else drank, but I caught Catty gagging on hers before I swallowed. I'd forgotten how she hated mead. I held a hand over my mouth, certain I was about to spray the table. Catty and Aodan noticed my struggle and laughed, making it worse.

I ducked away from them, collected myself, and swallowed. "I nearly doused the table in mead!"

"So we noticed." Aodan winked.

Catty's face crumpled. "I just hope no one thinks we're laughing at Lorcan's comment."

I wiped my mouth on my sleeve. "It was ye gagging on yer drink."

"The others don't know that." She glanced around at the other tables as if expecting to find judging eyes on her.

"Bah." Aodan waved it off. "Who cares what anyone thinks? If we thought Cahal and his family were traitors, would we have invited him to sit with us?"

That seemed to settle it, so we delivered our dishes for cleaning and sat on our usual patch of green. The bonfire bathed all in its vicinity in a warm orange glow. Sparks flickered into the night sky like fireflies.

Silvery melodies wafted from flutes, blending with angelic voices. Drummers joined in. Their tribal beats resulted in a haunting sound that pierced my soul. Many of our clan danced about the bonfire with light feet and joyous hearts, laughing as they twirled about wearing animal masks.

Something tugged me, urging me to join them. I'd never felt even the slightest temptation to dance. Did it have something to do with reaching my bian? We'd never danced before. What if I somehow called attention to myself if I started now? Difficult as it was, I had to wait until they reached their bians before sharing mine. Even if it took all my willpower. If that meant no dancing, so be it. I enjoyed sitting with my mates, soaking up the scene, allowing it to brighten my spirits. I'd focus on that. Only that.

"Why so jittery?" Catty placed a hand on mine, stilling it.

"Huh?" I scowled at my flattened hand as if it didn't belong to me. Had I been fidgeting? "Oh, I, uh—"

A shadowy figure walked up the hill toward us. A man, judging from the outline.

"I see we have a new clansman among us." Achaius. Though a few years older, he never treated us as insignificant the way other clan members a few years our senior sometimes did.

"Aye." I shuffled aside to make room. "Join us."

"Nay. Thank ye." He tipped his head toward Cahal. "I'm off to meet with yer mum and da, but I wanted to meet ye first and welcome ye to Notirr." He proffered an arm.

Cahal clasped his forearm. "Thank you."

"I heard tell of the Treasach babies." Achaius's winning smile dipped to a frown. "Did Cahal tell ye what his mum and da did for Duana?"

Duana? Who was Duana?

"Aye. They left Gnuatthara to save her," Catty said.

Ah. Cahal's baby sister. I'd forgotten her name.

"Aye. Did he tell ye? The poor thing lost her da to a fasgadair. Then her mum died in childbirth." Achaius clicked his tongue.

Now I was thoroughly confused. "Cahal's parents are here."

Achaius's shadowed expression was hard to see, or it'd betray the same confusion as I felt. "Cahal's parents? Oh, did ye think Duana was Cahal's sister? Nay. They risked their lives to save another's child. 'Tis inspiring." He straightened and tucked his hands behind him and rocked on his toes. "I hope I can do something to help."

Eyes narrowing, Catty cocked her head at Cahal. "I thought ye said Duana was yer sister?"

"She is... now." Cahal leaned back on his elbows.

So, his parents hadn't waited until their own child's life was in danger. They'd endangered themselves for an orphan? Whatever I had thought of Cahal and his parents before, I felt different now.

Catty frowned, then turned her thoughtful gaze on Achaius. "How do ye intend to help?"

He rubbed the black stubble on his chin. "I need to speak with his parents and the elders, but I'd like to rescue the babies. Perhaps we could bring them here for adoption into our families. Kylemore and Ardara might take in some babies, too."

I couldn't imagine giant babies toddling around. But they'd be the runts, so maybe they wouldn't be that big. Regardless, the plan sounded good.

Catty sucked in her breath through her teeth, giving off a slight whistle. "But it's so dangerous."

"Wouldn't that anger the fasgadair? Make you a target?" Aodan asked.

Achaius shrugged off the potential dangers. "What does that matter if it's God's plan?"

He waited as if we might answer. But what could we say?

"I'm in search of Sully to see if he has insight. Have ye seen him?"

We shook our heads.

"Well, I'm off. Pray for God to make His will clear. 'Tis an honor to meet ye, Cahal." Achaius waved and sauntered down the hill.

"You as well." Cahal's words came out in a rush.

I shivered. Achaius. So fearless. My already high opinion of him increased tenfold.

"Incredible." Catty pressed her fingers to her lips. "I wish I could help."

"Well, if it isn't the giant lovers." Tevin's voice chafed. Whatever warmth had soothed my soul in Achaius's selfless presence, Tevin sucked into his empty void. His shadowed eyes made him appear more menacing than usual.

Cahal's stoic expression was impossible to read.

Aodan waved a dismissive hand. "Away with ye."

"Away with me?" Tevin pointed to himself and balked. "*Me?* I was born here. *I* belong here. And *I'm* not some freakish, gigantic baby killer."

Cahal jumped to his feet. The boy was swift considering his mass. He rose to his full height, chest puffed.

Tevin's gaze continued to rise as Cahal closed in, his twisted smile fading in Cahal's shadow while his Adam's apple took a long dip.

I leaped between them and pressed my hand against Tevin's chest, keeping him at bay. "Don't get involved with him, Cahal. He's the village browbeater. Nothing more. He's not worth it."

Aodan stood beside me and crossed his arms in an unhurried, dramatic manner.

Tevin dropped open his mouth as if surprised and insulted by his status. Cahal drew in a sharp breath, then thudded himself onto the grass beside Catty.

"Get out of here, Tevin." I pushed him. "I mean it. Next time, I'll encourage Cahal to do whatever he wants with ye. God knows ye deserve it."

Tevin clutched his heart, feigning hurt. Then his expression morphed into a sneer. He waved before starting to walk away. "This isn't over. My father will chase those giants out of this village." The weasel always had to get in the last word. "So, watch yerselves, giant lovers."

I silently cheered as the numpty tripped in his haste to leave. When he disappeared into the shadows from whence he came, the air felt lighter. But the weight wouldn't lift entirely.

Tevin was right. This wasn't over.

CHAPTER SEVEN

CATALEEN

My discouragement grew with each passing day. The fifteenth anniversary of our birth had come and gone. First one moon, then two. Then fall. Then winter. Spring readied to give way to summer. In less than three moons, I'd be sixteen summers. Though the air warmed, my patience cooled. None of us had reached our bian. Not one. Or so they claimed. For all I knew, they kept it quiet for my benefit.

No, only Faolan would do that. Aodan would gloat. Sure as the morn arrived each day. I slathered jam onto my bread with more aggression than necessary. Red glops splattered across the table.

"Knock it off," Aodan grumbled, dropping his bread onto his plate.

"What do you care about some spilled jam? I'll clean it up." I fetched the dishcloth and mopped the splatters.

He gave me a hard stare. Clearly, the jam wasn't his concern.

"Oh!" I'd been projecting my thoughts onto him again. I closed the link.

"It's bad enough that I haven't reached my totem yet. I don't need all yer senseless thoughts invading my mind."

"I just... I—"

"Do ye really think so little of me?"

"Wha—"

"The images of me prancing around as a lion before ye." His face cracked, and hurt glazed his eyes. "Do ye think I'd do that to ye?"

I stretched across the table and grasped his hand. "My apologies, Aodan. I know ye love me."

Pulling away, he smirked. "I don't know that I'd go *that* far." He took a huge bite of his breakfast, then tucked his bite into a cheek like a chipmunk. "Just mind yer thoughts. Keep 'em in yer own head. I've got enough of my own."

"And ye shouldn't speak with yer mouth full." I chewed the inside of my cheek. Brothers.

"Quit yer squabbling." Ma stacked the dishes on the table. "I'll take care of these."

"Thanks, Ma." I planted a kiss on her forehead. I'd never get over being taller than her. "We'll bring home strawberries for ye."

Aodan shoved the rest of his bread in his mouth, puffing out his cheek, then fisted his cap, tipped it toward Ma, and plopped it on his head before tromping out the door.

I rushed to catch up, and we walked to the barn in silence. The MacLaughlins' hill home bathed us in its shadow as we passed. The rising sun met us on the other side. I shaded my eyes, only to pass through another shadow.

How many times had I walked this path, passed these homes? I hadn't lived a full sixteen years yet. Would I continue to walk this path twice as many times as I already had? Three times? Four?

Was this all there was? Sowing and harvesting, season after season, year after year?

There had to be more to life than this. Even if I reached my bian, what difference would that make? Villagers didn't prance about in their totems. Only those new to their animal forms did that.

Was I putting all my hopes in the wrong thing?

Achaius sprang to mind. The elders had just approved his plans to visit a refuge outside Gnuatthara to see how he might help save babies. *He* was doing something. *He* had a purpose. Yes, he'd face danger, but he didn't let fear stop him. His dreams surpassed his fears. *He* was truly living.

What was I doing?

"Ah, the demon twins have arrived."

I jumped as Tevin stepped out from an empty stable. I hadn't even realized we'd entered the barn. "Not now, Tevin. Go find someone else to snivel at."

Pieces of hay stuck to his rumpled clothes and tousled red hair. Dirt caked his bare feet.

"Did you *sleep* here?" A gloomy cloud filled my heart. Had he slept in the barn to be here when we arrived, waiting to catch us alone? Without Faolan? Or Cahal?

"Away and boil yer head." Aodan waved him off, grabbed my hand, and pulled me along.

Surprise, surprise, Tevin followed. What did he want? Why was he so determined to torment us? What demon possessed his soul to make him persist? Cahal and his family had proved their value in the community. None questioned their presence in Notirr any longer. They'd become official clan members, and the clan voted in Cahal's father, Evander, as an elder. Most of the clan approved of them. I'd hoped Tevin would relent. But no. He took every opportunity to aggravate. And his jeers were gaining intensity.

"What are ye all still doing in this village? Yer no gachen." Tevin's voice grated.

What was he talking about? Cahal wasn't even with us. And he *was* a gachen. Being a Treasach didn't make him less so. Or was Tevin suggesting *we* weren't gachen because we hadn't reached our bian?

I yanked my hand from Aodan's grip and whirled around to face him. "What's yer problem? Ye haven't reached yer bian either... and yer *older*."

Aodan grabbed me again and wheeled me around. An image of him putting a finger to his lips invaded my mind. But why should we remain silent? Why should we listen to this scabby dolt's ugly words and not defend ourselves?

"Ow!" Aodan's hand flew to the back of his head.

A rock thudded to the ground and rolled into a pile of hay.

Aodan brought a shaky hand from his head and inspected it. Blood covered his fingers. His eyes widened. "Why, ye—"

I gaped at the blood. *What happened? Did he—*

Aodan tried not to wince as he touched the back of his head again, fingering past his yellow hair, but I sensed his pain.

"What's this?" Tevin's gaze flicked back and forth between Aodan and me. "Yer doing that mind thingy again, aren't ye? I always wondered how ye did that. Now I know."

What is he talking about? I asked.

I don't know, but it's time to stop rolling over for this dunderhead.

I placed a hand on Aodan's shoulder. *Don't do anything daft.*

"My father did a little digging, wondering why ye'd be so keen to aid traitors. He found out all about ye, Demon Spawn." Tevin spat a thick wad onto the dirt floor.

Aodan shook me off and moved toward Tevin, fists ready.

Tevin's eyes creased, shimmering with glee as a grin overtook his scabby face.

"Are ye actually *enjoying* this?" My blood curdled.

Tevin reddened as he laughed.

Aodan lunged and punched Tevin. Blood spurted from his nose.

Tevin clutched his nose with both hands. Fear flashed in his eyes, but then he smiled again and cackled like a lunatic. Blood dripped into his mouth, and he spat it out. "My da will have yer head for this."

Tevin rounded the corner. Dread pooled in my gut. Next time we saw Tevin, his father would be with him.

I grew tired, and my back begged me to stop as we picked berries. I straightened, arching my back to relieve the pressure as I wiped the sweat from my brow. My concern for my brother had weakened my anger toward Tevin. That and all the images of Tevin being harmed in various ways that had assaulted me all morning. After hours of this, I'd seen him die a hundred deaths.

Rarely did I see Aodan so outraged that he lost complete control of the messages he bombarded me with. I could scarcely collect my own thoughts. But something had to be done. Tevin had grown violent, causing Aodan to respond in kind.

Someone approached. I shielded my eyes from the sun. A large man headed our way.

Lorcan. With Tevin at his heels.

I trembled at their swift approach, wishing the earth would open and swallow us.

Lorcan grabbed Aodan by the collar and yanked him off the ground. "Are ye responsible for this?" He pointed to the bandage on Tevin's nose between black eyes. "Ye broke his nose, ye useless nitwit!" Lorcan shoved Aodan to the ground as Tevin bounced out his excitement.

"Sir, I—"

"Save it." Lorcan grasped Aodan's collar again and jerked him to his feet. "Yer coming with me." He lugged Aodan across the field with Tevin practically skipping in the rear.

Faolan, Cahal, and I eyed each other, their wide eyes probably much like my own. We dropped our baskets and ran to follow.

CHAPTER EIGHT

FAOLAN

Catty and I huddled together behind the elders' cabin, hunkered in some bushes. We crouched below a window, facing each other with ears to the wall, listening. Aodan and Tevin were in there with Lorcan and Mirna. Da was probably off on a fishing boat. Because Aodan and Catty's wise Ma refused to speak to Tevin's father alone, two elders had joined them—Quin and Sully.

Cahal stood on the corner near the path, keeping an eye out.

Catty adjusted her position, jostling the bushes. I gripped her shoulder and shook my head, pointing to the wagging branches visible through the window. She cringed and stiffened. Staying like this wasn't easy. My thighs and calves begged for a chair. But we couldn't be found out. Not by Lorcan. Things were bad enough already.

I couldn't hear much of the conversation. Only Lorcan came through loud and clear with his enraged shouts. "That boy is the devil's spawn!"

Mirna responded, but the window muffled her words. I narrowed my eyes at Catty. Seeming to understand, she shrugged. She twisted her mouth to get a better grip on her cheek and nibbled away. Too bad she couldn't share thoughts with me as she did with Aodan.

"That's right." Lorcan's voice broke through. "I know all about their father, his blood churning with fasgadair poison when those blasted roasters were conceived."

Mirna spoke again. I strained to hear her words, but she was too soft-spoken and far away.

"Please accept our apologies, Mirna." Quin sounded as if he sat right by the window. "That information was confidential. I have no idea how it leaked. Yer children are well-behaved and a great help to the community—valued members of the clan. The state of their father's health at their conception is irrelevant to what happened here today."

Something rattled inside.

"Well-behaved? A help to the community?" Lorcan raged. "Look what those little roasters did to my boy!"

"Those? I believe only one clan member was involved in this situation." Sully's gravelly voice sounded far away, but he probably sat by the window near Quin.

"Violence is not acceptable under any circumstances, and the elders will deal with that matter..."

Catty and I exchanged grim faces. None of us had faced punishment before.

"... but I would like to know what transpired just before Tevin's injury," Quin said.

Good question.

"My son was provoked," Lorcan said.

"Oh? How so?" Quin asked.

"The very presence of demon children in this village provokes him! Isn't that what demons do? Cause strife?"

Sully chuckled.

Crackkk!

Catty and I both jerked, then fought to regain our footing.

"What is so amusing?" Lorcan's low voice came out like a threatening growl.

Catty stared at the wavering branches. Hopefully, if anyone noticed, they'd think it was windy.

But what caused that sound? Had Lorcan slammed the table? I couldn't imagine being so brazen with the elders, especially during a peaceful meeting.

Something creaked. Then Sully's voice filtered through the wall. "Take care with your words, Lorcan. One might think you're accusing your son of being a demon."

Catty crushed her mouth with her hand as I bit my tongue. I had to look away from her, or I'd bust out laughing.

"Accusing my son— How, in God's creation, did I do that?"

"You said demons cause strife. Isn't that what your son has been doing in this village for years?" Sully asked.

Skrrrt! Thrump!

Did he just throw something?

"I helped raise the children in this village." Whatever was happening in there, Sully didn't sound rattled. "The only bad character I've seen among them is yer son. And you."

"Shut yer gob!"

Thrump! Scuttle. Scuttle. Thrump!

"How dare ye claim to see *anything*, ye blind numpty!" Lorcan rasped as if someone held him back by the collar. "Git yer scabby hands off me."

"As soon as ye... can restrain... yerself, I will." Quin grunted a response.

Silence. Then shuffling. A chair scraped against the floor.

"Aodan, what have ye to say for yerself?" Quin asked.

Aodan cleared his throat. "I–I lost my temper, sir. I shouldn't have skelped him."

"That's fine, lad. We'll address that later, alone with yer mum. But what prompted ye?"

"T–Tevin's been taunting us our entire lives, but more so this past year. I don't know if it's because we're friends with Cahal or because we haven't reached our bian. But he's getting worse. H–he threw a rock at me."

"Is that true, Tevin?" Quin asked.

"I didn't do nothin'."

"Are ye suggesting you've lived quietly, minding yerself, and Aodan skelped—er, *struck*—ye unprovoked?" Quin asked.

"Aye."

"Let me see yer head, Aodan." Another chair scraped the tile floor. "Well, there's a scab forming here. Aodan appears to have been hit by something." Quin's voice grew louder as he returned to his seat. "How do ye suppose he received such an injury?"

"How should I know? Maybe he did it to himself."

"He stabbed himself in the back of the head to make it appear like he had an excuse to hit ye?" Sully laughed.

"How should I understand the mind of a demon?"

"Watch yer words, boy."

I'd never heard Sully sound so threatening.

"I trust my boy," Lorcan said. "If he says he didn't provoke him, he didn't. And I want to move that the devil's spawn be banished from the village."

Catty's eyes widened, and her mouth hung open. I shook my head, hoping she'd receive my silent message that they'd never banish Aodan. Before this, he'd never shown any kind of violence.

Her mouth closed. But her forehead still creased.

A chair squeaked, and Sully groaned. "I've seen yer boy. I've heard his taunts to the children over the years. The elders have spoken to ye on several occasions. Tevin is no longer a lad. Ye had yer time to correct his behavior and failed to do so. He's of age, and his insults have escalated to action. Therefore, I move that the elders intercede."

"Agreed. The elders will meet to discuss this situation. In the meantime, keep yer boy at home." Quin's voice strained on the last word as if he was rising. "That's an order, not a suggestion."

The meeting must be ending. The last thing we needed was to be caught eavesdropping. I motioned to Catty, and we shuffled away from the window. She snagged Cahal's hand, and we dashed down the path to her house.

CHAPTER NINE

CATALEEN

Faolan, Cahal, and I sat at my kitchen table, catching our breath. We waited for Ma and Aodan, hoping we appeared to have been here all the while. But we needn't have worried. We had plenty of time sitting there actually growing bored.

"What's taking them?" I chewed my cheek. "Do ye think Ma and Aodan stayed behind for Aodan's punishment? Do ye think they'd banish him?"

"Nay." Faolan patted my hand. "They wouldn't punish him for one infraction. Especially with Tevin involved."

I wiped the sweat from my brow. "What was all this talk about devil's spawn and demons? What has my ma been hiding about our da? About us?"

Faolan shrugged.

Cahal's large hand wrapped around my shoulder, its weight comforting.

"What's taking them so long?" Every bit of me jittery, I jiggled my leg under the table until I couldn't sit any longer. I sprang from the chair and paced from the dining table to the sitting area, peering out the window each time it came into view. Every time someone would walk by, I'd rush to the window. But nay, it wasn't them. On my return to the kitchen, Cahal pointed out the window.

"Is that them?"

I dashed to the window to check. "They're coming!"

I threw the door open. Ma shuffled through and tugged off her coat. Aodan closed the door and hung his cap. Both looked like they could sleep for a week and it wouldn't be enough.

"Have a seat at the table," Ma said. "I'd like to speak with ye both. Faolan and Cahal, ye should go."

The boys stood.

"No, Ma." I grasped Faolan's hand, rooting him. "They're our friends. They should stay."

"Aye." Aodan agreed. "We'll just tell them whatever ye tell us later. Better they hear it straight from yer mouth now."

Ma pursed her lips, then nodded. "Please sit."

Faolan returned to his seat.

"What's gonna happen to Aodan?" I tugged my lips. "Is he going to be punished?"

"They're letting me off with a warning." Aodan slipped into his usual chair.

"Oh, thank God." I aimed my thanks toward God in the heavens.

Ma's skin had developed a greenish sheen. "I need a drink. Does anyone else want water?"

We shook our heads. Everyone else must be as eager as I was to hear what she was about to say. We waited, barely breathing, as she grabbed a mug from the cupboard, then the pitcher from the table. Her hands shook while she poured. She then slid into the chair Cahal vacated and offered her. Lips set, she took a long sip.

Were those creases around her mouth and eyes new? The frailty of her slumped shoulders? Had she aged considerably since the morn?

"There are some things I need to tell ye." She reached for Aodan's shoulder and gave it a squeeze, and I winced at the sorrow dulling her eyes. "I'm sorry ye heard it from that wretched man's mouth."

"What, Ma?" My voice came out as a squeak.

Our ma consulted the heavens as she often did before delivering a tough message. "Yer father, God bless his soul, didn't die from an infection as I led everyone in the village to believe. He was in the forest felling trees with two men from the village. They stayed longer than they should have." She closed her eyes, shook her head, and took a deep breath as she did when Aodan or I displeased her. She must've warned Da not to tarry. "They were attacked on their return home."

"By what?" I hadn't even realized I'd spoken until the words hung in the air.

"Fasgadair."

Sharp inhales sounded from around the table.

Ma took another sip, and her teeth clanged against the stoneware. "Yer father was bitten. The fasgadair offered yer father the chance to live by becoming a fasgadair himself."

"What?" Aodan and I spoke in unison.

"At first, he said yes, but he didn't understand what he was saying yes to. As soon as he realized the fasgadair was feeding him its blood, he spat it out. He refused to be turned."

"So, what happened?" Aodan's whole body strained toward her, likely mirroring my posture.

"The demon blood—the little he ingested—healed him. He arrived home the following morn in perfect health. Or seeming so. Shaking with fright and battle worn, but physically well. He shared the story of the attack and surmised that his mates hadn't survived. They never made it home. But he neglected to mention what had happened to him... claiming the blood on his collar wasn't his. It wasn't until his health declined that I learned the truth."

We all stared at her, silent.

"The bite marks reappeared. Nasty black veins spread from the site. The elders sought a cure. None was found, but they learned yer da wasn't the first. It's uncommon. But others had ingested fasgadair blood, but not enough to transition into a fasgadair. None lived for more than a year."

Ma took a long drink, her mug shaking.

"The elders advised the village that the tree-felling incident that took the other men's lives had affected yer da, too. They claimed he suffered from a minor injury that resulted in an incurable infection. We kept him in seclusion to keep our secret safe."

"Why keep it a secret?" I asked.

"Because of no-good dobbers like Tevin and Lorcan," Aodan said.

"Precisely." Ma threw him a softened version of her typical hard stare. "Though I'd prefer such words wouldn't pass yer lips." She took a deep breath and consulted the heavens once more. "Ye were conceived whilst yer da was infected." She leaned across the table, reaching for Aodan's hand, then mine. "We knew that, if the villagers—particularly those who are superstitious or unkind—found out, they'd make all kinds of false accusations about ye two such as what occurred today. Lorcan claimed ye both were devil's spawn. But it's not true."

Fire lit her eyes. Her grip pinched my fingers. "Ye understand? I'll not have anyone feed yer heads with such nonsense. Yer children of God. With my own ears, I heard yer professions of faith. And I believed them because I know yer hearts. Yer imperfect yet beautiful hearts and yer love for God. So don't ye pay one bit of attention to any unholy words from ignorant lips, ye hear?"

"Aye, Ma." I squeezed her hand. She probably needed the comfort more than I did. The air seemed thick, compressing my head, making it difficult to absorb what I'd heard. Did demon blood pulse through my veins?

With his face crumpled and his eyes big, Aodan didn't look convinced either. He looked... scared. "How can ye know, Ma? What came over me in that barn? How do ye know it wasn't demon blood in me?"

She leapt from her chair and hugged him. "We all have a little of the devil in us, son. None of us is good. Not one. 'Tis why we so desperately need God. Ye made the wrong choice, but that doesn't make ye a demon. Understand?" She clung to him, rocking him, smoothing his hair. "And if ye ask me, that Tevin and his father have a bigger dose of the devil inside them than the entire village combined."

CHAPTER TEN

FAOLAN

I hadn't recovered from the news over the past weeks. It haunted me still. Stealing my joy. The elders wouldn't punish Aodan, but they'd yet to announce a decision about Tevin. Until then, he was loose. Available to torment the twins. So far, none of us had seen him, but we'd heard from others that he'd been spotted and sent home many times. If the elders continued to delay, we were bound to run into him. No warning was strong enough to keep Tevin at home.

I tried swallowing my fears with my porridge.

"Slow yerself, lad." Da reached across the table, stopping me from lifting another bite. "The harvest will still be there after ye eat at a proper speed."

"I know, Da." But no telling what might happen if Aodan and Tevin faced each other again. I had to be there. As protection and witness. As soon as Da freed my hand, I shoveled the rest of my food into my mouth, then threw on my cap, and dashed out the door to the barn.

I ran around the corner and crashed into someone.

"Whoa. What's yer hurry, mate?" Achaius caught me and gripped my shoulders.

"My apologies." I pointed to the barn. "I'm meeting my friends to help with the harvest."

"I'm sure they'll still be there when ye arrive. Take a breath."

I eyed Achaius. Had he lost weight? "Weren't you traveling to Gnuatthara?"

"Aye. It seems I've returned, but I'll be off again shortly."

"You've already gone and returned?" I had to pay better attention. "Did ye save any babies?"

"Aye. I brought three with me." His eyes sparkled with life. "Thanks to Cahal's parents, I met with other Treasach who've already begun organizing rescues. They lay in wait for the abandoned babies, then bring them to a hidden camp. I plan to travel back and forth to collect any children they don't have room for and bring them here or to another village that can take them."

"Isn't it dangerous?"

"We've set up camps at natural stopping points along the way to rest and switch out the horses. They're well-hidden—and fortified." Achaius gripped my shoulder and flashed a reassuring smile. "Not to worry, mate. God's in this. He'll see us through."

Achaius disappeared around the bend, taking the joyous atmosphere with him, leaving me wondering how he could be so calm in the face of danger. The threats I faced weren't nearly as dire, yet they drained me of peace.

I slumped and trudged back toward the barn. If only I had a smidgen of what Achaius had.

I met Cahal on the path, and we walked the rest of the way together. Having grown accustomed to his scant words, I found his silent presence comforting. Aodan was only silent for long spells when he was brooding. Chatty Catty was never quiet. So I basked in Cahal's calm.

We arrived at the barn as Aodan and Catty entered and disappeared into the dark entrance. A figure stole from the shadowed tree line across the field, toward the barn.

Tevin.

My stomach swallowed my heart as my hands turned to ice. Why oh why hadn't they waited for us? Cahal growled and broke into a run. I tore off after him. His footsteps pounded the earth by my side across the vast field.

"Hey, Demon Spawn." Tevin's grating voice taunted from inside, urging me to hurry.

We came up behind him and slowed. He tossed a rock in the air, then caught it.

Toss. Catch. Toss. Catch.

Aodan gave an almost imperceptible headshake, warning me to stay out of it. Cahal seemed to grow taller. He tensed, his meaty hands clenching. But he must've caught the warning. He stayed back, too.

Tevin fingered the rock, held it close, and smiled. He wound his arm back as if gearing up for a throw.

Without thinking, my feet rushed him. Blood surged through my veins, urging me to act before another rock hit my friend.

"No, Faolan!" Aodan held up a hand.

Tevin whirled around. A white bandage covered his nose, although the swelling had receded and his eyes weren't as black. I stopped, unsure of what to do. My heart hammered on though Tevin's attention was now on me. At least I'd distracted him. He hadn't thrown the rock.

"Let's get the buckets and get out of here." Aodan waved us to join them.

A sick sensation intermingled with my rage. I tried to swallow it... to allow reason to return. This was the first Aodan was trying to get *me* not to do something stupid. He was right. Tevin wasn't worth it. He wasn't right in the head. Violence wouldn't change that. It would only make the situation worse.

I pushed past Tevin, bumping his shoulder with my puffed chest. Tevin sneered. Keeping a wary eye over my shoulder, I followed my mates to the buckets.

The softheaded dolt followed.

"When will ye get the message? Yer not welcome here, Devil's Spawn. Nor is yer ogre." He spat a glop of something at our heels.

Catty yanked her hand from Aodan's grip and wheeled around. "What's yer defect, Tevin? We're all God's children!"

"God?" Tevin scoffed. "How can ye even say His name without bursting into flames, *Demon?*"

Hands on her hips, her mouth hung open.

He stepped closer, his eyes narrowing into slits. His upper lip gathered into a sneer. "I always knew something was off about ye. Was demon blood that birthed ye. And now the entire village knows it."

Catty worked her jaw, but nothing came out. It took a lot to steal words from Chatty Catty.

My fists shook, willing me to act. I wanted to do something, but what?

"Don't ye dare speak to her." Aodan seethed. His chest rose and fell in measured beats as he skewered Tevin with a look I'd never seen and never wanted aimed at me.

"I'll do whatever I please, Devil's Spawn."

Tevin's shirt erupted in flames.

All eyes widened further than seemed possible as our minds grappled to comprehend what happened. Tevin's shirt was on fire? How? I searched the ceiling as if fire rained from above. But there was nothing. No flames anywhere. Just Tevin.

He howled, smacked at himself, then yanked his shirt off and threw it onto a pile of hay. The bale ignited. Flames spread like an army of ants overtaking a fallen apple.

Pure horror encased my heart, cementing me to the spot.

"This is yer fault, Demon Boy." Tevin pointed at Aodan. "Ye'll burn for this." He then ran from the barn.

Tevin's disappearance snapped me back to my senses. "Get help!"

Catty waffled for a moment, then shot off toward the homes.

"Cahal, free the animals." I pulled Aodan's sleeve. "Help me."

We grabbed the nearest buckets, dumped their contents, and

darted for the well. By the time we returned to the fire, the flames had taken over an entire stall and were climbing the walls to the rafters. Flames licked several more stalls. Cahal emerged from the smoke with whinnying horses in tow. A cloth covered his mouth and nose.

I didn't have time to tear my shirt to do the same. The flames were too quick. The buckets were too small. And my feet were too slow. I tried covering my mouth with my arm. Smoke spilled in, searing my nostrils and coating my tongue. My lungs burned. I coughed, which only made me need to cough more.

We tossed the water into the flames, but it wasn't enough. Not nearly enough. We paused. The panic on Aodan's face mirrored my heart. As fire consumed the barn, we couldn't do anything to stop it.

I smacked Aodan's arm, pulling his gaze from the inferno. "We can't give up. Come on!"

We ran back toward the well. As futile as it was, we needed to try.

Cahal stormed past. Arms protecting his face, he jumped into the flames.

Masked villagers came running, armed with buckets. Catty followed. It was too little, too late. But their presence bolstered my waning hope. We weren't in this alone.

"Get in formation!" Quin yelled through his face covering to the reinforcements.

The volunteers formed lines from the well to the all-consuming inferno as if they'd been practicing their whole life. Everyone seemed to know where to go, except us.

"Put these on." Quin handed us each a cloth to cover our faces. "Move outside near the well or go to the infirmary."

We pushed our way outside, coughing and sputtering.

Evander's monstrous form crashed toward us. "Where's Cahal?"

"Freeing the animals." I pointed. "Inside."

His wild gaze trained on the door. He knocked into people, sending them teetering in his haste to get to his son.

We filled gaps in the line of villagers handing buckets of water down the line, losing precious fluid with each handoff. Sloshing water soaked our shoes. The forming mud threatened to knock me off my feet. My arms and shoulders ached. My fingers cramped. Blisters burned my palms. The handle threatened to slip from my weakening fingers. My body begged to slump to the ground. But the fire continued to spread, consuming everything in its path, toward the greens ready to be harvested, showing no signs of relenting. I couldn't relent either. Bucket after bucket. An endless parade of waterlogged pails teased me, telling me to give up. My efforts were in vain.

Coughing villagers fought their way outside and collapsed on the green. Others from the line in the fresh air moved in to replace them. Crashing met the continual crackle and pops as the barn broke apart inside.

I couldn't give up. I wouldn't give up.

Groooaaan.

The world seemed to stop as everyone fixed their gazes on the ominous sound.

Crraaaaack.

A section of the roof buckled. Everyone stepped back with a collective gasp. Villagers streamed from the entrance like bees from a disturbed nest.

"Everybody, out!" Smeared in black, Quin ushered people out.

Crraaack. C*RRAAAAACK!*

Half the barn caved in as the roof collapsed, sending sparks raining over the crops.

Disbelieving horror shivered through me.

CHAPTER ELEVEN

CATALEEN

Smoke burned my nose, and I coughed.
Fire. The barn.

I bolted upright. Where was I? Had I been sleeping? My heart raced, and I fought to catch my breath as I jerked my head one way, then the other. The fire was out. No embers shone in the darkness. Only a skeleton of the barn stood in the charred field.

My aching body groaned at the slightest movements as I took in my surroundings. Aodan's head rested on my arm. Faolan lay curled up beside him. Other villagers sprawled close by. Had everyone fallen in their exhaustion?

Where was Cahal?

I tugged my arm out from beneath Aodan as gently as possible, not wanting to wake him. Though my body screamed at me, I stood. Sharp pains settled into dull aches. My head seemed to expand and contract to an annoying beat, making me swoon. Ash covered my clothes, my arms... *everything*. The barn was nothing but charred boards, some still standing, and soot-covered residue.

I walked toward the remains.

"I wouldn't go in there, lass."

I jumped, then searched the darkness. Quin sat beside the well. My body resumed its protests as I lowered myself beside him. The night sounded eerily quiet.

"Is everyone—" My voice cracked.

Quin hung his head. When he lifted his gaze back to the barn, the moonlight betrayed him, revealing his glistening eyes. "Duffey, Rey, and… Evander are now in paradise."

Tears pooled, threatening to spill over. "Cahal's father?"

"Aye." He breathed the heavy breath of a man with the weight of the village on his shoulders. "The barn collapsed on him. Cahal tried to rescue him, but a beam engulfed in flames fell on his shoulder. Cahal's okay, but he's badly burned. Nurses are tending to his wounds, along with the other injured."

I choked on my breath. "How many are injured?"

"Four more—Keiran, Ewen, Jakodi, and Les."

I covered my mouth as tears slipped down my face, splashing my hands while each face flashed in my mind. "Are they—"

"They'll live." Quin rested a comforting hand on my shoulder. "Not to worry, lass. Ye did good coming for help." He dragged a hand down his face, smearing the soot. "Do ye know how the fire started?"

I wiped my tears and shook my head. "No."

"What do ye remember?"

"Tevin's shirt—"

"Aye?" Quin prompted.

"I don't know. It just… burst into flames."

✲

I DRESSED in my nice black dress—my most uncomfortable dress—and followed Ma and Aodan up the path to the elders' meetinghouse. I'd only ever attended village-wide meetings under the tent where we shared meals. Eavesdropping outside while Aodan met with the elders was the closest I'd ever come to a private meeting. This was the first I'd been called. I'd never been inside.

An image of a bird soaring high above the woods filled my mind.

With his typically unruly yellow hair slicked back, Aodan flashed a crooked smile. *You'll be all right.*

He rarely spoke to me in our minds these days. According to him, we weren't kids anymore and needed our privacy. I disagreed but tried to respect it. So, his response both calmed me and choked me up. My eyes blurred as I smiled back. *So will you.*

I believed those words, yet I didn't. Tevin caused the problems, but we were always involved. How much longer would the elders excuse us?

And now, after this? Devastation like Notirr had never seen.

I swallowed a lump in my throat as we neared the place of authority. The wooden structure's style was similar to the few other wooden buildings in the village. Simple. Unimposing. Yet today it loomed before me. The door hung open like a hungry mouth, waiting to devour me.

Why was my dress so tight? I tugged at the bodice and tried to breathe.

Quin appeared in the entryway. "Greetings, Mirna." His smile didn't reach his tired eyes. He probably hadn't slept. Only two days had passed since the fire. This was all too soon.

He held the door wide. "Aodan. Cataleen." He nodded as we passed. "Have a seat."

The room was much larger than those in hill homes. Windows on three walls overlooked the ocean on one side and the forest on the others. I watched the trees for signs of eavesdroppers, then moved to the imposing table. Two elders already occupied seats—Declan Cael II, the oldest elder, and Sully, the blind seer.

A warm smile rounded out Declan's cheeks above his white beard, crinkling his sparkling azure eyes, and my breath came easier. Something about him put me at ease—almost as if I stood in God's presence. Same with Sully. Though he couldn't see us, a genuine smile lit his face at our approach. They motioned toward the empty seats across the table. Aodan and I sat beside Ma with me in the middle.

Quin greeted someone else at the door as I peeked into another room lined with shelves full of books, reminding me of our schoolhouse. The similarity to our old school and the peace emanating from the older elders eased my anxious thoughts. *It's just a building like any other. The elders are the same kind, loving people who helped raise me. Nothing bad will happen here today.*

But the fire... What had caused the fire?

CHAPTER TWELVE

FAOLAN

Dressed in my scratchy wool trousers, I approached the elders' meetinghouse alone. I should have allowed my father to accompany me, but nay. No reason to put my da through this. I was just a witness.

Then why did I want nothing more than to shift into my wolf form and run away?

I swallowed a lump in my throat.

Before I knocked, Quin opened the door. "Thanks for coming, Faolan. We're just waiting on Lorcan and Tevin now."

I spied an empty seat next to Aodan and made a beeline for it. I winked as I passed Catty, hoping to ease her fears. We hadn't spoken since the fire. Mirna had locked the twins away—even from me. If only I could sit beside her, squeeze her hand, and be a calming presence.

All was quiet. I patted Aodan's back, then dragged out the chair beside him. It let out a horrific squeal. All gazes darted my way. Catty released a nervous laugh. I grimaced as I slid into the seat, not daring to pull it back to the table.

An elder, Malina, sat on my other side. She smiled politely. "Good to see you, Faolan."

I flashed a nervous smile.

Finnian, the youngest elder, scribbled something on parchment. What was he writing? Would he make note of my noisy chair?

Cracksh!

Like overtightened strings, we all snapped toward the entryway. Lorcan charged into the room, cane raised as if ready to strike anyone who got in his way, with Tevin close behind. Chin held high, he removed his cloak and hung it by the door. "Have a seat, lad."

Tevin skulked through the room to a seat next to Sully, almost directly across from Aodan.

Lorcan took his time seating himself beside his son.

"Thank ye all for coming." Declan Cael II motioned toward me. Somehow, his eyebrows hadn't aged. They remained red while white had overtaken his facial hair and what remained of the hair on his head. "Unfortunately, we're short two elders today. Evander is now with God—"

"Treasach giant had no business acting as an elder."

Every muscle within me raged, crying out to leap from my seat and smack some sense into that vile man. How could someone be so spiteful? So callous? So... cruel?

Judging by Aodan's clenched jaw, he was holding himself back as well. His temples pulsed.

Declan narrowed his eyes at Lorcan, raising one thick eyebrow, then dragged his gaze away in thinly veiled disgust. "And Keiran is among the injured. We've asked Faolan to join us as a witness to these recent events. Cahal is still in the infirmary and unable to testify. Before we begin, let's take a moment to pray. Sully?"

Sully cleared his throat. "Father, Almighty God, thank ye for extinguishing the barn fire and sparing our animals and most essential crops. While we mourn the loss of a valuable leader, we're grateful Evander is now with Ye along with Duffey and Rey. Please heal the injured and fill us, those you've chosen to oversee Notirr, with Yer wisdom and discernment. Reveal the truth of recent events and guide us as we decide what's best for the village Ye've entrusted in our care. Amen."

"Thank ye, Sully." Declan landed his gaze on Tevin. "Before we begin, please only respond if yer spoken to." He trained his gaze on Lorcan. "Parents are here to support their adult children and will be asked to leave if they interfere. Is that understood?"

Ma nodded. "Of course."

Lorcan scoffed and shifted his crossed leg to the other, arm draped over the back of the chair as if he were the village's sole overseer.

"I would also like to state that this is an official inquiry of the elders before God. He will judge any lies or omission of truth according to His perfect nature. Do you, Tevin, Faolan, Cataleen, and Aodan, submit yourself to God's judgment and swear to speak the truth throughout this meeting?"

We all replied with ayes.

"All confirmed." Declan flattened his palms on the table as Finnian's quill scratched the parchment. "Tevin, please share what ye recall in the moments leading up to the barn fire."

Tevin shuffled, appearing eager, frightened, and sick all at once. "W–we w–were in the barn"—his eyes flashed as he grew in his seat, and his voice strengthened while he spoke directly to Aodan—"when he lit my shirt on fire."

"And how did he start the fire?"

"With his demon eyes."

"Ah." Declan nodded as if it all made sense. "Is that correct, Aodan? Did ye set Tevin's shirt on fire with yer eyes?"

Aodan squirmed in his seat. "I–I don't know how the fire started, sir."

"Cataleen and Faolan, ye were present when the fire started, correct?" Declan pressed praying hands to his lips.

"Aye." Fingers shaky, Catty tucked her long hair behind her ears.

"We were there," I said.

"Did either of ye see what caused the fire?"

"It just—lit," she said.

"Nay. I didn't see anything."

As Declan cocked his head to one side, his red brows rose. "Were you unable to see what ignited the fire?"

When Catty glanced at me, I prompted her to go ahead. "N–nay." She wiggled in her seat. "We were all standing close by. I could see his shirt, but no one was near enough to Tevin to set his shirt on fire. I don't know what caused it."

"And what about ye, Faolan?"

"I saw the same thing. His shirt just... caught fire. I didn't see what caused it either."

Quin raised a finger. "May I interject?"

"Certainly." Declan motioned for him to speak.

"I spoke with Cataleen after the fire while she was still groggy and *before* she spoke with anyone else to come up with a story. That's what she said then too. 'It just started itself.'"

Declan rubbed his short beard, the sound rasping in our silence, and took a deep breath. "Let's put the cause of the fire aside as no one seems to know or be willing to admit what caused it. Everyone agrees Tevin's shirt caught on fire. So how did the barn catch fire? Tevin?"

Tevin shrank back. "I panicked. I pulled it off and threw it."

"I see." Declan paused as Finnian continued scribbling. "Is that what ye three saw as well?"

"Aye." Aodan, Catty, and I spoke together.

"And what happened once the barn caught fire, Aodan?"

"Faolan told Cataleen to get help. Cahal rescued the animals. We—Faolan and I"—Aodan's Adam's apple bobbed—"did our best to put the fire out. But it spread so fast. The well was so far away."

"And what about ye, Tevin? Did ye help put the fire out?"

Tevin's eyes widened. Nothing but fear lived there now. "I–I—"

"He didn't help. He ran away like a coward." Aodan sneered.

Tevin burst from his seat, sending it toppling behind him. "Now look here, Devil's Spawn—"

Sully snatched Tevin's hand. "Mind yer manners, lad." He lowered his sightless gaze at Aodan. "That goes for ye as well, son."

"Yes, sir." Aodan hung his head.

Tevin's now narrowed eyes pulsed with hatred. But he relented and stooped to retrieve his chair.

How had Sully known where Tevin's hand was to catch it with such accuracy? And how did he stare down Aodan? No wonder rumors ran rampant that Sully wasn't really blind. Despite the cloudy gray where his irises belonged and his walking stick, the man didn't seem to have much trouble with his vision.

"I'd like to add one more thing." Quin waited for Declan's nod before proceeding. "Sully and I met with Tevin and Aodan and their parents regarding a previous altercation. At that time, we advised Tevin to remain at home until we discussed the situation and gave our ruling. It appears he failed to comply."

Lorcan pounded the table. "You've no right to force my boy to stay home."

Beneath his beard, Declan set his jaw. "One more outburst and I will remove ye from this meeting."

Quin folded his hands on the table. "When the council has reason to believe a clan member is a danger to others, it is within our power to enforce the accused to remain home during the investigation. Ye know this full well."

A firm nod ruffled Declan's hair. "Tevin, why were ye at the barn?"

Tevin shrugged. "I was going to help with the harvest."

Though I was shaking, I couldn't hold back. "May I speak?"

Declan waved me on.

"Cahal and I were trying to catch up to Aodan and Cataleen that morning. They arrived at the barn first. We saw Tevin sneak in after them."

"Sneak in." Lorcan huffed. "The boy was going to help with the harvest."

"Lorcan"—Declan's warning tone and raised brow made me shrink back—"you've been warned about interrupting these proceedings."

"Pfft. You think you can stop me from defending my son from skewed perspectives?"

"Consider this your final warning." Declan raised a palm to silence Lorcan. "Cataleen, what happened when you first saw Tevin at the barn?"

"He threatened us with a rock, calling us demon children and devil's spawn... again."

"Is that true, Tevin?" Declan asked.

Lorcan stood. "If yer here to blast my son with accusations, I'll spare ye the need to remove me." He moved to collect his cloak. "We've more important things to do today." His eye twitched as he jabbed a finger at Declan. "I suggest ye do more digging into this 'mystery' fire. As any reasonable man can attest, fires don't start themselves. C'mon, lad."

Lorcan stormed from the building, his bewildered son trodding at his heels.

Quin slapped the table. "How much longer will the council tolerate his impertinent behavior?"

Finnian dumped his quill in the inkwell. "He's begging to be banished."

Holding up a hand, Declan silenced the others. "The council should hold all comments until we're in private."

"Bah." Sully waved off the concern. "Perhaps it's best the clan knows the council has some opinions about Lorcan's behavior."

Declan huffed. "We've gotten all we can for the moment, anyway. Mirna, ye and yer children may go. The elders will remain and discuss the situation. We'll contact ye shortly."

CHAPTER THIRTEEN

CATALEEN

Faolan and I spent the afternoon searching for Aodan. He wasn't home, on the pier, or anywhere along the coast—none of his usual places. Worse, I couldn't sense him. His overwhelming rage and images of a fist punching Tevin bombarded me when we left the meetinghouse. But then he ran off. It still rubbed me raw that Ma wouldn't let me follow.

And now, I felt nothing. That concerned me the most. In all my life, I'd never been so far from Aodan that I couldn't sense him.

How could I not fear the worst?

We searched the only place left—the woods. But it was growing dark, and I hadn't been to the woods since learning the truth about my da. Before that, I'd felt at home among the trees, especially at this time of year when the peepers heralding the spring soothed my soul.

Not today. Every crunch or rustle made me jump, both hoping it was Aodan and fearful it might be a fasgadair. But it was too light for that yet. Still, the woods didn't feel safe anymore at any hour.

"Catty." Faolan held an arm out to stop me. "We should turn back. Night is falling."

"Which is why we can't leave my brother out here."

"Be reasonable. What if he's already gone home?"

"What if he hasn't?"

"Then we can search for him in the morn. But I'll not risk ye both." He grasped my hand and pulled.

I dug my heels in and yanked my hand free. "Nay! I need to find him."

"Then let me do it. Why don't you check on Cahal in the infirmary?"

What was wrong with him? My brother needed us. Grinding my teeth, I shook my head. "I'll check in on Cahal in the morn. He's safe in the infirmary."

"Why are ye being so stubborn?"

Of all the... I jammed my hands on my hips. "*I'm* stubborn?"

He dragged a hand down his face. "For the love of all that is holy, Cataleen. Let me get you safe. I can find him faster alone."

He was pulling out my full name? He only did that with others—or when he was fed up with me. "What? *I'm* the problem? *I'm* slowing yer progress?"

"Nay, that's not—"

"*I'm* the one with the connection to him. *I'm* the one who can sense him." I jabbed a thumb at my chest. "And *I* will find him faster than you."

He gripped my shoulders and gave them a reassuring squeeze. His hazel eyes pleading. "You don't understand. I can—" He blew out a breath. "I can find him. Please—just trust me."

I narrowed my eyes. "I've always trusted ye. There's never been secrets between us. So why do I sense yer keeping something from me?"

His jaw worked, but no sound came out. He released me and diverted his gaze downward.

"You *are* keeping something from me." My heart squeezed. I

thought we shared everything. "What is it?"

"I didn't want to tell ye. I wanted to share the excitement together."

That could only mean one thing. "Have ye reached yer bian?" I held my breath.

"Aye." His hazel eyes glazed over. "A wolf."

Excitement soared within me like a hundred lit lanterns overtaking the skies. "A wolf!" I squealed. Then a strong breeze extinguished the lanterns, and they plummeted. "Why didn't ye tell us? We've all been waiting for this day. I wanted to share it with ye."

"We wanted to share it *together*. How could I be happy flaunting my new totem, knowing ye hadn't reached yers yet?"

"Sharing a major thing in yer life with yer friends—yer *triplets*—isn't flaunting. We would've been happy for ye."

"I should have told ye." His shoulders slumped.

"Aye." I smacked his upper arm. "Ye should have. Don't go holding out on us again, ye hear me?"

"Aye, miss." He smirked.

I rolled my eyes. "Right. Well then, let's get back and pack ye with some clothes so ye can sniff out Aodan."

✯

I STARED INTO COMPLETE DARKNESS. With no windows to shed any light to distract me, I normally snuggled into my soft bedding, breathed in the cold air, and drifted off into a deep sleep. But not tonight. Instead, the blackness closed in on me, making it hard to breathe.

Where was Aodan? Why couldn't I sense him?

God, please don't let him be...

I couldn't bring myself to say the worst, not even as a prayer. God knew what I feared most.

Why was I even trying to sleep? That would never happen.

I lit the lantern on my bedside table. The unsteady flame cast flickering shadow monsters along the walls and ceiling. My toes sought my slippers beside my bed, and lantern in hand, I left my room to sit by the window and await the boys' return.

As I strode across the small room, a bloody deer carcass invaded my mind. I tripped on the rug, catching myself on the chair. I took a deep breath, grateful I hadn't dropped the lantern. We didn't need any more fires. I sat in the rocker to use the anxious energy building up within rather than pace.

The image must've come from Aodan. He was alive.

I tipped my face toward the ceiling as I rocked. *Thank Ye, God. Now, can Ye just bring him home?*

The tension in my muscles eased, but a lingering worry pricked the back of my mind as I recalled the dead deer. What on God's green earth prompted him to project *that* image?

CHAPTER FOURTEEN

FAOLAN

I raced through the woods, my pack full of clothes bouncing on my back. I'd have to find a way to tighten it in the future. Until then, I tried ignoring its constant slipping, focusing instead on keeping the scent of Aodan's shirt at the forefront of my mind. I sniffed the ground, searching for it. If he'd gone to the woods, he must've come this way.

What if I couldn't find his scent? The forest was alive with so many smells. Trees, flowers, mushrooms, moss, shrubs... Rodent trails zigzagged in every direction, along with frogs and insects. Bird pathways dissipated in the air. Even rocks had a distinct essence my human nose would never have noticed.

How would I find Aodan amongst this cacophony of smells?

A fragrance triggered in my wolf brain. I paused, then shoved my nose to the ground and sniffed, rustling leaves. A match! I snuffed in multiple directions to catch the strongest whiff. The scent strengthened, and I darted off, following the invisible trail, excitement mounting while I surged ahead.

As his scent thickened, a breeze carried smoke along with another, stronger odor. A coppery scent.

Blood. Lots of blood.

I slowed my steps, lowered my head, and peered into the darkness. Another wolfy benefit—enhanced night vision. I stalked to the glow up ahead. Smoke and crackling intensified when I approached the fire. With one eye, I peeked around a tree. Orange firelight cast an eerie glow over Aodan's slumped form. Something black covered his face. I sniffed. Nay, it couldn't be. Why would he be covered in blood?

A little way off lay a deer. A dead deer.

I skulked away to transform and throw on my clothes, then stepped out from behind the tree.

Aodan jumped to his feet.

"If I were a fasgadair, you'd be dead," I growled.

"What are ye doing here?" He glanced about as if I might have brought a search party. "How'd ye find me?"

"Never mind. Let's get out of here. 'Tis not safe."

"I can't go back." He slinked back down along the tree onto his rear, his eyes glazing and losing their focus on the flames.

"What are ye saying? Of course, ye can."

"Tevin was right." He tipped his face my way, tear-shiny eyes reflecting the fire. "'Twas me. I started the fire."

"What, in God's creation, are ye blatherin' on about? Don't let that sad sack of wasted flesh get in yer head. Ye didn't start any fire."

Aodan picked up a stick and stared at it, and the tip blazed. He ground it out in the dirt, then tossed it into a pile of sticks with charred ends.

The ground beneath my feet wobbled. Arms splayed, I lowered myself before I fell. Firelight flickered over his numb expression while I dragged a hand down my face. "Y–ye set Tevin's shirt on fire?"

He nodded.

"With yer mind?"

"Apparently."

Well, I never expected to hear anyone say *that*. Ever. How did one respond to such news? I waved toward the deer. "What happened to that poor creature?"

"I happened." Aodan dropped his head.

"But the beast isn't scorched. Ye didn't set it on fire."

"Nay, I turned into a mountain lion. In my anger, my instincts took over."

A thrill rose within me. Aodan had reached his totem, too? A mountain lion. Just what he wanted. "Yer a—" I stopped, squelching my excitement. This wasn't the time to celebrate. "Mountain lions only kill to feed. They don't kill out of anger."

"Aye. But then, I'm not fully a mountain lion, am I?" Raising his chin, he stared at me through glazed eyes. "I'm part man, part animal... and part demon."

CHAPTER FIFTEEN

CATALEEN

"What are ye—" My voice was getting loud. Too loud. I tiptoed across the stone floor to Ma's cracked door and peeked inside. No movement. I pulled it shut, holding the latch upright until the door was closed, then lowered the catch in place so as not to make a sound. Then I took a deep breath and returned to my seat.

Faolan poured a mug of water and pushed it across the kitchen table at me.

"Are ye trying to say Tevin was right?" I scoffed, shaking my head as if to shake his words from my mind. "How could ye suggest such a thing? And how could Aodan believe it? That dobber, Tevin, has gotten himself into his head, convincing him he's a demon."

I jabbed an accusing finger at Faolan. "You should be talking sense into him, not encouraging such horrible notions. No one starts fires with their eyes, least of all my brother. He's no demon."

Faolan grasped my hand as he did when he had no words. Under normal circumstances, the gesture comforted me, but now, it annoyed me. I shook my hand free. I needed to see Aodan and put an end to this nonsense. "Where is he?"

"Cataleen." Faolan's eyes pleaded. "There's more to tell ye."

How I hated it when he used my full name. He reserved it for rare occasions, like this, when he thought I was being unreasonable. I jammed my hands on my hips and jutted out my jaw. "You're telling me my brother, my *twin*, starts fires by looking at something. What more could ye possibly have to say?"

Faolan breathed as if a boa constrictor squeezed his torso. "Will ye please sit down? Yer making me nervous."

"Ha!" I tipped my face to the sky, grinding my teeth as if I might gnaw my emotions away. "What more?"

Everything from his slumped shoulders to his pained eyes screamed that he was hurting. And I wasn't making it easier. I blew out a frustrated breath and forced myself to sit beside him.

"He's reached his totem. He's—"

"What?" I'd barely sat before I was up again as if my seat was burning hot. "When? What is he?" My excitement dimmed, and the frustration returned. "Why didn't he tell me? Why doesn't *anyone* tell me?"

"Will ye let me speak?"

I made a stirring motion in the air to speed him up.

"He's a mountain lion."

A squeal rose within me, but Faolan's appearance and accusation reminded me this wasn't a joyous occasion. The warning in his eyes held my tongue.

"He–he killed a deer."

An image of the deer carcass reemerged. "That explains the image he sent me." Though it didn't explain why Aodan sent me the image. He usually had better control. He must've been distraught. "Why is that a problem? Isn't that what mountain lions do?"

"Aye. I imagine I could kill an animal if I were in my wolf form and hungry. But Aodan claims he didn't kill the poor beast to feed. He was scorching mad."

I worked my jaw, but nothing came out. I didn't know what to say. What to think. Except that Aodan was off his head.

"Before ye approach him, ye must understand he's vulnerable right now. Whether ye believe it or not, *he* believes he started that fire. *He* believes he killed the deer out of anger." Faolan aimed his hurt eyes at me. "*He* believes he's a demon."

✬

WE FOUND Aodan leaning against a tree by a bed of dying embers not too far from the deer carcass. I tugged a sleeve over my hand and covered my nose to block out the horrific stench. Aodan's head lolled as he blinked, reminding me of clansmen when they drank too much mead. Nay. This was worse. Much worse. With his blood-smeared face and his yellowy hair, crusty with red streaks, sticking up in every direction, he looked like he could be a demon.

How could you even think something like that, Cataleen? Even for the briefest of moments. This is Aodan. Yer twin. I prayed my thoughts hadn't leaked through the mind-link or he'd be too out of it to notice if it had.

"Cathalee?" He slurred my name, sounding like he'd drank numbing elixir meant to be applied topically.

"Aye." I approached him as if he were a cornered animal. "Faolan is telling me some tall tales. Set him straight, will ye?" A nervous laugh escaped, betraying my true feelings.

Aodan rubbed his face as if washing it without a cloth, though the bloodstains remained. He narrowed his bloodshot eyes and groaned. "Nay."

A torrent of images assaulted me—Tevin's shirt igniting, the barn ablaze, men pulling hurt bodies from the fire, harsh stares from Tevin and his father in the meetinghouse, racing through the woods on feline paws, lunging at a deer, then the dead deer. The words *devil's spawn* and *demon child* in Tevin's voice accompanied each visual.

I staggered back, my legs threatening to buckle beneath me as I struggled to process all Aodan had shown me. He was in worse shape than I'd feared. The last time he'd bombarded me like this he'd been delirious with white fever. I tried to ignore the foul smell as I knelt at his side and gripped his hand in an attempt to siphon the errant thoughts from him. "Ye are no demon, hear me?"

Aodan's face crumpled. He buried his face in my shoulder, wetting my dress as sobs rocked his body.

When had I last seen him cry? Had I ever? I pulled him closer, holding him to keep him from falling apart. His tears moistened the dried blood, staining my dress. The moment I caught Faolan's injured gaze, he dropped to Aodan's other side and crushed us in his embrace.

"Well, well. If it isn't the demon twins and their empty-headed numpty follower." Tevin's voice sent every hair on my body standing on high alert. My imbalanced emotions soured, hardening into a dark sensation I'd never experienced—hatred. Pure hatred.

I peeled myself away from my brothers and glared at Tevin, who was wielding a thick stick. Was his head full of mince? Who would be so cruel as to interrupt three grieving people with more hate? And what was he planning to do with that branch? I rose, keeping my death stare trained on him. "Away with ye."

Faolan and Aodan stirred behind me. I dared take my focus off Tevin to check on them. Faolan stood with a protective arm splayed before Aodan.

"And what are ye eejits going to do to me?" Tevin held the stick like a sword. "Set me on fire? Good. Ye'll be run out of Notirr for sure."

I wanted to smack the sneer from his ugly face.

Aodan staggered forward, pushing Faolan's resistant arm aside. "Yer fight is with me."

Tevin's gaze flickered between us all, then fell on the deer. His eyes widened, and he stepped back, lips twitching between a sick smile and a frown. Both fear and horrid glee cavorted on his face. His reaction sickened me, sending a thick sludge of hate-laced dread churning from my gut through to my extremities.

Aodan closed in on Tevin. "Ye want to have me banished? Fine. But I'll take ye out with me."

Tevin crouched, winding the club as if preparing to strike.

An image of fire filled my mind.

The stick in Tevin's hand flared. His jaw slackened. His stunned gaze flickered between us and the fire. Then he flung the flaming weapon away. Head still down, he looked up at Aodan, his sickening smile returning, making me shudder. "They'll banish ye fer sure, now."

Faolan sprinted to the flaming wood and stamped it out.

"See? Did ye see that?" Tevin screamed into the woods. He tore off into the woods, screeching. "Did ye see?"

Some village kids emerged from behind the trees and dashed through the forest on Tevin's tail.

I felt like I was drowning in ice. So that was his plan. Get Aodan to reveal his ability in front of witnesses. A new sickness pooled in my gut, sending it churning. They were sure to banish him now.

Enraged, I wheeled back to my brother. "Why? Why'd ye do that?"

Aodan, wide-eyed and innocent-looking, opened his arms. "I didn't, Cataleen." His Adam's apple bobbed. "Ye did."

CHAPTER SIXTEEN

FAOLAN

Fire-hot heat flared within me. "How can ye turn on yer own sister? Ye admitted to starting the fire with yer mind. And I believe ye. I've seen it twice now! Why drag Catty into it?"

She stared off into the empty woods, eyes wide like a deer sensing danger. Her hands shook. "I–I couldn't have." She blinked frightened purple eyes at Aodan. "Could I?"

"Of course ye didn't." I jabbed a thumb her way. "Tell her, Aodan. Tell her the truth."

Aodan's mouth gaped like a fish in need of water.

I gritted my teeth and growled. "Tell her."

"I'm telling ye it wasn't me. I've been honest about everything. I can start fires as I've shown ye. But Cataleen can, too. She showed me fire in my mind, and then the stick was in flames. She did it."

I searched Catty's frightened face. She peered through me as she sometimes did when deep in thought or speaking to Aodan through the mind-link. I waved my hands. "Are ye talking right now? Ye promised to stop doing that with me around. And especially now. I need to know what's happening."

She blinked rapidly as if returning to the present.

"We weren't using the mind-link," Aodan said.

Catty limped to a rock, lowering as she went, as if she might collapse before reaching her destination.

I rushed to her side and helped her to sit. "Are ye hurt?"

She blew a puff of air, disturbing a tuft of blonde hair. "I think Aodan's right. We're twins. If he has this strange ability, it makes sense that I would, too."

"Argh!" Every part of me tensed as I yelled through clenched teeth, fists shaking in the air. "It wasn't ye! Don't let him make ye believe it!"

"There's only one way to know for sure." Aodan squatted before her and held up a stick.

She gaped at me, her fearful eyes piercing my heart.

I flung myself between them and swatted the stick away.

"What'd ye do that for?" Aodan asked.

"Are ye daft?" I pointed a finger in his face. "What if more of Tevin's bootlickers are watchin'?"

Aodan gave a sniff. "They've all gone. We're alone. But if you'd feel better, I'll turn away. You hold the stick for her."

"Nay." I slashed a hand through the air. "That's not happening. I'll not have ye fillin' her head—"

Catty picked up another stick. "Let me try."

If only she'd listen to reason. But nay, she looked at the stick as if to set it ablaze. She squinted, glared, then slumped. "I can't. If I did it, I don't know how."

"That's because ye didn't do it." I glared at Aodan, hating myself for being so irate with my best mate. But why was he doing this? Wasn't it bad enough that he was in trouble with the elders and would likely be banished? Was he doing this in hopes they'd banish Catty, too? So he wouldn't be alone?

Aodan grasped her hand, raising the stick. "I felt yer mind. Ye sometimes use the link without meaning to when yer emotional. And ye were scorching mad... and scared. Ye sent an image of fire. Then the dobber's weapon erupted in flames." He jostled her hand, making the stick wag in her face. "Try recalling how ye felt. Imagine Tevin threatening us."

"Ugh!" I tipped my head toward the heavens as if reasoning might fall from above and restore us all.

Catty gazed at the twig with renewed fervor.

"Wait!" I marched over to Aodan and covered his eyes. "If ye want to entertain this preposterous idea, fine. But I'm not taking any chances he might start the fire."

Aodan yanked my hand down. He looked at me as if I'd ordered his execution. "You think I'd trick my sister into thinking she could do it too?"

My hand shook, and guilt nagged me like a child starved for attention. "I–I just... Humor me, will ye? If we're going to test this, let's rule out all possibilities."

He snarled and returned my hand to his eyes.

She focused on the stick. Her face twitched as her eyes morphed between squinting in intense anger and widening in complete horror. Her expression settled somewhere in between, and the tip blazed.

I lowered my hand, staring at Catty and Aodan.

He twisted the stick in the dirt, snuffing out the flame.

Tears streamed down her face. "What does this mean, Aodan? Are we truly demon spawn?"

"'Twasn't ye." But even as the words escaped me, my belief in them dwindled. "Was it?"

"It was me." She choked on a sob. "I did it."

Something inside me broke. I drew her into a tight embrace, her face against my chest as if I might squeeze the evil thoughts from her mind. Her tears dampened my shirt.

"At least *your* instinct was to go for the weapon." Aodan crouched beside the rock, pulling his knees tight to his chest, his eyes shining with unshed tears. "*I* went for his tunic."

How had things gone so terribly wrong? It seemed like just

yesterday we were dreaming of our bians. And now, Aodan was on the verge of banishment. That was almost more than I could endure. But Catty—? If she were banished, that would be the end of me.

I searched the woods in the direction Tevin had gone. What if they returned with guards to capture Aodan? What if this was the last moment I would get with my friends? My *family*.

I disentangled myself from Catty and caught her face in my hands. The despair in her eyes tore at my heart. "Listen to me. Yer *not* demon spawn. Ye understand? As yer ma says, yer children of God. We were all baptized in the Bàthadh Sea together. None on God's green earth knows ye better than I. Yer not evil. Yer the best mates a lad could ask for. More than mates. My brother and sister. If ye ask me, *Tevin* is the devil's spawn. He's doing his father's work right now. Don't let him get a foothold." I stared into Catty's wide eyes as if to force my thoughts beyond their purple depths and into her soul. "Ye understand?"

When she nodded, I released her.

"And ye?" I awaited Aodan's response.

He buried his head in his knees.

I sighed. I'd have to work on convincing him later. Right now, we needed to get out of here. "We should go. That clipe will fetch his father."

Aodan's head snapped up.

The sun was rising through the trees.

"Let's go to the meetinghouse." I rolled my neck side to side to release the tight kinks, then scrubbed a hand over my face. "Someone should be there. 'Tis better to bring this situation to the elders than to have Lorcan and his bootlickers drag us through the village."

Aodan gripped his hair as he ran his hand through it. "What if they catch me on the way? Should I transform into my totem and meet you in the woods by the meetinghouse?"

"Good idea." I retrieved my satchel from behind the tree. "Take the path through the north woods. I'll take yer clothes and meet ye at the gate."

Aodan held up a hand. "Listen, they're only after me. Tevin thinks

I started that fire. He doesn't know about Cataleen. Please... Let's keep it that way. We'll tell the elders the truth. But let's not share that little detail? Let them think I started the second fire, too."

Catty stepped toward her brother, her arm reaching for him. "But they—"

Aodan dodged her. "I mean it, Cataleen. If ye want me to meet the elders, those are my terms. No one finds out about yer ability. If ye don't agree to this, I'll leave now."

She lowered her arm. "Fine." She then pointed a finger, her eyes fierce. "If they ask me directly, I'll not lie."

It must be true. She must've started the fire for Aodan to insist she not tell. I should have known better. My friend would never betray his sister. I cursed myself for believing the worst, even for a spell.

I pointed toward the stream. "Wash up first. As best ye can."

Tevin's complaints were nothing but hogwash. But now, with the fire and witnesses, who knew what the elders might do?

CHAPTER SEVENTEEN

CATALEEN

I struggled to force my feet down the path to the elders' meetinghouse. The building repelled me like a reverse magnet. The nearer I drew, the greater the force pushed me away. I couldn't face the judgment that was sure to meet us there. What would the elders think of Aodan's appearance? We'd gotten most of the blood off his skin, out of his hair, but his clothes... If only we could have gone home to change first. But we couldn't risk being found by the wrong person.

God, please don't let the elders judge us wrongly.

Faolan climbed the steps, raised a hand to knock, then turned back as if waiting for us to stop him. While his hand remained poised midair, the door opened.

Quin rubbed his short red beard and gave us a half smile. Weary eyes, slumped shoulders, and mussed hair aged him. He widened the gap to let us through.

I followed the boys inside, then plowed into Aodan's back. When I peered over his shoulder, all the elders sat around the table appearing exhausted. Each plastered their face with a reassuring smile. But it failed to work on me. What were they all doing here? Had they been here all night?

Something was up. Warning fires blazed throughout my body.

I didn't remember sitting, but there I was, with Aodan beside me and all the elders around us. As an invisible weight pressed against my chest, I fought to breathe. I squeezed my brother's hand beneath the table, hoping I provided comfort. But I needed *his*. My other hand felt empty. Cold. Though I could've used Faolan's comforting presence, Aodan needed him more. Faolan draped a protective arm across Aodan's shoulders.

Sully smiled, and the air cleared, making my breath come easier. Peace and calm emanated from him, and I soaked up what I could. But even Sully couldn't eliminate my anxious thoughts.

Quin closed the door without a sound. "Yer mother should be along any moment. But I want to ease yer minds by telling ye Tevin and his father will not be at this meeting."

"How did ye know to be here?" Faolan asked.

The door squeaked on its hinges, and Ma appeared in the entryway. Her crooked shawl tumbled from her shoulders. She took a deep breath and threw us a worried smile as she approached.

Quin rose. "Mirna, so glad ye made it." He motioned to a seat at the end of the table. "Please have a seat."

"You've never posted guards outside before." Her smile morphed into a nervous thing I'd never seen on her face. "Is that necessary?"

"I'm afraid so." Quin took a seat beside Sully.

Guards? I hadn't noticed guards. Judging from Aodan's and Faolan's faces, they hadn't either.

Ma's nose twitched as if stifling a sneeze... or tears.

Sully cleared his throat. "First, let's pray." He folded his hand and closed his eyes. "Father, Almighty God, thank Ye for being here with us during these difficult times. Please open our hearts and minds to understand the plans Ye've set before us and be willing participants in those plans. Protect us from the evil one. Amen."

Quin steepled his freckled fingers. "None of this comes as any surprise. God has a plan to deal with the fasgadair. This is part of that plan."

Fasgadair? What did this have to do with fasgadair? I searched Aodan's and Faolan's surprised expressions.

"Aye." Sully nodded.

"Last night, each elder had a dream that roused us from our sleep and prompted us to meet here." Quin searched the other elders and received a wide-eyed nod from each one. "Sully was already here." He laughed. "Waiting for us. This is the first I've experienced or heard of such an occurrence. God gave each of us a dream, affirming what Sully has been attempting to get us to believe. He's known about this for a long time. When did this revelation first come to ye, Sully? Since yer twenty-first year?"

"Aye." Sully tugged his long, whitening beard.

I sucked in a breath. How, in God's creation, was our battle with Tevin and an ability to start fires part of God's plan? What did it have to do with the fasgadair? And how did Sully know about it for so long? Since before our birth?

Quin scratched mussy hair. "Yesterday, the elders unanimously decided to banish Lorcan and Tevin."

A weight I hadn't realized had been pressing down on me lifted, and I felt as if I might float away. Aodan's and Faolan's eyes reflected similar feelings.

"But"—Quin sliced a hand through the air as if to cut off the relief connecting us—"regardless of the provocation, Aodan started a fire that resulted in casualties. And he possesses an ability that rightfully concerns many villagers and causes excessive discomfort among the community."

The weight returned, pressing my shoulders down. My brothers blanched.

Quin closed his eyes and heaved a heavy sigh. "For these reasons, we must banish Aodan as well."

I SAT ON THE PIER. My place of solace. But I found no relief. My heart ached more than I'd ever thought possible. It throbbed as if something had smashed it.

But then, something had.

They knew how awful Tevin and his father were. They banished them. Why banish Aodan too? He didn't throw the flaming shirt onto a bale of hay, then run away like a coward. He fought the flames all night. He'd had no idea he could start fires, or he would have controlled his ability. Plus, there would be no fire, no deaths, if Tevin hadn't provoked him. None of this would have happened.

Tevin. This was all. His. Fault.

And what about me? Whatever Aodan was, I was too.

Where was he? Why had Faolan stopped me from following him when he darted off after the meeting?

The sun dipped below the tree line at my back, casting a gray hue over the ocean.

Gray... like my heart.

This was our last night together. Aodan's banishment would come in the morn. How could we spend our last moments apart?

Footsteps sounded on the boards, rocking the pier.

"I thought ye'd be here." Faolan stooped beside me with two packs over his shoulders and two cloth-covered plates.

"Have ye found him?"

"Aye. He missed dinner. So, I'm bringing him some food." He thrust a plate toward me. "I've some for ye too."

I had no appetite. And the packs Faolan carried made my stomach threaten to regurgitate my last meal. I pushed the plate away. "Why do you have packs with you?"

"He doesn't want to wait until morn and leave with an audience. He plans to slip away tonight."

"Tonight?" I jumped up. Tears I thought I'd used up sprang to my eyes. "He can't. It's—"

"Shh." Faolan set the plates down and gripped my arms. "Do ye blame him?"

I recalled the only other time I'd seen a clan member banished. Roarke. He'd nearly killed his wife. He *had* killed their unborn child. Most of the village attended. Some as witnesses. Some, like me, out of curiosity. But all celebrated his departure.

Would those Tevin and Lorcan infected with their hate-filled words show up to celebrate? To sneer? I shuddered. I didn't want that for Aodan. It would break me. More than I'd already broken.

Hot tears burst through my sore, puffy eyes. I covered my face in my hands. "Why is he being treated this way? Aodan isn't a murderer."

"I know." Faolan wrapped his arms around me. "But if ye want to see him before he leaves, ye best come with me now."

CHAPTER EIGHTEEN

FAOLAN

Catty and I found Aodan on the log where I'd left him.

"Here." I handed him the plate.

He uncovered the food and picked up a buttered roll. Based on his pale face and listless eyes as he took a bite, he didn't want to eat. But he didn't know when his next meal would come.

"Yer mum let me gather some things." I dropped the satchels, then sat beside him. "There's clothes, extra food, a knife, hatchet, rope, and other things she thought ye might need... balms and such."

Catty gave a strangled sound, her tear-streaked face twisting up. But, surely, she wasn't upset with me for overstepping my bounds by gathering his things rather than asking her to do it. It was the right thing to do. She was strong. But not that strong. Not when it came to being separated from her twin.

"Yer ma wants me to plead with you to see her one last time."

He shook his head. Tears slipped down his face, wetting the bread lodged in his mouth.

"I knew ye wouldn't. Deep down, she knows it, too. She's also concerned how villagers might treat ye. But she wanted ye to know she loves ye. Her heart and prayers are with ye." I tried to shake the image of their ma in her broken state. "Sully approached me and said the same. He knew ye wouldn't be there in the morn."

Aodan let out a huff of a laugh—a good omen. He gulped his food. "Why are there two packs? Did my ma make ye bring me that much? I can't carry both."

I threw Catty a sideways glance and steeled myself for her response. "I'm going with ye."

"What?" Her puffy eyes gawked.

Here it was. The moment I'd feared more than heading out into the unknown fasgadair-infested world. I gripped her shoulders and skewered her with a look that begged her understanding. "Think about it, Cataleen. Ye have yer mum. Yer clan." I nodded to Aodan. "He's all alone. I can't leave him."

"I agree."

Her calm unnerved me. Still, I relaxed my hold. She wasn't going to fight?

She stiffened. "I'm coming too."

Aodan nearly dumped his plate in his haste to set it aside and rush to her. "Is yer head full of mince? Yer not coming with us, ye hear? 'Tis not safe out there."

"Aye. Yet ye expect me to let ye go out there without me?"

"Faolan and I can handle whatever comes our way together. Besides, I can start fires with my mind. If fasgadair attack, they're dead. I'll burn them, then chop off their heads. We can defend ourselves."

I expected Aodan to be grateful for my companionship. But he sounded a bit too confident. Far more confident than I felt, which was not at all. But the two of us facing the world together eased the sting of his banishment, for me anyway.

"I can too," she said.

"Be reasonable, sister. Would ye be able to set anyone on fire? Even a fasgadair?"

"I almost set Tevin on fire."

"No, ye didn't." He laughed. "Ye set the stick on fire. And ye didn't know what ye were doing. Do ye think ye could set any living thing on fire... on purpose? Even if it is partially dead?"

Catty turned her pleading eyes to me as if I'd fight for her to join us. Not a chance. "What if everyone finds out I can start fires, too? What if they banish me and yer not here to leave with me? What if I have to leave... alone?"

Sake! I hadn't thought of that. I raked a hand through my hair. If only I could split myself in half and leave part of me here.

"What if... what if... what if... Life is full of what-ifs." Aodan clutched Catty's head as if to squeeze out the mince. "That's not gonna happen. Tevin will be gone. Nothing will prompt ye to start a fire."

"What if I start one accidentally?"

"Ye won't."

She yanked her hands from Aodan. "How can ye be so sure?"

He clamped his forehead. A sure sign he was losing his patience. "We're twins! Ye don't think Lorcan's supporters will hassle me?"

Aodan growled. "I swear it, Cataleen—if ye don't let me go, I'm going to run away from ye when ye turn yer back."

She stepped back as if stung. "Ye wouldn't."

"Would you like to put a wager on it?" He dipped his shoulders. "And I hate to say this, but ye haven't reached yer bian. We may need to switch to our totems to survive. What will we do with ye in human form?"

Her wounded look deepened. I wanted to comfort her, but if Aodan's biting remarks kept her home, I couldn't minimize the wound.

"Just do as I ask and stay. Ye can't leave Ma. She needs ye."

"She has the village." Catty's weak voice revealed her heart. She was giving up the fight.

"'Tis not the same, and ye know it. She's already lost Da." Seeming to sense his win, Aodan moved in for the kill. "Do you think she can bear to lose both her children in one day?"

Fresh tears pooled in her bloodshot eyes.

He pulled her into a hug. "I love ye. Yer my sister. That'll never change. But I can't have ye following me. Yer needed here."

CHAPTER NINETEEN

CATALEEN

The agony of everything breaking within me had settled into a numbness. I no longer felt like me. Rather, I floated outside myself, yet somehow maintained some control.

It wasn't fair. Either Ma lost her entire family or I lost my brothers. Once they were gone, I'd never know what became of them. Where would they go? No other clan would accept them. Would they survive on their own? Would they survive the fasgadair?

I couldn't keep thinking about it. As desperately as I wanted to go with them, they were right. I couldn't leave Ma. She needed me more.

If only I could stay connected to them. A shard like broken glass pierced the numbness. "We should have tested the mind-link. We don't know how far it reaches."

Aodan kissed my cheek, something he never did, making this feel like a real goodbye. "I'll reach out to you every day. I'm stronger than you. I'll practice. Even if you can't reply, I'll keep talking to you, in case you can hear me."

The way his eyes shone killed me. Why did he seem confident, like he was excited to leave, as though it was an adventure and not a banishment? "This isn't a vacation to some exotic land, Aodan. Yer leaving me, yer leaving Ma. Forever. We'll never see ye again."

The pain returned to his eyes. I kicked myself for doing that to him, but I also needed to know he wasn't happy to leave me.

He hung his head. "I know."

"So why do ye seem so eager to leave?"

"I'm not. I–I have to make the best of this, Cataleen. Ye understand, don't ye?" Head still ducked, he peered up through tousled yellow hair, pleading with me.

I was being selfish. This was bigger than us. Bigger than Tevin and Lorcan. Bigger than the elders, even Sully. This was God. For whatever reason, God was allowing this to happen. This was harder for Aodan than for me. I had to make this bearable for him.

I threw my arms around him and clung as if I could hold him there forever. Then I let him go. "This is God's plan. You'll be okay."

Aodan finished his meal, and Faolan helped him clean my plate, too. Faolan replaced the coverings on the empty plates, then shoved them into his pack. We skirted the border of Notirr through the woods in silence until the main gate came into view across the clearing.

Faolan nodded toward it. "You should go back now."

No! Not yet! Tears spilled down my face as my brothers hugged me. "I–I'm holding y–ye to yer promise. Reach out to me e–every day."

I will. Aodan caught hold of my shoulders, and images of shared memories bombarded me. Me covered in porridge after I'd tripped while carrying my bowl. Ma doing a little dance in our kitchen. Faolan racing about a field trying to catch a chicken that escaped the coop. Cahal's baby sister taking her first wobbly steps. And the three of us—me, Faolan, and Aodan—splashing each other in the ocean. I remembered that day. We'd just finished our chores, and it was so hot. We jumped in, fully dressed, off the pier into the cool ocean without stopping home for our bathing clothes. I said something that set Aodan off, and he used both his hands to make a wall, pushing the water at me in a gigantic wave. Then Faolan and I retaliated. That's always the way it was—Aodan and me fighting and Faolan jumping in to aid me. But we were all having such fun dousing each other, it didn't matter. I would remember this day. I would remember them all and keep them close to my heart no matter how far they traveled, even if Aodan could no longer reach me. He was with me.

After one last hug, I kissed them both on the cheek, then ran toward the gate, sobbing.

CHAPTER TWENTY

FAOLAN

Aodan and I had never ventured far from Notirr's gates. Occasional hikes to help fell trees or hunt. We'd done all these things within mere cubits of our home. We'd never even traveled as far as Kylemore, barely more than a day's walk north. Though the fasgadair threat was minimal this far north, people rarely traveled between the villages.

If only Kylemore were an option now. But, as part of the Co-Cheangail, allowing us in would be like harboring criminals, threatening the alliance.

No, Kylemore wasn't a choice. Neither was Ardara. We were on our own.

We walked in silence, increasing the distance between ourselves and our home, Catty, their ma, my da. My heart sank further with each step.

I wanted to put as much distance between us and Notirr before Lorcan and Tevin's banishment in the morn. But my calves burned, and a hitch formed in my side. "What's yer plan?"

Aodan glanced over his shoulder. "I'm heading east to the Somalta Caverns."

That came as a surprise. We'd never talked about going there. "Why?"

He shrugged. "I don't know where else to go. We can't go to any gachen villages. Gnuatthara is too far. They wouldn't accept us anyway, scrawny as we are. The fasgadair have taken over Diabalta. They must occupy the City of Nica, too. At least in the caverns, we might find shelter. There's running water from the river, so there should be plenty to hunt."

Impressive. "You've given this a lot of thought."

He shrugged again.

"How do ye know which way is east without the sun? Yer granda?" I remembered little of the twins' granda. But, as a fisherman, he knew how to navigate using the stars. Catty and Aodan had tried teaching me, but I couldn't see patterns in those random lights like they could.

"Aye." He stopped and pointed to the sky. "Do ye remember the stars Cataleen and I taught ye... the saucepan?"

"Aye." I stared at the stars, uncertain how to find that pattern.

"It's easy to find. See the handle?" His fingers traced the stars.

I tried to follow.

"It connects to the pan. It's high in the sky, facing down."

The pattern emerged. "I see it."

"See the two stars at the end of the pan? Not the handle."

"Aye."

"Use those two stars to form a line. Follow the line. See that dim star they point to?"

"I think so."

"That star never changes. It always points north. If we keep that star to our right, we know we're traveling west, straight for the Somalta Caverns."

"Incredible."

"Aye." Facing west, he resumed his trek. "That also tells me it's just after midnight. See how much you could've learned from us if you'd paid attention?"

We'd never needed such tricks before. We'd never traveled by night or ventured too far from home. But explaining how to read the stars seemed to lighten his mood. I didn't want to say anything to dampen it again.

I fell back in line behind him, dreading the long walk ahead. Then it clicked. "Ye know, this might be easier in our totem forms. As a wolf and a mountain lion, we can hunt and travel much faster."

As my excitement grew, Aodan stopped. "Right. I don't know why I didn't think of that."

"Probably because we've hardly had time with our totem forms. And we've had a lot on our minds." A thrill coursed through me at the idea of running as a wolf with my best mate, a mountain lion, by my side.

He must have felt the same. A grin crinkled up his cheeks as he pulled off his shirt.

We undressed, tossed our clothes into our packs, slung the satchels across our backs, then shifted into our animal forms and took off through the woods on all fours.

CHAPTER TWENTY-ONE

CATALEEN

I sat on Aodan's cold bed, ran my fingers over his folded bedding, and reached out for him—again.

Nothing.

Aodan had never been so far or so shut off that I couldn't sense him. Never. Had he tried to reach out? Was he too far away? He promised.

Ma came in and sat beside me. The mattress sank, tipping me toward her.

She wrapped an arm around me and kissed my head. "Ready to go, me bairn?"

I would never be ready, but I allowed her to guide me out of the house. My feet plodded after her along the path to the crowd gathering within the main gate—to the banishing. I struggled to see through puffy eyes. My weary mind screamed, begging my feet to stop, desiring nothing more than to turn around. I never wanted to see Tevin or his nasty father again, even to watch justice delivered. The elders' justice didn't bring peace. My enemies' banishment wouldn't bring Aodan or Faolan back. They were—

Gone.

A fresh wave of sobs threatened to overwhelm me. Welling tears blurred my already poor vision.

Ma's hazy form paused. She grasped my hand and guided me through unrecognizable people. They faced me with muddled expressions. Hands patted my arms, my back. Voices carrying words meant to comfort jumbled together, forming incoherent sentences.

I wanted to scream at Aodan. Why hadn't he reached out to me? I sought him out, yet again. Nothing but emptiness met me.

Everything reminded me of my loss. And now, I'd have to face the culprits who were as good as murderers. No punishment would soothe my aching soul.

A sizable crowd made it difficult to get any closer. I pressed my sleeve to my sore eyes to clear my vision. Had the entire village made an appearance? Never had I seen so many people at once, not even for meal gatherings. Ma pulled me through the crowd to Cahal.

The sight of him was like a salve, soothing the sting of my fresh wounds. "Cahal."

He wore a sleeveless tunic, torn to fit a bandage across his shoulder. Wounds that hadn't quite healed yet covered his face and arms. He looked like I felt—battle worn.

"They released you from the infirmary?" I wrapped my arms around his wide waist, hoping I wasn't hurting any unseen injuries. "I'm so sorry we didn't visit more. You were always asleep when we did. So much has happened."

He patted my back with his giant hand and offered a comforting smile that held no bitter feelings.

"But ye?" I leaned back to see his face, my heart breaking that we hadn't consoled him after his father's death. And now, he'd never get to say goodbye to his mates. I buried my face in his tunic as he rubbed my back, the rough linen muffling my words. "I'm so, so sorry."

"Here they come!" someone shouted.

I peeled myself away from Cahal and swiped at my tears. We were close enough to hear. Yet far enough away and at a high enough elevation to see over the horde. The elders stood together outside the open gate.

The murmurs rose to a deafening rumble. Head held high, Lorcan sauntered toward the gate with Tevin in tow. Tevin cowered, stepping on his father's heels as if attempting to jump into his shoes and hide. Lorcan sneered at Tevin each time his son trod on him, but otherwise held it together. The mass parted as they neared, then filled as they passed, like beò feur.

A memory intruded of us as children, mucking about a field of beò feur, trying to stomp on the creatures that looked like blades of grass. An impossible goal. Those wee critters were swift. They'd sink into the ground just before we landed. If only we could make the sun go in reverse, shrink in age, reclaim those times when we had no other cares and nothing was of any real consequence.

I cast the image out like a worm on a hook, searching for Aodan's mind. But I came back with nothing. Again.

I choked on a rising sob. Fists clenched, a fierce desire to destroy the offenders washed over me. Cahal rested his arm on my shoulder, the weight of it somehow comforting.

Lorcan clasped his hands behind his back. Chest out. Chin high. Oh, how I wanted to smack that haughtiness from his face.

Tevin disturbed the dirt with his toes.

I almost felt pity for him. Almost.

"Notirr clan," Quin shouted, then waited for the crowd to hush. "We, yer appointed elders, have the unfortunate task of following through with three banishments today—Lorcan Grear, son of Shanley Grear; Tevin Grear, son of Lorcan Grear; and Aodan Tuama, son of Brayan Tuama. As you can see, only two of the three are present. We've received word that Aodan Tuama left last night."

"Coward!" someone shouted.

My neck snapped toward the shout. Who would dare say that? These were Aodan's people. Aodan's clan. Where was their remorse at losing an innocent member?

As if sensing my desire to smack the inconsiderate fool, Cahal pressed down on my shoulder, keeping me rooted.

"We shall begin with Aodan Tuama, who stands accused of igniting the fire resulting in the death of three clan members with several injured, the barn destroyed, and crops lost. Firsthand witnesses cannot account for the fire, but the limited evidence and an accusation point to Aodan. No witnesses have come forth to discount this accusation. Though he aided the village in extinguishing the fire, the indication that he was the initial cause cannot go ignored. After consulting God, we, yer elders, have found him guilty."

The crowd erupted, shaking their fists and shouting ugly words. What if I accidentally started a fire? I had the same twisted ability. And less control. I should have left with them. I wasn't safe here.

Quin pumped his palm in the air as if to squash the noise. "Next to face banishment is Tevin Grear, son of Lorcan Grear. Tevin stands accused of spreading the fire and fleeing the scene. After consulting God, we, yer elders, have found him guilty."

The decision revived the crowd's ire. This time, I shared their animosity toward the accused.

Quin waited for the villagers to quiet once more. "Last is Lorcan Grear, son of Shanley Grear. Lorcan stands accused of failing to control his son, resulting in the fire, and for behavior rendering him a danger to the clan. We have witnessed and listened to accusations regarding hateful speech, harmful rumors spread, and violent behavior. We have met with Lorcan several times over the years. During such meetings, the elders have seen no repentance nor remorse for any damage caused. Such damage includes poisoning minds within our community against other members and violent behavior, which led to the barn fire. After consulting God, we, yer elders, have found him guilty."

Malina stepped forward. "God, who oversees us, the elders whom you have appointed, has made His will clear. Therefore, we proclaim our united decision before the accused, before you, and before God. Aodan Tuama, Tevin Grear, and Lorcan Grear are henceforth without a clan. Unlike visitors who we'd treat with hospitality which pleases our Lord, we are not to allow them to return, even as guests, until true repentance is revealed."

Declan straightened to project his voice. "Let their banishment serve as a warning. Those who torment others or spread hateful rumors, thus poisoning our peaceful community, will not go unpunished."

Quin and the elders turned to Tevin and his father. "Do ye understand the terms of yer banishment?"

"Aye." Lorcan gave a firm nod. His prideful smirk widened.

Eyes downcast, Tevin wobbled a nod.

"Then our sentencing is complete." Quin held a fist over his heart and bowed. "God be with ye."

The elders moved through the open gate. Two guards closed it behind them with a clang. The crowd parted as they passed. The villagers followed the elders in eerie silence.

Faolan's father passed by, hunched over, hobbling as if a horse had thrown him. When his gaze fell on me, the weary sadness pooling within crushed my already broken spirit. He grasped my hand, squeezed it, and half smiled... probably the most comforting smile he could summon, then released me, and shuffled away.

Quin approached. "I know this is a difficult day, and I'm loathe to ask for anything more of ye. But Sully has called a meeting of the elders. He'd like us to meet in my home with both of ye."

"Of course." Ma reached for me.

I dodged her hand. "Can I... have a moment?"

She tipped her head as if about to argue, then changed her mind. "Don't be long."

Tevin followed his father down the road, daring a glance to his former home over his shoulder. Did he see me standing with Cahal on the hill? Did he care that he'd torn my family apart? Taken Cahal's father from him? If my heart weren't too broken over my brother and Faolan, I might have felt sorry for him. What kind of kid would he be if someone other than Lorcan had raised him? Perhaps he wouldn't have turned out so rotten. And what would life be like for him now, the only person left for Lorcan to torment? There would be no one for Tevin to take his frustrations out on.

Had Aodan and Faolan gotten enough of a head start that they wouldn't come across them? Who knew what they'd do without the village holding them accountable.

And how Aodan might respond.

The criminals made their way around the bend. Out of my life forever. Just like my brothers.

※

I CLUNG to Ma on the wooden couch. Undignified. Yes. But I didn't care. I was broken. Only her grip held me together. My heart ached more than I'd have believed possible. My brother and my best friend—nay, my *brothers*—were gone. Just gone. Forever. Insufficiently armed, venturing dangerous, unknown territory where only God knew what would happen to them.

Sully sat in the rocker by the window. His calm body melted into the curved back. The other elders filed in, one at a time, each sharing their condolences and apologies.

Cahal's massive form passed by the window, casting a shadow across the room as he went. The bandages over his shoulder flapped like a flag, heralding him.

I flinched. Here I was feeling sorry for myself when he was nursing physical wounds from a fire that had taken his father's life. And Cahal had been powerless to save him despite his heroic efforts.

His heavy fist rattled the door.

"Pardon me." Quin rose from his seat to open the door. "Cahal, I see you've brought me a visitor. To what might I owe this pleasure?"

"He asked to see an elder."

"I have a gift for you," came a gruff voice with a strange accent.

"Well, let's have a look, shall we?" Quin opened the door, and a small man with long red hair and a beard to match strolled into our midst. Although the size of a child, he appeared to be a full-grown man. I'd never seen such a small adult in my life.

Cahal's shadow fell on us once again as he turned back down the path.

"Cahal is a man of few words and an intimidating sight, but he is a kind soul," Quin said. "I hope ye don't mind. The clan elders are here."

"My apologies." The wee man bowed. "I don't mean to intrude."

"No worries, my friend. 'Tis no imposition. Join us."

The stranger squinted as the elders greeted him. He bowed and thumped his chest twice.

I tensed as he approached, tightening my grip on Ma. She replied with silent assurance by stroking my hair and kissing my head.

"Please have a seat." Quin dragged another wooden chair into the room.

The chair was too big for the tiny man. He had to hoist himself up to sit, and his feet dangled above the floor.

"Welcome, Pepin," Sully greeted him. How did he know his name? I had never seen him in the village. "I'm called Sully."

Now I was even more confused. If Sully knew him, why was he introducing himself? The wee man's face twitched, appearing as confused as I was.

Quin handed Pepin a drink and sat in a chair across from him. "What is this gift you speak of? It must be important. Pech keep to themselves. I've only met one once."

A pech? I hadn't heard much about pech or given them much thought. They weren't a myth? An invented creature to straighten up wayward children like giants, selkie, or the Bogle? Pepin tugged something—a stone—from around his neck.

"Is this the amulet?" Quin took the stone.

"Aye." Sully's voice came out thin, as if he barely breathed. "'Tis Drochaid."

Drochaid? A tingling sensation swept over me as if countless feathers tickled me at once, making me itch. Was I witnessing one of

Sully's prophecies come true? Was I in the midst of a momentous event in God's plans?

"This will allow travel between realms?" Quin asked.

"It should, but I haven't tested it yet." Pepin tipped his head to further show his uncertainty, then narrowed his eyes at Sully. "Nor have I named it."

"God named it. And I'm sure it will work. We'll need Pepin to show us how to use it to save Cataleen from Aodan." Sully nodded toward me, and my breath caught.

Save me... from *Aodan*? That was the most preposterous thing I'd ever heard. My brother wouldn't hurt me. What, in God's creation, was Sully blathering about?

"Well." Folding his hands in his lap, Quin leaned back. "I don't know why these things still amaze me. Pepin, you must be an important man of God for Him to use you like this."

Pepin smiled, relaxing in his seat.

"If Sully is correct"—Quin gave Sully a knowing smile—"and, as a prophet who speaks for God, he usually is, we need your help. Will you join us?"

As Pepin looked each elder in the eyes, his countenance grew as if he'd just received a boost. "I'd be honored."

What were they all talking about? I released Ma and pushed my hair from my face. What did the elders and Pepin seem to understand? Was this how others felt when Aodan and I used our mind-link?

I reached for him once more. But he was either too far away or blocking me. Either way, I couldn't handle not finding him. Again. Without his continual presence beside me or in my mind, I felt dead. Just dead.

"Cataleen." Sully rocked forward, his gray, pupil-less eyes trained on me. "You must have many questions."

Did I? I loved and trusted Sully. He'd proven himself to me and my clan over and over again. He was a man of God. A prophet. He knew things no created being could know. If he believed Aodan was a threat to me, did I want to know?

CHAPTER TWENTY-TWO

FAOLAN

A cave? I hardly dared hope this one might make a suitable shelter for the long term. After we'd traveled for weeks during the rainy season, the constant precipitation was dampening my mood, along with my clothes. I wanted nothing more than a dry place to sleep and air out my things.

"This is perfect!" Aodan rushed toward the craggy opening in the rocky wall. Unlike mine, his attitude seemed to improve every day.

"We don't know that yet. It's off the ravine. There could be water inside. The roof might not be stable. There might be something else occupying it already."

He scowled at me. "Well, aren't you the pleasant traveling companion?"

Set back from a beach with an opening high enough water shouldn't be an issue, this *might* be habitable. Before entering, I pushed to ensure it was as solid as it seemed. The last thing we needed was to be crushed in our sleep. Inside, it opened up, providing plenty of space. We couldn't stand upright, but we could crouch or walk on our knees and have plenty of headroom. Aodan lit a stick to search the back of the cave, proving it dry and unoccupied, with no visible openings where anything worrisome might hide. In the flickering light, his face radiated, and I allowed his optimism to indwell me.

"What's this?" Aodan shuffled to the front of the cave beside the entrance.

I hurried to his side.

He pushed the burning stick into a hole and peered inside. "A stove?"

I swept my fingers along a flat surface above the hole. They came back black, grimy with soot. Aodan stuck the blazing stick toward the back of the stove, above the cooking surface. The stick disappeared into another hole. We gaped at each other, then jostled in our haste to search outside the cave and confirm our suspicions. Sure enough, we found a small opening, a chimney.

Was this good fortune to find a place with a stove to cook? Or bad luck to happen upon someone else's dwelling? The stove was cold, and the place was empty. No evidence indicated it had been occupied recently. Still, it belonged to someone.

Aodan set about unpacking his bag. "After we lay out our things, let's gather some wood for a fire so they can dry."

I dropped my pack and worked at the straps. "What if the owner returns?"

He groaned. "You're becoming a crabbit old man."

"Am not. Just concerned."

"Well, shove yer concern. This is God's provision."

I studied him as he unrolled his bedding. He seemed serious. I hadn't heard him mention one bit about God in a good while. Was that where his confidence came from? God? When had we switched roles? When had he become the trusting one?

And what had happened to my faith?

I dared allow a small portion of his faith to take root. How else could we have come across such a perfect dwelling? It had all we needed. And fresh water in the river outside our door meant fish. "Perhaps you're right. Maybe it is God's provision."

Aodan's grin faltered as his gaze flicked to the entryway. "We should make a door and attach something to alert of intruders."

We finished unpacking and set about looking for wood for a fire and a door. Small twigs and branches strewn about the banks meant there must be trees nearby. Or the river carried them. Most were wet.

"We'll need more wood than this to keep a decent fire. We need to find trees... and a place to hunt."

"We can fish," he said.

"Aye, but if we're to make a home of it here, we should find other sources of food." I searched above, but all I saw were walls of rock. "I didn't see any paths off the ravine along our way, did ye?"

"If someone else found this to be a suitable place to build a stove, there must be something." He beckoned me. "Let's follow the ravine a ways."

We continued along the winding river and neared a break in the rocky ledge. Were those stairs? Sure enough, someone had cut the rock into steps. I crouched to inspect one. "Do you see this?"

"Who made this?" He raked a hand through his blond hair.

So my vision wasn't failing me. Nor was my mind... yet. I rubbed my face, unsure what to think of such a bizarre and unnatural phenomenon, like the stove.

"Some of our clan have abilities to manipulate soil. The Arlen have abilities with trees. Can any clans manipulate stone?" he asked.

"So close to Notirr?" I mentally flipped through all the information I knew about the clans. "Not likely. Besides, we'd have learned of it in our schooling and the history of the Co-Cheangail."

"Then who could have done this?" He touched the stones. "They're mossy and worn."

The moss appeared undisturbed. "Doesn't look like anyone's been here in some time."

He made his way up a few steps. "Let's see where it leads."

I held back. "'Tis going to be dark soon. We should get to the cave and explore this in the morn."

"Nah. I want to see this." Aodan bounded up the steps, slipping on the moss, then disappeared around the corner.

"Aodan!" Groaning, I followed my headstrong friend. I had to skip steps as I climbed. They were too small to take one at a time. The moss added some traction, except when it gave way, making me slip. We kept rounding corners only to find more stairs. "How far does this thing go?"

Birdcalls sounded up ahead. The rock wall opened to a wooded area. Exactly what we were looking for. But how? Even if this place existed to serve someone else before us, how, in all of Ariboslia, had we happened upon it?

This was no coincidence. God was looking out for us.

Excited, we tore off our clothes and shifted into our animal forms to hunt. We raced through the rocky forest at speeds my human form could never achieve. Aodan matched my speed, appearing in my periphery in breaks in the trees. Though our totems weren't animals that got on well together, because of our humanity, we'd learned to stifle our totem's instincts so we could join forces and take down larger prey, something a wolf couldn't do on its own. I needed a pack. As a mountain lion, Aodan didn't rely on others to help him hunt. But he was kind enough to assist me.

I caught a familiar scent and stopped. Deer. Saliva dripped from my jowls. I motioned to Aodan with my head, then tracked the animal. It was close.

Crouching low behind the brush, we watched the animals graze. A small herd. He circled around, dragging his belly along the ground in his low crawl. I gave him a few minutes to get into position, then darted into the clearing, snarling. The herd shot off, bouncing like neas in their annoying zigzag way. I nipped at the heels of one. Then Aodan burst from the trees, soaring through the air in an impressive leap, claws ready. He landed on the poor creature, sinking his jaws into its neck.

I sat by the fire, inhaled the wonderful aroma of cooking meat, and chomped down on my steak. I chewed and wiped the dripping juices from my chin. This place was too good to be true. Shelter with a stove. Running water. A nearby forest with deer. "Don't you wonder how the deer found their way into the woods? They're surrounded by mountains. It's almost as if they're penned."

Aodan shrugged as he ripped meat from bone.

A strange scent wafted my way, intermingling with the savory scents. It straightened the hairs on the back of my neck. I felt sluggish—woozy. Was it from the smell? I stiffened, searching up and down the ravine. "Do you smell that?"

Aodan stopped chewing and sniffed. He raised an eyebrow and gulped his half-chewed mouthful. "Smell what?"

"It smells like—"

Something crunched the ground behind us. "Smells good. Mind if I have some?"

Alarm bells rang throughout me, but my body refused to respond. Something rooted me to the spot as if the air had wound itself around me, pinning me. I fought to reach my knife's hilt at my hip, but my hand wouldn't move.

What was happening?

A cloaked figure slipped from the shadows, appearing as a pale face hovering in the darkness with grotesque eyes showing no whites at all. Nothing but a deep blue that almost appeared black.

A fasgadair. It had to be. Did it have me under some kind of spell?

My heavy feet shuffled away at a pathetic pace. A newborn could outrun me.

"Or perhaps not." The creature sneered, licking its thin lips. "Gachen blood tastes much sweeter."

I hadn't seen the creature move, yet powerful arms wrapped around me, squeezing my lungs. I fought to breathe. Demon breath moistened my neck. Something sharp touched my skin. This was it. The beast was going to bite me. This was how I'd die.

Orange light blazed. The air warmed. Too warm. Flames licked the creature's back. It screeched and released me, its wide eyes glowing yellow.

Aodan had set it on fire.

Scorching pain radiated from my arms and chest. I peeled my gaze from the fiery demon to find flames licking me as well. The force immobilizing me lifted, and I dropped to the ground, squashing the fire in the dirt.

The monster's screams cut short. It fell to its knees, then pitched forward, sinking its face into the pebbly beach.

I stood and dusted myself off. My tattered shirt was nothing but singed holes. My skin was a little red, but nothing the twins' mum's balms wouldn't cure.

Aodan and I closed in on the charred fasgadair remains. A breeze swept through the ravine, sending most of the pile scattering until it no longer resembled a human form.

"Well done, you!" I meant the compliment, but it sounded sarcastic as I touched my torn shirt. Somehow, my olive skin was healthy. No hint of a burn.

"I saved your life, mate!"

"Aye, but what of this duddie?" I pinched my sleeve, lifting it to reveal one of the burnt holes. "'Tis not like I have a chest full of shirts."

Aodan stared at me, slack-jawed.

I shuddered, then shook off the bells still sounding in my body. I pulled him into a hug. "Looks like you don't have to behead fasgadair to kill them. Fire works, too."

He grinned. We laughed ourselves to tears, then settled back by the fire. Once our anxious laughter dissipated, the seriousness caught up. The fasgadair had always been a threat, but they were a distant thing. Now reality sank its teeth in. I'd never been so close to death.

"What was that?" I tested my limbs as if they might betray me again. "I couldn't move."

"Nor could I." He released a shuddering breath. "But I didn't need to move to light it on fire."

If not for his ability, we'd both be dead. I shivered, expecting a horde of them to come streaming through the ravine. "Don't they live in nests? What if it had friends? What if they come looking for the one you cremated? We should move on. Find another place to settle."

"Are ye off yer head? Didn't ye see what I did? And besides"—he twirled his finger—"this place is a godsend."

"But what if there are more?"

"What are we going to do, travel through the Cnatan Mountains to Bandia? Or do ye want to take yer chances on the seas without a crew?"

"Or a ship." I puffed a fake laugh and shook my head. "And those mountains are unpassable."

He pointed to the ash that remained of the fasgadair. "I can protect us from those peely-wally beasts."

I knew that look. There was no changing his mind. Perhaps he was right. And I didn't doubt Aodan could protect us after what I'd witnessed. But what if a swarm overwhelmed us? How many beasts could he roast while frozen in place? And how many times could he set beings on fire—evil or no—and not have it affect him?

CHAPTER TWENTY-THREE

CATALEEN

A cloaked creature with inhuman eyes had someone in its grip. Faolan? Teeth bared, it closed in on Faolan's neck.

"Nay!" I screamed. "Nay, nay, nay!"

An orange glow lit up the sky at the demon's back. Fire. It released Faolan when flames engulfed it. Its eyes glowed yellow as it shrieked.

I bolted upright in bed and screamed, the monster's wail still sounding in my mind. My chest heaving, I fought to catch my breath. I broke out into a cold sweat while a torrent of emotions overwhelmed me. Then I sobbed.

Ma burst into my room and gathered me into her arms, holding me as if to keep me together. "Hush, my leanabh."

I couldn't remember the last time she called me that. It was meant for babies. I'd balk, but it soothed me like nothing else. I melted into her, breathing in her lavender scent as she rocked me and squeezed almost tight enough to wring all my bad feelings from me like water from a sponge. "You're safe."

What was that thing? The horrific face, frozen in a scream with glowing yellow eyes... The strange scent lingered still—fire and lightning. "Do you smell that?"

"Smell what, lass?" She sniffed. "'Tis a mite musty in here. Could do with an airing out."

"Nay. Never mind."

She smoothed my hair. "'Twas a bad dream. Your mind purging some bad feelings. Nothing more."

"Are you sure? It seemed like... like..." I peeled myself from her.

Ma tensed. "Aodan?"

I took several shaky breaths to steady my emotions. "I saw someone wearing a cloak. It looked like a man, but it wasn't. It couldn't have been. Its eyes—"

"What did its eyes look like?" Her voice came out thin, as if she weren't breathing.

"Dark with no white. Until... until it caught on fire. Then they seemed to glow—yellow."

She brought a hand to her mouth.

I shivered. It was no dream, and Ma knew it. "What is it, Ma?"

She covered her mouth. "'Tis nothing to concern yerself with. Yer safe. 'Tis all that matters. " She stood, kissed my head, and moved to leave. "Get some rest."

"Nay!" I grasped her wrist. "Please. Do you know what it was? Was it a fasgadair? Did Aodan set it on fire?"

"I cannae tell ye. 'Twas most likely a dream."

"I've never seen a fasgadair. Have ye? Is that what one looks like?"

Sniffing, she cupped a hand to my cheek. "I've never seen one either. But what ye describe... It could be."

My chest squeezed with a pressure tighter than her hug had been. It *was* Aodan then. He shut me out except when something overwhelmed him and leaked. That had to be it. He'd just killed a fasgadair. Were there more? Had he survived? I strained to reach out to him, but encountered nothing.

I should've reached out when the channel was open. If it opened again—I would.

I couldn't shake the dream. Nay, the vision. It had to be a vision. If I was just tortured by my brother's loss, wouldn't such dreams have tortured me every day since his leaving? But nay, only last night. And it seemed so—real.

If Sully was right, if this was all part of God's plan, what was my part? I had to go see him. As soon as the sun peeked out from its slumber, I left for his house. Was Pepin still there? What did they know? Was I prepared to hear it?

The flaming fasgadair... I shuddered, shaking my head as if to knock the image loose. What if something I learned from Sully could help me help Aodan? He was out there. If he'd lit a fasgadair on fire, he was in danger. Either from the demons or from himself.

And what of the prophecy Sully alluded to? What, in God's creation, could he have meant? Aodan would never harm me. What spirits was Sully conversing with to get such an idea? Certainly not God.

Sully's house peeked through the trees, and I stalled. I'd come all this way, and Ma didn't want me home anytime soon. Might as well see if he was in. I walked the rest of the way to his house, squared my shoulders, and lifted my hand to knock.

The door opened, and Sully's gray eyes peered down at me as if he could see me. "Come in, lass. I've been expecting you."

His calming presence melted my anxieties and disarmed me. I should have come here sooner. "How do you do that?"

Chuckling, he motioned to a stuffed chair. "Have a seat."

The humble space reflected him so well with only the essentials—a cookstove, cabinets likely holding just enough, a dining table, comfy seats for long chats with visitors, and small tables for drinks. When I sat, he presented me with a mug.

"Thank you." I took a long drink of the refreshing water, then set it on the table.

He sat across from me, clasped his hands together, and tilted toward me, eager for conversation. "What would you like to know, child?"

"I–I had a dream. Nay, a vision. From Aodan."

"And what did you see?"

"A fasgadair. Aodan set it on fire."

"Aye." Sully unfolded his hands, clasped the arms of his seat, and pushed back as if settling in for a long chat. "It has begun."

"What?" I pushed myself closer. "What's begun?"

"Your brother's descent." He tipped his head and frowned. "Or his ascent. Depending on how you look at it."

I'd forgotten how infuriating conversations with Sully could be when he knew things no one else was privy to.

"My apologies, dear one. Allow me to explain." He pulled his whitening beard. "Though ye won't like what I'm about to tell ye."

I rubbed at sudden shivers on my arms. My desire to help Aodan had led me here. But that's probably not what Sully offered. What if I couldn't handle what he had to say? I was still in such a fragile state. "Will it help?"

"Willingly taking part in God's plans always helps, but it doesn't always feel good."

How much worse could it get than the hollow life I lived now? Then again, wallowing in misery wasn't living. Whatever Sully had to share, perhaps it would prompt me to do something. I took another long drink, staving him off as long as possible.

Not that Sully minded. He appeared quite comfortable to sit in silence with me.

"Okay." Gripping the arms of my chair, I steeled myself for anything he might say. "I'm ready."

"Pray for your brother's soul, lass. Until a thing happens, there's always time to beseech God. Otherwise, Aodan is heading down a dark path indeed."

The world seemed to spin around me, darkening, while I clutched the chair. His words sounded far off as if he'd moved a great distance away. "What?"

"I know that's not what you want to hear. But 'tis true. You know of Morrigan, aye?"

"The original fasgadair?" My vision returned to normal.

"Aye." He nodded. "As the original, she has a link to all the fasgadair."

"Like Aodan and me?"

"No. They can't communicate with one another. I don't know how it works, but she can sense them… somehow. She knows where they are, when they're created, and when they die."

"What does that have to do with A—? He killed one." I snapped my head up. "Does Morrigan know what Aodan did?"

"Right now, she knows a fasgadair has passed. A fasgadair death is a rare thing, typically carried out by her. She will seek answers by sending more. When she does, she'll learn of Aodan's ability with fire. She will seek to recruit him."

My grip on the armchair tightened. "She'll turn him into a fasgadair?"

"Or kill him." Sully let out a series of sorrowful huffs. "That is why I beseech you to pray. Only God can save him."

I jumped out of my seat. "We have to warn him!"

Sully motioned for me to sit back down. "We cannot."

"But why?" I lowered myself, my heart thudded in my ears.

He patted my hand. "You'll only get yourself killed. You won't save your brother."

I eyed Sully, searching for anything that might give something away —a facial tic—anything. "Just yesterday you told me Aodan would turn on me. Yet today, you say to pray. Why?"

Hands folded in his lap, he rocked his chair. "God has plans. No one can thwart them, and He never changes His mind. But He wants us to pray. Sometimes, it seems He even changes His plans based on our prayers. But, if you ask me, that's all for show. His plans were just waiting for our prayers." His gaze had drifted upward. Did he just wink at God? "In my experience, you either take part in God's plans or get out of the way and suffer the consequences. And quite often, situations worsen before they improve."

"But this involves Aodan, my brother, turning into a demon! Or d..." I couldn't bring myself to say the word. Not about Aodan. Although death would be better than eternal damnation. "How can that be part of God's plan? I thought God used all things for good?"

Sully opened his palms, then spread his hands. "For those called according to His plans. Aye. 'Tis true."

"Does that mean Aodan isn't one of the called?"

Frowning, Sully tugged his beard. "Not necessarily."

My knuckles had whitened, so I eased my grip. "I don't understand."

"Nor do I, dear one. But... 'tis not our job to understand God's ways, but to trust."

Tears spilled down my cheeks. "But how? This is my brother we're talking about. How do I trust God with this? How do I let Aodan go to this dark, dark place?"

Sully leaned forward and covered one tense hand with his. "You pray. Beseech Him. And if He says no, ask Him to help you accept that and trust He knows best." He threw me a small smile. "Years ago, I attempted to thwart God's plans. The result was this." He pointed to his eyes. "And my efforts were in vain. Events transpired as God showed me. Now, even when I don't understand, I don't interfere. I do as God directs. But I always pray."

"But you're blind now. How is that good?"

"His ways are too good for me to understand. I'm merely a servant. For all I know, my disobedience was part of His plan, too. Now I'm certain He intended for me to be blinded. Truth be told, I see better without my eyes."

That made no sense. None of this made any sense. "What of Faolan? What happens to him in all this?"

"God has not revealed Faolan to me."

He reached into a drawer in the table beside him and pulled out something. The thing Pepin had brought. "This amulet will bring you to the human realm."

Sully must be losing his head. Wasn't he a little young for that? Was he even fifty yet? "The realm God rescued us from?"

"Rescued?" He loosed a full, hearty laugh. "What have they been teaching you children? God removed us from that realm because our abilities to shape-shift into animal forms led the humans to believe we were gods."

I squirmed in my seat, struggling to keep up with this bizarre conversation. "That's foolishness. We're no gods."

"Of course we aren't. But some, such as Morrigan, enjoyed being treated as such and encouraged them to revere her. And, as you know, there is only one God, and He is a jealous God. That is why He brought us to Ariboslia."

"So, Morrigan was a gachen in the human realm?"

"Aye. She died there. But then those women resurrected her."

"I know the story." The last thing I wanted to do was rehash old lessons from school. I was more concerned about his prediction. "Do they speak Ariboslian in the human realm?"

"No." He waved the amulet in the air. "But Drochaid will translate."

"What if I don't want to go?" I *didn't* want to go. Even if I did, how could I leave my ma after staying behind for her?

"Not to worry, child." He returned the amulet to the drawer. "In due time, you will."

CHAPTER TWENTY-FOUR

FAOLAN

An uneventful week passed, and I relaxed. Perhaps that fasgadair had been alone and no others would come after us. We'd grown comfortable in our new dwelling. Summer had settled in, and we now stood in a shallow part of the river, armed with spears with our pant legs rolled up.

Aodan thrust his spear into the water with a splash. "Whoop! Caught one!" He righted the spear, revealing a good-sized fish.

"Well done, you!" I patted his back as he passed. Fishing with spears was tricky work. It had taken us some time to understand how the water altered our view of a fish's location. But we were getting the knack.

He pulled the dead fish free. "This isn't so bad, is it? I like it here."

"Aye." It would be better if Catty were here, but I didn't dare dampen the mood by uttering her name. I missed her. Aodan didn't say so, but he did, too. This place would be heaven in Ariboslia if she were with us. My heart saddened. I knew her too well to think she was living well. We had something to occupy us—learning to survive on our own. She was stuck as a ghost in our old haunts. Was she miserable?

If only I could console her.

✵

That night, as we sat beside the fire eating our catch, I caught the unusual smell again. Lightning. I jumped to my feet and prodded Aodan.

"What is it, brother?" He followed my gaze into the darkness.

Three cloaked figures emerged. Fasgadair. Dread infested my stomach like squirming maggots.

The demon on the right caught fire. His screams poisoned the night sky.

"Stop!" The middle fasgadair held a pale hand out to Aodan. "We're not here to harm you."

Aodan stood, calm even in these circumstances. Perhaps, like his confidence in his ability to catch fish, his confidence in defending himself against fasgadair had grown, too. "What difference does that make? Yer demons. Why shouldn't I kill ye?" He pointed to the dust pile beside the remaining monsters.

Aodan might not be afraid, but I was. If only I could make him shut his gob. I kept waiting for the trapped sensation to overtake me.

"Morrigan sent us."

"Morrigan?" He snorted a laugh. "The original fasgadair? For what purpose?"

"She sent us to investigate a fasgadair's death."

"You mean the one I dusted a week ago? Tell her I did the same to yer friend and I'll do the same to any others that dare disturb us." He stepped forward, and the fasgadair backed away, keeping an equal distance between them. "Tell her to leave us be and no other fasgadair need die."

The fasgadair nodded. "I'll relay the message." Then they were gone, taking the strange smell with them.

As much as I enjoyed our new home during the day, I despised it at night, especially during our evening meal when unwelcome visitors might arrive. Every night, as we settled down to eat, my eyes strained to see beyond the firelight, my body taut as a tripwire, ready to spring.

Aodan seemed as comfortable as a pig in mud. If I wasn't concerned for him the night he killed a deer and declared himself a demon, I was now. Something was happening to him.

"How can ye be so calm?"

He placed his meat on the makeshift plate of bark and slumped his shoulders. "Must we have this conversation again, mate?"

"I don't understand. Morrigan knows where we are. Ye know... *the* Morrigan?"

"I know who Morrigan is. We attended the same classes, and ye've been reminding me since the fasgadair departed seven suns ago. Yer endless and repetitive arguments chafe like a cheese grater on my bum."

"Sake! Must ye be so crass?"

"If it gets ye to cease yer incessant blathering, aye."

I recoiled. What personality-changing parasite had wormed into my friend's head?

"My apologies, brother." He reached across the void between us and rested a hand on my shoulder. "Please just *trust* me. I sent those fasgadair away, didn't I?"

I stiffened. Sure, he had more confidence, but this was a notch or hundreds of notches beyond. Did he think himself a match for Morrigan? I held up three fingers. "Three Aodan. Three. There are thousands, possibly hundreds of thousands more in Diabalta and the City of Nica. And now you dare threaten Morrigan? She decimated two entire armies by herself!"

"None had my ability. If they come back, I'll light them all up. I could light up hundreds at once if I have to. It will be their fault. I warned them." He smiled a confident—*terrifying*—smile. "Trust me."

"That's another thing... Why should I trust *you*? Where's God in all this? Shouldn't we be trusting *Him*?"

Aodan's face darkened like a snuffed candle. "Where was God when I was banished? Huh? He turned His back on me. Or was my banishment part of His plan? Either way, He's rejected me, so why would I trust Him?"

Where was my friend, and who was this stranger wearing his skin?

I should return home. I'd joined Aodan because I couldn't let him face banishment alone, but he'd made it beyond clear he could protect himself. Perhaps he'd be better off without my constant nagging. And Cataleen... What must she be going through right now? She needed me more than Aodan did.

The thought stamped my mind like a signet in wax. I'd give it a day or two. Then I'd return home to Cataleen.

CHAPTER TWENTY-FIVE

CATALEEN

Seven suns had risen and set since my visit to Sully. I had yet to digest all he'd said. And I couldn't shake the fasgadair from my head. If only I could feel Aodan. But nay, I hadn't felt anything from him since. But I couldn't sit around here anymore, thinking the worst.

But where would I go? What would I do? Go to the ocean where my brothers and I liked to swim? Sit on the pier where we liked to fish? Hike in the woods where we liked to explore together? Walk through the cornfield to the shack and speculate about what happened there by myself? Look for a field of beò feur and try to stomp on the creatures alone?

There was nowhere to go and nothing to do that wouldn't invoke memories of them.

And make me wonder if they were still alive...

Ma still wasn't forcing me back to chores with the clan, but she was running out of things to find for me to do at home and tiring of my sulking, releasing my pent-up energy on the rocking chair. I hadn't noticed the incessant squeaking until she placed a hand on my shoulder, stilling me.

"Go see if Achaius and Cahal have returned yet. They're due to arrive today."

"Do you think they've brought more babies?" This was the only thing that excited me anymore, Achaius and Cahal's heroic rescues from Gnuatthara.

"Only one way to find out." She swatted me with the dishrag.

I donned my shoes and shawl and slogged through the village. I was beginning to hate this place. Everything was tainted. I couldn't stand to look at it. So, I put my head down and focused on my feet.

Would I ever recover? No place brought me solace. And I couldn't outmaneuver Sully's words. They followed me everywhere.

Nothing he'd said made sense. How could Aodan hurt me unless he returned? But he couldn't. The elders wouldn't allow it. Not unless he showed true repentance. And if he repented, he'd never hurt me. If he returned, I'd only have more reason to stay. If I left, he wouldn't know where to find me.

Nay. Aodan couldn't hurt me. I'd never leave.

But what if he became a fasgadair?

My stomach gurgled, rejecting the idea. Aodan would never allow that.

Sully had to be mistaken. Perhaps he was beginning to misunderstand God's messages. And he said to pray. That meant his prophecies weren't infallible. He must've been wrong at least once.

I stopped on the hill near the main gate, far enough away that the guard wouldn't expect me to speak with him. But this was the worst place to sit. The last time I'd stood here, the elders declared their doom upon my brother.

Were Aodan and Faolan all right? Had they happened upon Lorcan and Tevin? Or worse, a fasgadair nest? Morrigan? Were they still alive? Still gachen?

Stop it, Cataleen! I pounded the side of my forehead with my palm. *Stop think—*

Stomping horse hooves and creaking wooden wheels interrupted my thoughts. A carriage made its way to the gate. Achaius.

I ran to meet them. Hopefully, they had babies to distract me. Watching the helpless babes who'd been tossed out of their village—left to die—because they didn't meet the Treasach's standards of growing into an inhuman-sized gachen broke my heart, yet filled me with purpose. I hadn't known my da, but I'd had my ma's love. God had spared these children. Our clan would raise them. But they'd always feel a hole. Like something was missing. Just as I had without a father. And now, without my brother, without my best friend, that hole was wider.

Guilt soured my mouth, oozed down my throat, and pooled in my stomach. How could I wander about feeling sorry for myself when others more in need existed and I had the means to assist? If I could do anything to help them grow into well-adjusted, God-loving, content members of our village, I would do just that. With a new determination in my step, I strode down the path as the carriage passed through the main gate, kicking up a cloud of dust in its wake.

Achaius brought the horses to a stop and sprang from his seat. The carriage door popped open. A man I'd seen before ducked through the small door and jumped to the ground without waiting for the step, sending the carriage rocking. Something about him was different, aside from his hair, which was clipped so short by his ears it was nearly shaved with the rest sticking up and brushed back.

"Let me get the step for ye." Achaius rushed to the door. He blocked my view as he unfolded the step from beneath the carriage.

"Thanks." Another man stepped down with care, cradling an infant tight to his chest. No, not quite a man. He appeared young, perhaps about my age. Something in his face made me suck in my breath. He, too, had an unusual haircut. His thick mass of black hair stuck up in places like spikes, but it was too perfectly tousled, too beautiful to be accidental or the result of negligence. And his strange clothes... Blue pants of a material I'd never seen before. And a fitted black shirt with small buttons running from his unusual collar, past his chest, to his waist where the shirt disappeared. Who wore their shirt inside their pants? He carried himself differently, too. He squinted in the sunlight as he spun about, scanning his surroundings.

Something about him was—unreal, making me feel faint.

He was the strangest, most beautiful thing I'd ever seen.

Achaius elbowed me. "Ye all right, lass?"

Had I been gawking? "Oh. Uh." I pressed my hands to my warm cheeks to push the blush away. "I've been running." *Since when did lies spring so easily to yer lips, Cataleen?* "I, uh, came to see if ye had any babies. Need any help?"

"Only one this time. But I picked up a couple of travelers along the way." He removed his cap and aimed it at the two men.

"Oh?" I said as if I hadn't noticed them.

"Ye may know Nathaniel. He grew up in Notirr and returns from time to time." Achaius pointed to the older man. "The lad is his son."

I giggled. Why it struck me as funny that Achaius would refer to the young man as a lad, I wasn't sure. Perhaps something else made me laugh so uncharacteristically. Whatever it was, Achaius was only three summers older than I was. From what I could gather, the young man was somewhere in the middle.

The "lad" adjusted the baby in his arms and held a hand out to me. "The name's Josh. Nice to meet you." He trained his hazel eyes on me and flashed a smile that sent my stomach rolling. What kind of accent was that? And what was wrong with his words? Something was off.

I glanced at his hand. Did he intend to grasp forearms as the men did?

His smile wavered, and he lowered his hand, wiping it on his foreign pants.

The older man stepped forward. "My apologies. My son isn't familiar with the local customs."

"Oh? From where do ye hail?" I asked.

Josh scrunched his thick eyebrows and consulted his father, as if unsure how to answer. Why the hesitation over a simple question? And why did every move he made make me light-headed?

Achaius stepped between us. "This is Cataleen."

Josh smiled.

"Cataleen?" Nathaniel coughed into his fist. "Mirna's daughter?"

"Aye." He seemed to know me. Did I know him? Maybe. But I couldn't place him.

"I grew up with yer mum. Ye have a brother, too. A twin. Aodan?"

The mere mention of his name brought tears to my eyes. I forced them back, along with a fake smile.

"Uh-oh. That doesn't look good. Has it begun?" Nathaniel asked.

"Has what begun?" Did he know about Sully's prophecy?

"Perhaps it's best we meet with Sully." Nathaniel started toward the gate, holding out a welcoming arm. "Would you join us?"

Part of me wanted to bask in Josh's presence a little longer, but another part feared what their visit meant in God's grand plans. "Are ye sure ye don't want to settle in first? Ye just arrived. Ye must be exhausted."

"Bah." Nathaniel waved his hand. "It wasn't that far."

"But I thought—"

"Let's go meet Sully and explain." Nathaniel offered his arm.

So I was right. Something bigger was happening here. They would only want to include me if I were involved. Ignoring the warning signals screaming within me, I accepted his arm and allowed him to lead me to Sully, ready or not.

✭

SULLY'S DOOR OPENED, and his face popped through the opening. "Nathaniel? Did I hear yer voice?" His gray eyes scanned the area as if searching for us. "And I believe I heard sweet Cataleen, too. Come in. Come in." He held the door wide for us to pass through. "Have a seat. Can I get ye anything? Have some water." Without waiting for a response, he poured water from the pitcher on the table into mugs always ready and waiting for visitors.

"Thank ye, Sully." I placed a hand on his. "Allow me to help."

He kept pouring, so I removed my hand. He pushed the mugs to different spots around the table and sat. How'd he know to pour four? "What brings ye to Notirr? Another mining expedition?"

"No, I–I... God told me to come." Nathaniel sputtered and lowered himself across from Sully.

As Josh sat beside his da, I claimed the seat beside Sully.

"Why do ye say that like 'tis something only a crazy person would say? You know who yer talking to? Don't tell me America has changed you that much."

America? Where in Ariboslia was that? Nowhere on our continent.

"It's more difficult to be a believer there. And my Ariboslian is getting rusty since Fiona refuses to speak it. But that's not it. H–He told me to bring Joshua."

"I thought I sensed another with ye! Yer so quiet, lad. Do ye breathe?"

"Ha!" Josh's laugh seemed to surprise him. He covered his mouth and reddened. Even his embarrassment was endearing. "I've heard a lot about you, sir. It's an honor to meet you."

What was wrong with his speech? His lips didn't match his words.

He caught me staring at his lips, so I averted my gaze.

Crow's-feet deepened around Sully's eyes. "I've wanted to meet ye for some time. How's yer ma? I know she's not happy about yer da's ventures home. How's she handling letting her son go?"

"Uh." Josh's Adam's apple bobbed. "She's handling it okay, I guess." His wide-eyed gaze darted to his da.

Nathaniel's face twisted. "I promised to keep him safe, assuring her we won't leave Notirr."

"But the megalith," Sully said. "It's outside the village."

"Less than a day's walk. I promised to get him here before nightfall."

"But she never trusted Notirr either. That's why she left after her brother's death—"

"I know." Nathaniel rubbed his troubled face. "But there hasn't been a fasgadair attack within these gates in all these years. It took some heavy convincing. But I assured her God wouldn't put him in harm's way."

Sully cocked his head. "Was that wise?"

Nathaniel shifted. "He *will* be safe, right?"

"He is in God's will, but are any of us ever truly *safe*? And is it wise to advise someone with a weak faith that God doesn't put His followers in harm's way? He calls us to face danger more often than I'd like. And sometimes, He calls us home."

Nathaniel let out a long breath as if pushing out every negative emotion along with it. "I didn't know what else to do. As you said, her faith is weak and has only dwindled over the years since her brother's death. It's gotten bad, Sully. She tries to deny Ariboslia's existence. When I told her where we were going, she lost it. She said to tell her we were going camping. So I did. Just like I pretended to be in the military and gave her prewritten postcards to send to herself. I fear it's unwise to give in to her denial of reality."

I'd listened in on private conversations before, but this was too much. I didn't understand half of what he said, and I didn't want to listen to a man talk about his wife's weak faith. I squirmed, eyeing the door. Maybe I could slip away unnoticed.

He huffed. "Everything I do seems to make it worse, but God called us here. I always do what I have to do to follow His will and provide for my family. I try to tell her the truth, then give in to her demands to say whatever she's willing to hear." He ran a hand over his weird hair, puffing it up further. "I don't know if it's so she can have a ready excuse for my absence for the neighbors without feeling like she's lying or if she's losing touch with reality."

Sully quirked his lip. "I wish I had answers for ye. How long does she expect ye to be on this so-called camping trip?"

"I have to get him back before school starts in the fall. It's his senior year."

I was so confused. What were they talking about? What had his mother lost? What was the military? What was a postcard? What was a senior year? Why'd they have to return before school starts? Surely no one continued a formal education at their age. Were they teachers? And why was I here, eavesdropping on a personal conversation? I glanced at the door again and picked up my mug with a shaky hand and peered at these strange people over the rim as I took a long drink.

"Joshua, has yer da taught you much about Ariboslia?"

"Some. I know a few words."

How was he speaking to us if he only knew a few words?

Sully chuckled. "Has he taught you about the world, not the language?"

"My dad hadn't told me anything until I shifted into an elk when I turned fifteen. That was awesome!" He smiled a wide smile. Then it faltered. "But also scary in Maine during hunting season. I know you're all shape-shifters, too, which is supercool. And you sent my dad to America to prepare the way for her." He motioned to me.

I sprayed my sip of water back into the mug, wetting my nose.

Sully handed me a cloth.

"I don't think she knew that yet, son." Nathaniel nudged Josh's arm with his elbow.

"Oh. Sorry." He threw me a sheepish look.

"She knows there will probably come a time in which she'll need to escape her brother, though she's not yet convinced."

Why was everyone talking about me as if I weren't present?

Sully swiveled in his seat to face me. "These are the people ye'll stay with in America—the human realm."

I was fighting so hard to contain myself, but I couldn't hold back any longer. "What is happening here? I don't understand most of what you're saying." I pointed to Josh. "And why don't your lips match your words?"

Josh reached under his shirt and pulled out a stone on a string.

"He has an amulet, like Drochaid?" I scooted closer. His amulet didn't have Drochaid's arrows or the strange markings in between. Rather, a symbol like three diamonds with a line through the middle, the one in the center bigger than the others. Or a mirrored mountain range.

"Drochaid is special," Sully said. "One of a kind. This is a more common pechish amulet that allows inter-realm travel through the megalith and acts as a language translator."

"That's why your words don't match?" I stared at his lips, though he wasn't speaking. "You're not speaking Ariboslian?"

"I speak English." Josh studied the amulet before tucking it back into his shirt. "This is my dad's. He hasn't needed it as a translator in a long time, though his English still needs some work." His teasing grin made my stomach do that strange flip again.

"Well." Sully leaned back, folding his hands across his chest. "This is a pleasant surprise. The good Lord saw fit to give ye a chance to connect before leaving for the human realm. That will make the transition much smoother indeed. Cataleen, why don't ye show Joshua around the village whilst I chat with his da."

I scanned Josh, my stomach twisting under his intense hazel gaze. Why did I feel like this was a bad idea?

CHAPTER TWENTY-SIX

FAOLAN

Aodan and I killed another deer. Rather than eat most of it raw in our animal forms, bringing scraps home to cook, we dragged the skinned deer carcass on our makeshift sled through the woods. The tricky part would be getting it down the stairs. There was enough room for us to sit behind the deer if Aodan rested its head in his lap. Once he settled in at the top of the stairs and latched onto the rope, I kicked the sled over the edge and hopped on.

When it hesitated, Aodan and I rocked to get it moving. Then it took us for a bumpy ride. My teeth chattered as my brain scrambled, then jerked to a stop as the sled wedged on a turn too tight for its length.

I readjusted the deer, yanked the sled free, then hurried back on. The sled careened down the remaining steps, then cracked, folding in half as it slammed to the bottom.

"I guess we'll have to come up with something better." I wiped sweat from my brow and readjusted the animal once more, hoping we could still pull the sled back to our cave in its broken state.

How would Aodan handle this on his own? Perhaps my leaving wasn't a good idea. Though he could just stay in his feline form and eat the animal where it lay.

We dragged the animal back to our camp. As we neared, the lightning scent drifted my way, strengthening with each step.

I stopped. "There's a fasgadair in our camp. I can smell it."

Aodan wiped his hands on his trousers. "I smell it too. Not to worry. I'll handle it." He pulled the sled, then stopped when I failed to move. "What are ye doing? I said I'll take care of it."

"Have ye ever stopped to think who these creatures are that ye kill so easily? They were human once. What if they could be saved? But yer just killing them with no concern for their souls."

Aodan's face morphed, disbelief and disgust snarling up his features. "Are ye off yer head? They're demons. Murderers. They feed off people. Or worse, they make more of the blasted things. They're the killers. Not me."

He was right. But something in my gut couldn't allow me to partake in killing them without regard. They were destined to go to hell. What if there was another way? How could Aodan curse these people to an eternity of misery without blinking?

As he shook the rope, not hiding his impatience, I gave up the fight and followed his lead.

A woman sat on the log by our campfire. She looked out of place, somehow sitting with perfect posture in an elegant gown. Her eyes closed, she seemed at peace, beautiful even, with flowing dark hair and a perfect complexion.

But this was no woman. I didn't need to see her eyes. The telltale scent radiated from her, stronger than any other fasgadair. The air enveloped me into a cocoon, stilling me.

Then she stood before me with my neck in her grip. I hadn't even seen her move! Her frightening eyes with nothing but black, fixed on me, without blinking. Horror excited my every sense, but I was powerless to do anything. I couldn't even speak. What little breath I got was only because she allowed it. She could cut off my air or snap my neck with ease.

"Think twice before setting me on fire. Ask yerself what I can do to yer friend before I burn up. *If* I burn up." Though she spoke to Aodan, she never looked away from me, her freakish black eyes inches from my face. Her lightning breath burned my nostrils.

"Morrigan." Aodan wobbled out her name, his confidence vanquished. "What do ye want?"

She laughed. The sick sound reverberated off the ravine walls, chilling my soul. "You."

"Me?" He gasped. "What on God's green earth for?"

A shudder rippled over her, flowing through her hair and dress. "You start fires with your mind."

What had caused her to shudder? That Aodan could kill vampires with his mind-fire? Or was it the mention of God?

"What of it?"

"I want it." Dark fire flashed in her coal eyes.

When would we ever have another opportunity like this? If I died, so be it. "Light her up!" I choked as Morrigan's grip tightened. "K–kill h–her." Helpless in her grip, I gurgled, straining to breathe. My vision darkened. If this was the end, so be it, as long as she died, too.

Her grip loosened. I sucked in air as my vision cleared. We were now a few feet from where we'd been. When had we moved?

"Should anything happen to me, yer friend will die first. Then you. Then my servants will attack Notirr—starting with yer family—all of them will die." She released me, and I fell to the ground.

I landed on my side, still incapable of moving other than to suck in air. Why did it still feel like her fingers squeezed?

Aodan stepped toward Morrigan, his now blotchy-red face twisted. "If ye do anything to my family, I'll—"

"Restrain yourself, and they'll stay safe."

He dropped to his knees. "What do ye want with me?"

Morrigan materialized before him. She brought her fingers to his chin and lifted his face to hers. "To offer you my kingdom."

He goggled as if she'd spontaneously combusted without his help. "Pardon?"

She caressed his face as one would a long-lost son. "Fasgadair roam Ariboslia without purpose. Be their leader. Give them purpose."

He moved to swipe her hand away, but she'd already stepped back. He rose to stand before her. "Why would I want to do that?"

"Because you can." Her laughter ricocheted along the rocks, as hard and cold as they were. "Imagine it, Aodan. Imagine being immortal. You're already powerful. I can make you more so. You've seen what fasgadair can do. Speed. Healing. Strength. You can have it all. Be their ruler. Rule all of Ariboslia."

I couldn't read his face, but his eyes roamed as they did when he was deep in thought. My insides liquefied. He couldn't be considering this.

"Cataleen and my ma would be safe? My village?"

I gurgled, straining to speak. "N–n–n—"

His gaze flicked to me.

Morrigan appeared beside us. "If you rule, you can guarantee their safety, but without you in control, who knows what will happen? My minions are outgrowing their space, longing to stretch out. And I'm tiring of watching over them." She tipped her head in a slow, eerie way. "Sleep on it."

I jerked as the unseen power holding me let me go. She was gone, along with her fasgadair stench.

"You can't, Aodan." My voice cracked. "You can't."

CHAPTER TWENTY-SEVEN

CATALEEN

I led Josh to the tent where the villagers ate our evening meals together, introducing him along the way. When he sat beside me in Aodan's spot, I shoved down the rising emotions. "So, what do ye think of our village?"

"It's cool. All the little homes in hills look like something out of *Lord of the Rings*."

His sideways smile soothed my emotions. But his speech confused me. "Who is the lord of the Rings, and why are you cold? 'Tis summer. Is it typically warmer where ye live?" I'd hate to live somewhere hotter than Notirr in the summer.

He laughed. I was getting used to the sound. He laughed a lot. Did I amuse him, or was he nervous?

"*The Lord of the Rings* is a book. There's a movie, too. And cool just means I like it. It's nice."

I shook my head, still not understanding. "Cool means nice in yer world? And what is a movie?"

"Ah... It's a—it's like a picture that moves and tells a story."

"I still don't understand."

He waved his hand. "Never mind. I'll take you to see one when you come to Maine. There's a great theater in—"

Cahal bumped the bench as he sat beside me. "We have a visitor?"

"Cahal, this is Josh. He's from—" Wait. Was I supposed to say where he was from? No one had mentioned if this should be kept quiet or not.

"The north." Josh reached a hand out to Cahal. "Nice to meet you."

Cahal reached in front of me to grasp Josh's arm.

Josh's hand dangled in Cahal's grip before understanding set in and he latched onto Cahal's forearm. I should have explained Ariboslian greetings before bringing him here. Nay. His father should have prepped him. How much didn't he know about his culture?

"Bandia?" Cahal gripped a tureen of salad, scooped some onto his plate, and held it for me. "Did you travel through the mountains or by way of the seas?"

"Ship," I said.

"The moun—"

We looked at each other as we contradicted one another.

I piled my plate with salad. "Were you about to say the mountains are still unpassable? That's why you took a ship?" It wasn't a complete lie. The mountains were still unpassable, and the megalith was kind of like a ship. It transported him from one place to another. Wasn't that what a ship did? I passed the tureen to Josh.

"Ah, yeah." He dropped a scoop of salad on his plate.

"Are there many fasgadair in the north?" Cahal asked.

Why was he so atypically chatty? Or was he trying to get Josh to talk so he wouldn't have to? "There's really nothing up there for them, is there?"

Josh's dark brows pinched together. "Uh, no."

I needed to change the subject. Quick. "Cahal is from Gnuatthara. 'Tis in the south. He had to travel through fasgadair-infested lands to get here. Cahal, why don't ye tell Josh about how yer family made it possible to rescue Treasach babies?" Getting Cahal to talk might be almost as hard as stomping on beò feur, but once Josh started talking crazy about things like gods of rings and moving stories, there'd be no hiding the fact that he's not from anywhere in Ariboslia. I'd have to ask Sully if was okay to share the news about the human realm with others. Until then, if Cahal persisted in feigning interest, I'd steer the conversation to something safer.

※

AS WAS BECOMING THE NORM, I tossed and turned in my bed. Aodan's and Faolan's absence, Josh's presence, and Sully's predictions overwhelmed me, spinning like a top in my mind. Aodan wouldn't betray me. Sully was wrong. And nothing could make me go to the human realm. But Josh... Was this God's way of assuring me these weren't mere predictions but actual prophecy? Was I going to America? Would I live with him and his family?

Nay. Nay, nay, nay. It would never happen. None of it would *ever* happen. Aodan would never betray me. I would never leave Ma. And Josh? His face with his uncertain smile... My stomach did a flip, sending little thrills throughout.

What was that? What was happening to me? Could it be the beginnings of reaching my bian? Was Josh the trigger? Why else would my body betray me, acting so out of sorts?

Josh was handsome... in a strange, foreign kind of way.

Nay. Nay. Nay! *Stop thinking like that, Cataleen!*

Had someone put a spell on me? What kind of witchcraft had come over me?

I pushed Josh's face from my mind and focused on Aodan. My brother. My best friend. He would never turn on me. Never. Nothing Sully could do or say would convince me otherwise. Even if something strange came over Aodan, Faolan would pull him out of it.

But how could Josh just accept this news? He didn't know me. He seemed content with the idea of bringing me home.

Why did he have to be so beautiful? So mysterious?

How old was he? Fifteen at least. He'd reached his bian. I huffed. A foreigner from the human realm was more gachen than I was.

My stomach rolled again as if unsure whether it needed to eliminate the small meal I'd forced down or raid the kitchen for any pastries Ma might've left cooling on the counter. I didn't want to leave the only home I'd ever known. My clan. Ma. It would be like giving up on ever seeing Aodan or Faolan again. Nay. I would never give up.

CHAPTER TWENTY-EIGHT

FAOLAN

Sleep on it. Right. As if sleep were possible now. I twisted in my bedding. The hard cave floor hadn't bothered me before. But between my discomfort from the unforgiving stone and images of Aodan with fasgadair eyes, sleep would not happen.

I ran through all I'd learned of Morrigan from our lessons—the War Queen. The Battle Crow. Two foolish women resurrected her, thinking she'd help their husbands win the war. Morrigan was frightful before she died. But partially revived? Undead? She was a walking, flying nightmare. She killed almost everyone on the battlefield—legions of armed warriors—by herself! Aodan was as big a fool as those women if any part of him thought he could trust her.

Images of her slaughtering thousands of men flashed through my mind.

Aye... sleep was *not* happening.

So I prayed.

Night was gone, and early morning rays illuminated the cave's mouth. Had I fallen asleep while praying? I peeled the blanket away, careful not to disturb Aodan. His soft snores echoed, sounding as if a bear slept in the depths. How could he be so peaceful with the Battle Queen's threats still lingering in the air? Didn't they disturb his thoughts as well? The stone walls seemed to squeeze in on me, along with my biggest fear—the offer might intrigue him.

"What are ye doing?" He grumbled and wiped his eyes. "'Tis early."

"Couldn't sleep." I escaped the confinement, hoping the new sun and open air would alter my perspective and relieve my sour gut. I breathed in the wind as it rushed through the ravine, rubbed my chilled arms, and prayed.

Pebbles kicked behind me.

"Thinking about Morrigan?" He covered a wide yawn, then stretched.

"Praying." I grumbled. "Something ye should be doing. Something we both should have been doing all night."

Aodan sat beside me and threw his blanket over my shoulder, along with his arm.

I shoved his arm and the blanket away. "What are ye doing, Aodan?"

"I'm just trying to warm ye. There's a chill—"

"What are ye doing with Morrigan?"

His defensive countenance sagged. "I don't know."

"Ye slept soundly for a man with a threat from the War Queen looming over his head."

He jumped to his feet. "Ye heard her threats. Not just to my family, but to our entire clan. Ma and Cataleen would be enough to sacrifice myself. And yer da. But she's gone and added the entire clan!"

I stepped back, watching Aodan as if he were second-in-command to Morrigan already. "So yer going to accept her offer?"

"Do ye see another way?"

I needed more than one sleepless night of prayer to seek such an answer. How could I come up with something to free my mate from an ancient evil that rulers hadn't succeeded against in hundreds of years?

"But yer so calm." I couldn't express nor contain the dread and foreboding now plaguing my every sense. It was like lying on a bed of needles, but the sharp points penetrated every area of skin, urging me to rise and act. Do something. Anything to end the torture.

His impassive face belied no emotion. "'Tis my fate."

"Says who?" He wasn't just off his head. His mind was gone, floating off somewhere far away.

"I don't know how I know—I just know. When Morrigan comes, I'll be ready. I'll accept my fate."

"Sake! Yer off yer head. You've heard the stories. Ye know what she's done, what she's capable of. Do ye think ye can stand up against her?"

Maybe I should leave now. But then, how could I explain to Cataleen what happened to her brother? That I'd abandoned him to Morrigan and his so-called fate. She'd forgive me. Eventually. But our relationship would never be the same. And could I ever forgive myself?

His teary eyes blinked up at me. "Ye think I want this?"

I softened, but not enough. "Search me. Only ye know what's going on in that thick skull of yours. But I think ye think yer more powerful than ye are."

He sneered. "Trust me. I know my limitations. Do you know how many times I tried to light her on fire? She seemed to sense it coming. And did you see how quickly she moved? Nay, ye didn't. Cause she was too fast to see!"

My shoulders sagged.

"She's too powerful, Faolan. Don't ye see? If I don't go with her, she'll kill our entire clan."

I toed the pebbles at my feet. If I were Aodan, wouldn't I do the same? Wouldn't I willingly sacrifice myself, hoping to save our people? So why was I being so hard on him?

"I'll go with her. I'll do as she asks, pretend to be on her side, and hope I'm enough of a distraction to keep her away from our clan. If she kills me, she kills me."

"But what she's asking ye to do is worse than killing ye. She's planning to take yer soul... turn ye into a demon. There's no coming back from that."

Aodan lurched forward, dropping his head into his hands, then tipped his tear-streaked face to me. "Right now, all I can do is trust God. He has to have a plan, right?"

"He always has a plan, but—" I couldn't bring myself to voice the possibility that God's plan involved Aodan losing his soul—forever. Would God do that?

He swiped at his eyes. "I have to trust that, if I sacrifice myself for my clan, God will honor it somehow. Without that wee bit of hope"—his voice broke—"I've nothing."

I pulled him into a fierce hug, wishing I could purge the demon from his soul even now.

"Will ye come with me?"

I heaved a heavy sigh. "Of course, I'll come with ye. I'm not abandoning my best mate."

Nay. I couldn't abandon my friend when he needed me most. When Morrigan arrived, I'd be here too. But I would *not* become one of them.

God, I hope Ye have a plan.

CHAPTER TWENTY-NINE

CATALEEN

I woke with an eager thrill tingling in my belly, pushing out through my extremities, urging me to rise. I'd promised to go on a hike with Josh today. His smile invaded my mind, and I bounced out of bed, humming an Ariboslian hymn whilst I brushed my hair. Had I ever woken so eager to face the day? Definitely not since Aodan and Faolan had left. Perhaps the morn of our fifteenth anniversary when I expected to reach my bian.

Which I still hadn't.

Both Aodan and Faolan had reached theirs. And now my sixteenth anniversary was nearly here and still nothing. And I'd be celebrating without them for the first time. The first of how many?

My enthusiasm waned. Was it wrong to experience happiness without them?

Nay. I refused to give in to the sadness. I'd spent much too long there. I imagined Josh's face again, kicking my stomach back into the strange cycle between illness and ravenous hunger—a rush of nervous excitement.

I readied myself and went to the kitchen. Ma stood over the stove, back to me, spurtle in hand, stirring. "I've a fresh batch of porridge, and I expect ye to eat, hear me?"

"Thanks, Ma." When she served some into a bowl and placed it on the counter next to a bowl of cream, I grabbed a horn spoon, scooped the porridge, and dunked it in the milk. It tasted better than it had in weeks. I chewed my mouthful of comfort. "Mmm."

Ma doled some into a bowl for herself and scraped the rest into the porridge drawer to harden for later. She eyed me askance. "Everything all right?"

I exaggerated my chewing and pointed to my mouth full of her masterful cooking.

She dropped the pot and spoon with a clang, then jammed her hands on her hips. "What's happened?"

I swallowed, scraping the sticky remains from my teeth with my tongue. "What do ye mean?"

"Ye've been moping about looking peely-wally for weeks. I've practically had to feed ye like a wee bairn. Now, look at ye." She motioned up and down my figure. "Yer eating like ye haven't had a proper meal in years, with yer face shining like the sun. So, I ask ye... what's happened?"

"I'm just hungry. As you said, I haven't been eating. And I need to get my energy up. I'm going for a hike."

She raised an eyebrow. "Alone?"

"Uh. No. With Josh." I mumbled his name.

"With whom?"

I groaned. "Josh."

"Josh? 'Tis an unusual name." With the way her eyebrows knit above her narrowed eyes, she must be completely confused.

"It's short for Joshua. He's Nathaniel's son. They were at dinner last night. Didn't you see them?" I shoved another spoonful into my mouth.

"Nay, I was a bit under the weather."

"Are ye unwell?" I searched her for signs of illness.

"Bah." She waved off my concern. "Nothing a good night's sleep couldn't cure. Nathaniel, ye say. Urchardan?" Her face relaxed. "I saw him in the market yesterday. He brought his son? With Fiona's blessing?"

I shoved my mouthful into my cheek to speak. "I think they changed their surname to Webb."

She puffed out her cheek and pointed to it, imitating me from earlier and reminding me not to talk with my mouth full.

I rolled my eyes and swallowed. "I'm to meet him for a hike this morn." I kissed her forehead, dunked another large spoonful of porridge into the cream, and shoved it into my mouth. Cheeks full, I plunked the dirty spoon into the basin and waved to Ma on my way out the door.

※

JOSH LEANED AGAINST THE GATE, chatting with the sentry. My heart sped up as my legs slowed. He was so different. Not only the way he talked and walked. Sake, everything he did oozed foreigner. But beyond that. Something was different about his core being. Was everyone from America like that?

"Hey!" He peeled himself from the fence, a smile crinkling his eyes as I neared. "I was beginning to wonder if you'd show."

"My apologies. My ma wanted me to eat." I slid my tongue over my teeth to ensure no porridge was lodged there. The sentry allowed us passage, and we made our way up the hill into the woods.

"It's so nice here. There's nothing but woods and ocean. No highways or factories. I've never seen the ocean without buildings everywhere. I mean, where I live in Maine is pretty nice. But the beaches are cluttered with houses. There's a lot of woods there too. But the colors here. What's that even called?" He pointed to a toradh tree.

"The green leaves? Or the measach?"

"Measach?" His lips matched his word, and his pronunciation was terrible. When I laughed, he arched an eyebrow. "Is that the name of the fruit? Or the color?"

"The fruit. The color is called aotrom."

"Aotrom."

I giggled at his pronunciation again.

"We don't even have a word for that color. It doesn't exist in my world."

I couldn't imagine a world missing even one color. What was his world like? If God's plan was to get me to go willingly, this wasn't the way. "Is your world... drab?"

"No." A twig snapped under his weight. "But it's not like this. We don't have that color. And the colors we have aren't as bright." He eyed me askance. "My world is beautiful, too. In its own way. And we have a lot of modern conveniences such as electricity, indoor plumbing, cars—"

He spoke the foreign words so fast I couldn't absorb them. I latched onto the last one. "What is cars?" My pronunciation better not be as bad as his.

"A car? Um. It's like a carriage, but without horses. It has its own motor and goes much faster."

My hand flew to my chest. Whatever that was, it sounded terrifying. Again, not helping me want to leave home. "A horseless carriage that travels *faster* than horses? That doesn't sound safe."

"It is. Well, there are seat belts and stuff." He grimaced as if trying to eat his words and realizing how awful they taste. "Even carriages get into accidents, right?"

"Aye. But at a faster pace, it would be a miracle if anyone survived."

Josh rubbed his face. "Well, I guess you'll just have to see it for yourself."

"What were those other things you said? E–lec—"

"Electricity? It's power that's available all over your house so you can have lights that don't need oil. We also have refrigerators to keep food cold so it lasts longer. And microwaves to heat it up in minutes. Washing machines so you don't have to scrub clothes and dryers to dry them. And coffee makers. My dad and I brought instant coffee, but it's just not the same as fresh-brewed—"

I touched my forehead, pressing my thumb and fingers to my temples.

"Sorry. It's a lot to take in. But you'll get used to it. I'm sure you'll love it there."

He spoke like my going was inevitable, but the more he talked, the less I wanted to go. Couldn't we just stay here?

I eyed him. He was handsome. But I'd let him walk away before I'd abandon my clan. My village. My world. Maybe I could convince him to stay here.

CHAPTER THIRTY

FAOLAN

We spent the day fishing, not that we needed the food. We had plenty of dried deer meat left. But we needed something to occupy our minds. At least, I did. Spearing the poor creatures satisfied my need to strike something, even if I'd never hit my true target —Morrigan.

I shuddered at her image. Those creepy eyes. The unearthly way she moved. The War Queen. I could almost smell her now. I glanced around, up and down the ravine—again. But she wasn't here. It was still daylight. She would wait until night, right? Did daylight affect her?

Aodan should've burned her, even with me in her grip. She'd been the start of the fasgadair. What if she was also the end? If she died, would her minions attack our village or would they scatter?

Something stabbed my toe. "Ow!" I dug my spear into the ground to steady myself and grasped my dripping foot from the cool river to inspect it. Just a scratch. No blood.

"Ye all right?" Aodan splashed through the water toward me.

"Aye. Just stepped on a rock or something."

"Ye seem tense."

I yanked my spear from the rubble and armed myself. "Tense doesn't begin to express how overly wound I am right now. As soon as that sun goes down, Morrigan is going to reappear expecting an answer from ye. How are ye not tense?"

"Ye think I'm not!" He armed himself with his spear as if ready to do battle. His face reddened.

Recalling our conversation from that morning, I took a deep breath. "My apologies, mate. It's just—She's going to be here sooner than we'd like. She's going to turn ye into a fasgadair, and we're just fishing like tomorrow will be a normal day. It won't. Shouldn't we be doing something, like coming up with a plan to kill her?"

He narrowed his eyes at me. "Weren't ye the one telling me there might be a way to save them?"

"Not her!" My face felt as hot as his looked. "How many undead has she created since her unholy resurrection? How many might be spared by killing her? She was dead. She should've stayed dead. We should put her back where she came from. Where she belongs."

"I already told ye—I tried. She's impossible to kill." He used his weapon as a walking stick and trudged through the water to our log. He hunched over.

I took my spot beside him.

Elbows braced on his knees, he plunked his chin in his hands, then nudged me with his shoulder. "What makes ye think *I* can kill her when so many others have tried and failed over the past hundreds of years? Sake! Her first act this side of death was to fly into battle and decimate both sides! She's unstoppable."

"So why didn't she kill us, too? Has she changed over the centuries?"

He shrugged. "Has she ever offered her kingdom to anyone before?"

If only I could look into his mind and understand whatever was going on in there. "It's not her kingdom. She stole it."

"On the inside, maybe I can find a way to destroy her. To destroy them all." His bloodshot eyes waited for my response to fill them with hope. "Could that be God's plan?"

"Maybe." I rubbed my chin. What he said made sense. I didn't like it, but I didn't see another solution. Other than to run... but to where? And what trouble would we bring upon our families if we did?

"This is the only way to save my family. And I have to hope it will somehow lead to Morrigan's end. To the end of *all* the fasgadair."

I struggled to believe God would allow Aodan to become one of those monsters, no matter the outcome. But maybe he was right. I grabbed his hand and pulled him to kneel on the pebbly bank. "We should pray."

✡

I STARED INTO THE FIRE, pushing my trout with my spoon until it no longer resembled fish. The ravine walls hid the moon. No light spilled from above. Only our campfire offered light. Beyond was complete darkness.

If only God would have spoken. But we'd both felt confident this was the solution. God must have a plan, even if only to save our clan.

Something splashed in the water. I snapped my head toward the sound and waited. Listened. Strained to see beyond the fire. Nothing. Probably a fish. I sniffed the air—again. I needed the smell to alert me... to prepare myself for Morrigan's return. Even if only by a snap of my fingers.

Aodan wasn't eating either. But he wasn't destroying his food like I was. His bowl waited on the ground beside him. He remained perfectly still, as if in a trance.

Was he all right?

I closed in on him to see if he'd notice me staring. He didn't move. I waved a hand in front of his eyes. "Ye in there, mate?"

Aodan blinked at me like he didn't recognize me. My stomach lurched as if I'd fallen from a great height. Was Morrigan nearby? Was she doing something witchy to my friend with her unearthly powers?

Life returned to his eyes. "Aye. I was trying to reach Cataleen. Send her images of Morrigan. In case word gets back to her, I want her to know why I'm doing this—to save our clan. I don't know if anything got through. She didn't respond. I'm too far away. But what if—what if this is the last—"

"Don't talk that way. This isn't the end. Ye hear me?" I wrapped my arm around his shoulder and squeezed. If only I believed my own words.

The scent permeated the air. I stood, pulling him with me, searching in every direction.

There, opposite the fire, a shadow moved. Morrigan's pale face appeared. Everything else, from her dark hair to her cloak, blended in with the background... even her black eyes. Only a floating face remained, like a mask. Shuddering, I gripped Aodan tighter.

"Have ye thought about my offer?" She seemed to float toward us, hovering above the ground like a wraith.

"I—" Aodan gulped. "We will go with ye."

A sly smile slithered across her face.

"But." Aodan held a hand out. "Faolan will not be turned. Can ye promise me that? He remains with me under my protection."

She leaned her head back. Sickening laughter flowed from her dead core and echoed through the ravine. I expected anything airborne to drop dead and rain down on us. Not a line appeared on her unnatural face. Her laugh cut short, and she trained her lifeless eyes on Aodan. "Whatever ye wish, Commander. Anyone who lays a hand on Faolan will die by my hand. Or yours." She motioned toward me, her smile twisting like a snake shedding its skin. "Unless he is harmed by your hand."

My gaze snapped to Aodan. He was about to allow himself to become an undead monster. Who knew what he'd be capable of with demon blood coursing through his veins? When we prayed, why hadn't we prayed about that? Might he kill me? Or worse... turn me into a fasgadair against my will?

Pain darkened Aodan's eyes. My thoughts must've been visible on my face. I tried wiping them away. But I couldn't project reassuring thoughts when I was anything but confident about how all this would turn out.

✡

How COULD we have been so foolish as to trust Morrigan? Nay, we didn't *trust* her. But we somehow thought we could trick her. We, fifteen-year-old gachen, would somehow fool a being that had already lived a lifetime in another world and existed for centuries in whatever state her body was in now? How could we be so daft? What if she said whatever it took to get Aodan to follow her? He had a strange ability no one had seen before. Did she want to keep him around for that reason? Or had she lied about everything to get him to this place—vulnerable?

She was a demon.

Demons lied.

I hugged my arms around myself by the dark cavern. Vomit-inducing squishy noises echoed from within.

What if she was killing him whilst I stood by? My entire body felt as if it were numb and feelings were returning. That nasty sensation of countless sharp projectiles rushing through my blood. I pumped my fists while groaning and sucking sounds ricocheted in the dark abyss.

I dropped to my knees, clutching my abdomen. My stomach twisted as if I'd swallowed a drop of Morrigan's blood, and it grew like an undead thing with unholy roots and branches shooting in every direction, threatening to break through my skin. With the pain unbearable, I clenched my teeth, then loosed a guttural cry to purge the ugliness from my soul before the roots burrowed deep and turned me into something else. Something not too far from what Aodan was becoming.

I bent over and vomited.

After I emptied my stomach, I spat and wiped my mouth. *God, please protect him. Keep our village safe. Protect Catty. Protect our parents.*

The nasty fasgadair scent strengthened, pushing me away from the entrance like a tangible thing. Morrigan emerged, and I stumbled, falling back onto my rear. Again, her feet didn't appear to connect with the ground as she passed me.

Was she weakened? Could I try to kill her now? My gaze darted to the spear leaning against the entrance. Why hadn't I been carrying it? I'd never get to it now.

"When he wakes, tell him to meet me in Ceas Croi."

"Ceas what? Where—?"

Morrigan was gone. But I caught a faint whiff of her scent wafting from the cave. I half expected Aodan to materialize like Morrigan. An image of him with fasgadair eyes sprang to mind. A full-body shudder racked me as I tried to purge the image. I wanted to go inside. To help. But what could I do? I didn't want to go near him. What if his first act as a fasgadair was to eat me?

I stood by the black hole, waiting for whatever emerged.

CHAPTER THIRTY-ONE

CATALEEN

Josh and his da filled the empty spots at our kitchen table.
Nathaniel braced both hands on the table, leaning back in his chair. "I'm sorry I've never stopped to speak with you, Mirna. I typically go straight out to the mine and return home to Fiona as soon as possible."

"'Tis all right, Nathaniel. Does she ever come back with ye?" Ma took a dainty bite of mutton.

He flattened his palms to the wood, his lips flattening as well. "She prefers to pretend Ariboslia doesn't exist."

Ma stopped chewing. Hand over her mouth, she choked down her bite. "Pretend it doesn't...? Ariboslia is her home."

He chewed his lower lip. "I know you weren't close. But surely, you saw how she was after her brother died. The entire village saw."

"I know she was afraid of the fasgadair after that." Ma laid her fork beside her plate.

"Right. She wouldn't leave her own home, never mind the village. She was eager to join me in America when Sully suggested I go."

"Sake, I'm glad fer that since ye were betrothed."

"Yes. But I worry for her. She won't acknowledge her brother at all. Or her parents. It's like they never existed. When we moved to America, she learned as much as she could, then invented a background to explain our accents and lack of understanding. I'm beginning to think she believes it. When I mention Ariboslia, she shuts me up and tells me what to tell her. She explains my absences by telling everyone I'm in the military. Becomes mighty awkward when I run into anyone who has served.... She goes as far as to send postcards to herself from wherever I'm supposedly stationed. Good thing no one else looks at them." Nathaniel scoffed. "They'd see they're all postmarked from Maine."

Ma placed her elbows on the table and clasped her hands over her plate. "I don't follow. What is a postcard?"

"It's a short letter." He waved as if swatting a bug. "Doesn't matter. The point is—she lost her mind when that fasgadair killed her brother. Sending her to America didn't help. She's only gotten worse."

"Hmm. I'll pray for her. Please remind her she is loved."

"I try to, but—"

An image invaded my mind. A female with black hair. Her eyes opened, revealing nothing but black, as if there was nothing inside. They flashed in the firelight, glowing yellow. Then another image of her appeared in a different location. A series of images of her flashed in rapid succession, along with feelings of frustration. A creepy voice accompanied the images as if they were echoes of something she'd said. "Rule Ariboslia. Be their leader. Guarantee Notirr's safety." In an endless loop. I slumped against the back of the chair, catching myself before I fell.

"Cataleen!" Ma raced to my side. She pushed my hair aside and felt my forehead. "Are ye unwell?"

I straightened. Aodan. He must've sent this, but why?

Aodan! Aodan, where are you?

I reached out, but came back empty. Tears streamed down my face. I swiped at them, my face warming. Why couldn't this have happened when I was alone? "Please forgive me."

"What happened? Was it Aodan?" She glanced at our visitors. "Cataleen and Aodan can…"

"We know about their connection, Mirna." Josh's da gave us a reassuring smile.

I had to collect myself. Now, with Josh and his da, was not the time to fall apart. I took a deep, shuddering breath. "He sent me pictures of a fasgadair. A female. It might have been Morrigan."

Ma's hand flew to her mouth. She stared at me as if I were a ghost.

I pressed a splayed hand over my heart as if to keep it in place. "It sounded like she was asking Aodan to rule Ariboslia to keep us safe."

Ma fell against the backrest and clutched her chest.

I eyed our guests. Each stared, wide-eyed and slack-jawed. Aodan. My beloved twin. One of those demonic creatures? My heart felt as though someone had tossed it into the winepress and trod upon it, mashing it to a pulp.

But if this was true, he was doing it to protect us. Not kill us. If anything could make Aodan agree to become one of those blood drinkers, protecting his clan was it. He could never harm us.

But if this part of the prophecy came true, if he became a fasgadair, what about the rest of it? He would never harm me with his right mind. But as one of the undead, how much would he change? What would he be capable of?

CHAPTER THIRTY-TWO

FAOLAN

Hours had passed, and still, Aodan hadn't come out. Crouching at the cave's entrance, tensed, armed with my spear, ready to spring into action the moment the baby demon appeared had exhausted me beyond anything I'd felt before. I crawled to our log and leaned against it, clutching my weapon across my chest.

Morrigan, the War Queen, had turned my best mate into a demon. Even if Aodan *could* keep Notirr safe, would he still want to?

Would he be bloodthirsty? Would he kill me?

I should run whilst I had the chance. Warn my da. My clan. Catty.

But my time to escape had passed. This night had wrecked my body. I was in no shape to hobble away, never mind run. And I'd come too far. I needed to know what had become of Aodan. I couldn't go back to our clan without answers.

The cave was silent as if my transitioning friend weren't in there.

I was nothing. Powerless. Dirt. I needed help. I released my weapon and clasped my hands. "God, I don't know what Yer plans are. I don't know what's happening to Aodan or why. But help me trust Ye through it all. Protect me. Protect my clan. Show me what to do, God. I don't know what to d—"

"Faolan?" Aodan stood at the cave entrance. The fasgadair stench oozed from him. His purple eyes were as I'd imagined. Nay... worse. I saw nothing of my mate in those eerie irises that took over his entire eye. If normal eyes were windows into a person's soul, these showed nothing. I backed away.

"I won't hurt ye." He spoke as if approaching a wounded animal he had no intention of harming, and he held out his hands to prove he had no weapons. But his voice. Something changed. It slithered through the air, making my ears itch.

Aodan needed no weapon. *He* was the weapon. I continued my retreat, stepping into the water.

"Please, I couldn't bear this if ye left me." He sounded tired. Which he must be after dying and partially returning to life, weighed down with demon blood. "Ye said ye'd come with me."

I couldn't see my old friend in his eyes, but I heard him—just a faint whisper beneath the prickling sound, but it was something. Taking a deep breath to still my racing heart, I forced myself to stay put. "H–how do ye feel?"

"Tired... different." He wrinkled his nose, raising a lip to reveal a sharp canine.

I backed away, angling along the shoreline.

His freakish eyes widened, and he felt for the wayward tooth, then rubbed his upper lip as if to stretch it out, hiding evidence of his new nature. But there was no hiding those eyes.

"Will ye stop backing away from me? I'm telling ye—I won't hurt ye."

I stilled. "She said to go to Ceas Croi."

Aodan nodded. "Yer coming with me?"

Bile burned my throat. *God, please tell me what to do.* Aodan's scent alone urged everything within me to flee. And his eyes. Could I ever look upon him without shuddering, listen to him without wanting to scrape the sound from my ears, or stand by him without wanting to heave? Without feeling as if I were breaking in two?

And yet... Aodan was still in there, keeping the monster at bay, or I'd be dead already. He wanted me by his side. What if he needed me, with my soul intact, to advise him as he "ruled" Ariboslia? Could I keep him in line and ensure he kept Notirr safe? What if I had a chance to save him?

Or was I delusional?

Now would be a good time to tell me what to do, God.

I had never heard God out loud. And I'd never felt a certainty about what to do after seeking His advice, so I wasn't sure why I expected anything now. But I knew much of God's writings to His people. Surely, something from His word would tell me the right thing to do.

Flee from evil. That was in His words of instruction, was it not? But then, so was "love your enemies." So His writings weren't helpful in this situation.

Why oh why won't You speak to me?

One thing was for certain—there was no way out of this without losing my mind.

I faced my unnaturally still friend, his face devoid of emotion. Waiting. *That* was unlike Aodan. But he wasn't moving to kill me. And what good would I be to my clan if I returned home, hunkered down in fear, waiting, wondering if Aodan would keep his word or attack? And what would I do if he did attack?

Die. I would die.

Be courageous. That was also in God's holy writings. Wasn't retreating to my village the cowardly thing to do?

Joining Aodan. Facing other fasgadair. Risking my life. That took courage. And following Aodan provided the unique opportunity to learn of the fasgadair from the inside. To know their plans. Perhaps, with inside knowledge, I could keep my clan safe.

Be courageous.

God wasn't speaking to me, yet He was. It was written over and over in His word. This was the courageous move.

Something changed within me. My gut settled. My spine straightened. "Do ye know where Ceas Croi is?"

A smile crept over Aodan's face, revealing his fangs, and I stifled the rising revulsion. "No, but I can get us to Diabalta. We can find answers there."

How did he know how to get to Diabalta when he'd never been? Did he have a strange connection with the demons who knew? A witchy understanding that defied reason? Or had he done a better job paying attention to our geography lessons? I eyed this half demon, half friend. I'd have to keep a wary eye on him and never sleep again. "Pack yer things."

Aodan moved inhumanly fast to the cave, nearly colliding with the rock. Arm outstretched, bracing himself, he ducked and disappeared into the darkness.

I threw my meager belongings together. I'd made my choice and stood by it, but I'd never have a moment of peace in the presence of this undead version of my friend. There was a fine line between courageous and stupid.

CHAPTER THIRTY-THREE

CATALEEN

Time dragged like a pregnant sloth. Three days had passed since Aodan sent the images of Morrigan. Only three. Somehow, it felt like weeks. I'd thrown images to him, hoping something got through—Ma, the orphan babies, Cahal, our favorite spot on the pier—anything that might ground him, give him reason not to give in to whatever temptation he faced. Or to keep his humanity had he already made the wrong choice.

But I didn't know if anything was getting through. Aodan had always been the stronger one. If only we'd thought to test our mind-link across distances while we had the chance.

I occupied myself by helping care for the growing orphan population. Dolan strained against the straps in his chair, then clapped his pudgy hands. I shoved another spoonful of porridge into his mouth. His uncooperative tongue pushed out more than he swallowed. Gruel dribbled down his chin. He smacked what fell on the table, sending porridge raining over the table, himself, and me. He squished what remained. It oozed through his fingers. He then stared at his hands as if wondering what the strange substance was and how it had gotten there. Then he laughed, clapped, and repeated the process, being sure to tug his blond hair and touch everything within reach so he wore more porridge than he ate. This boy was going to be a crusty mess to clean. Good thing cream and oats were good for bathing. There would be plenty in his bathwater.

He stuck out his tongue and made a razzing sound, sending more gruel spurting.

Backed away to a safer distance, I threw the boy an unimpressed look. "Are ye done spitting yer food all over me?"

He laughed and worked his tongue to repeat what he'd done before, but couldn't stop laughing long enough to stick out his tongue. Then he raised his arms, clenching and releasing his hands.

"All done?"

He nodded and tried squeezing his way free from his chair, mashing more porridge on the wooden rails. I doused a cloth in water and freed him from as much grime as possible. "You are such a mess!"

"Mess. Mess. Mess," he sang.

"You're quite the little myna bird."

"Mess. Mess. Mess." Dolan didn't speak much, but he liked to pick one word, usually the last one spoken, and turn it into a song. Everyone learned not to call anyone names in his presence lest it became his song for weeks. The more you tried to change the word, the harder he sang the one he'd already clung to.

Thank God for these babies. What would I have done without them? I couldn't imagine trying to do something mindless like helping in the gardens, leaving my mind fertile for weedy worries. Something I'd done since I was a wee lass with my brothers. I had too much time. But the kids distracted me, and their need, greater than mine, put things in perspective and kept me from worrying... much. Anchoring myself to them, I could keep from falling back into the pit of self-pity that seemed to move before me at every step, hoping I'd trip, ready to catch me in its unfathomable depths.

And Josh. Now I had him to worry about, too. He was so eager for me to return to America with him. I hated to tell him I wasn't going. I couldn't leave my ma, my home, and now these orphans to go gallivanting in a foreign realm with people I'd just met. And even if my messages weren't getting through to Aodan, I had to keep trying. I'd never reach him from another realm.

Besides, who was Josh to me? Sully's prophecies had me so confused. On the off chance that he was right and I went with Josh's family to America, would I live with him? Would he then be like a brother to me? What if he liked me in a different way? Like, the way a husband liked his wife?

My face burned. Nay. Nay, nay, nay. I pressed the back of my arm to my cheek, trying to avoid touching my hair with my filthy cloth. Blowing out a breath, I scrubbed away my errant thoughts like the oats between Dolan's fingers.

Dolan blew out a breath as I had, making me laugh. I wiped his face, and he squirmed away from the offending cloth. When most of his body was clean enough not to destroy the furniture or the other children, I reached to free him.

"There you are." Josh's voice made me jump. Tiny little bubbles burst throughout me. Why was my body constantly betraying me in his presence? So infuriating.

I tugged Dolan free, and Josh's face appeared in my periphery, a huge smile crinkling his sparkling hazel eyes. His eyes reminded me of Faolan's. But Josh's had more green, whereas Faolan's were more gold. But a mere look from Faolan didn't warm my cheeks like one from Josh did. So, so, so infuriating.

"This little guy is getting heavy." I groaned as I moved him from one hip to the other. Perhaps, if my face was as red as it felt, he'd think it was from the strain. "When did ye return from yer mining trip?"

"This morning."

His messy hair, even more so today, worked for him. He still looked irritatingly beautiful. "Have ye been home? Have ye eaten?"

"Nope. Came straight here."

"Why?" I wiped down the high chair as Dolan clung to me.

"I wanted to see you."

Something in the purity of his voice and his unapologetic confession sent my stomach tumbling, reigniting the heat in my face. What was he doing—confessing his feelings? If he wanted to court me, this wasn't how it was done. Had his father taught him nothing? Or, perhaps where he was from, there was nothing unusual about a boy running to see a girl before doing anything else and admitting to wanting to see her. But here? In Ariboslia? Nay. But how should I respond?

Best to pretend it was nothing. I tossed the porridge-ridden cloth into the bowl and nested it into the one that still held the remains of Dolan's breakfast. I picked them up and headed to the basin. "Ye should get something to eat. We can talk later."

His face fell, and my stomach dipped as I walked away. Perhaps I'd made the wrong choice. But what was he doing? If he was interested in me romantically, he'd best learn to court me properly. If the prophecy was true, I'd end up in his world. In the meantime, we were here, in my world. Even if we weren't, I wasn't about to embarrass myself by responding inappropriately to advances I didn't understand.

But then, if he approached me properly, how would I respond?

CHAPTER THIRTY-FOUR

FAOLAN

We hadn't made much progress since leaving our camp. I was still exhausted. It wasn't safe to sleep at night as we neared fasgadair territory. And the sun weakened Aodan. So we hunkered down during the day. We took turns trying to sleep in our animal forms. But I couldn't sleep. Even with him in his animal form, I didn't trust him. And he'd yet to talk to me. Perhaps there was no way to express what he was feeling? Or maybe demons weren't talkative.

The canyon grew increasingly narrow. I clung to the mountain wall. Sweat beaded on my forehead. A cool wind swept through the ravine, chilling the wet spots. I stretched my leg farther than felt comfortable, feeling for a foothold, and nearly lost my balance. I yanked my foot back—heart racing, chest heaving, feet itching. Pebbles pinged down the wall, crashing into the water below.

Why had we come this way? We should have split up. I should have come alone in the daylight.

"There's a break in the ledge about a cubit long." Aodan's slithery voice came from the darkness up ahead. "You'll have to reach. Do ye have a good fingerhold?"

"Aye." I strained the word out. Breath didn't come easy with my chest pressed against the unforgiving stone. Sweat dripped into my eye. I couldn't wipe it away. Not that it made my vision worse. The moonlight didn't reach us here.

I tested my fingers to ensure I still had a good grip, then shimmied to the side, feeling for the edge with my foot. When I got to the end, I moved as far as I could, then stretched my leg, searching for the ledge once more.

"That's it. Just a little further."

My fingers ached. My nails dug in to keep their hold as I strained to reach. They tingled, sure I'd lose my grip and fall into the river below.

"It's just there. Lower your foot a little, you'll step on it."

To do as he said, I'd have to release my grip. This was such an exercise in faith in my new demonic best friend. Would he toy with me rather than kill me? Just how twisted was he now?

My heart thundered in my ears as sweat dripped down my back. I released my handhold and stretched my foot, my fingers feeling for anything else to hold me as I slid down. My foot caught.

Thank You, God.

My labored breath came out in harsh puffs as I collected myself, praising God that I was still alive. When I calmed somewhat, I felt for new handholds to get my other leg onto the new ledge. Once they were secure, I thrust myself to the side. But my right foot had no place to land. I pressed it to the sliver of rock beside my secure foot, then shimmied until both feet were secure.

"You made it! That's the worst of it. There's a few more cubits of narrow ledge, but then it widens."

As much as I despised fasgadair, I'd give almost anything for their night vision right now. He was right. I struggled for the next few steps, but the path widened so I could walk normally.

Still, we were high above the ravine, and it was dark. I took my time.

"Sun's coming up," he said. "Let's shift. The ledge lowers up ahead. If we find someplace wider, preferably on the ground by the water, let's sleep."

The ledge brought us back down to ground level where we attempted to sleep on pebbles beside the water. Sleeping conditions weren't ideal, but we had water, fish, and relative safety. By the third day, the seemingly never-ending chasm opened, and we emerged into an open plain. I ran to the grassy field, discarded my pack, and fell onto the grass.

I breathed deeply as I tipped my face toward the starry sky. How much nicer it would be to see this during the day. To feel the sun on my face. But I was no longer constricted. Nothing walled me in. I could breathe.

I would never come this way again. If the time came to return to Notirr, I'd find another way.

I ran my fingers through the grass, but my relief only lasted so long. The presence of my best-mate-turned-monster confined me still. I was growing immune to the strange lightning smell, but something about him now made me feel... imprisoned.

Despite his help in the gorge, the creature traveling with me wasn't my friend. He was still there. But he wasn't alone.

As much as I appreciated solid ground and wide-open space, it brought new dangers. We were visible to any fasgadair that might happen upon us. We should have a few hours of night left. I shouldered my pack. "We should get moving."

The way he moved still disconcerted me. He didn't move too fast to be seen, like Morrigan. Nor did he seem to float above the ground. Rather, he was jerky, like he had speed he didn't know how to use yet, so he had to keep stopping and starting.

If he was amazed by his new abilities or haunted by his demon blood, I couldn't guess. We were brothers-turned-strangers growing stranger with each step. Was there a way to save him? Was it too late? I needed to get him talking. Perhaps something he'd say would make it clear if I should turn back toward Notirr whilst I could still leave with my life.

"Are ye getting tired? Or finally got yer fasgadair legs?"

Aodan wrinkled his nose as if he'd caught a foul smell.

"Ye used to race ahead of me and cycle back, but now yer keeping pace. Is it because yer getting tired? Or have ye learned to pace yerself?"

He shrugged.

Had he forgotten how to hold a conversation? Maybe he needed to feed. The thought made me feel like I'd jumped into leech-infested waters. I shuddered, then stopped.

Aodan nearly ran into me. He bounced back as if he'd hit an invisible wall, his face twisted in pain and disgust. Did I repulse him as much as he disgusted me?

"Why'd ye stop?" He growled. He buried his nose inside his elbow.

"We can't go on like this."

"Like what?" He stepped back and lowered his arm.

I scoffed, shaking my head. "Like ye don't know." I ran a hand through my hair and held, clutching a fistful.

"Know what?" His freakish purple eyes widened.

Bile burned my throat. Should I say it? "Yer a demon."

He waved me off. "Aye. I'm aware."

"I'm walking into a fasgadair nest—nay, an entire city *full* of fasgadair *with* a fasgadair. I must be off my head. How will this not end *very* badly for me?"

Aodan blew out a sharp breath, tousling the hair falling into his eyes. "Yer meant to stay with me."

"Says who? Why?" I moved toward him.

As expected, he wrinkled his nose and stepped back.

"See? We can't stand to be near each other. You know that smell that charges the air during a lightning storm? The smell that ignites every sense, causing ye to flee for shelter? Ye stink of it. It's tough to stay by yer side when every part of me is crying out to flee from yer presence. And where is my friend? I don't know. Other than your help in the ravine, I haven't seen any hint of his existence behind those grotesque eyes."

He opened his mouth.

"And ye can't tolerate being near me, either. I see how ye recoil when ye get too close."

Aodan closed his mouth and took a deep breath. "I didn't realize I was so disgusting."

What? Was he offended? "Ye jest. Don't ye recall the fasgadair we'd met whilst ye were still gachen? And judging by yer face when ye get too close to me, ye feel the same."

"Ye don't disgust me." He pursed his lips together and huffed. His unreadable eyes trained on me as if he had something to say, but unsure if he should. "Ye—that is, yer *blood*—attracts me. When I get too close, I can smell it. Sake! What repulses me is my desire to feed on ye."

I took a giant step back. "Isn't that all the more reason for me to leave? If ye, my friend, want to feed on my blood, what about the countless fasgadair we're about to meet?" I threw my arm out, aiming toward Diabalta. "How can ye save me?"

"I don't know. But I will. I have to. Yer *supposed* to join me. I need ye."

"Ye don't need me. Ye'd get to Diabalta much faster without me. Then ye could get a proper meal." Oh, why did I have to add that? My stomach rolled.

"Don't ye think I know that?" Aodan's skin sallowed. Or was that just his new peely-wally face? "I know what I am. I don't deny it. But I"—he pounded his heart—"yer mate is still in here. Together, we can save our home. I had a dream—"

"Oh, ye had a dream, did ye? Well, that beats all, don't it?" I tipped my head up to the heavens and laughed at the absurdity. "What happened in this *dream*?"

"I don't remember exactly. I just know 'tis all part of God's plan and we would keep Notirr safe—together."

"Ye were *dreaming!*" Every tendon in my neck tensed as I stressed the word, attempting to drill it into my thickheaded evil friend's head.

"Angels appear in dreams."

"Aye. But to my knowledge, they don't advise gachen to become demons. Doesn't seem holy to me. If anything spoke to ye, was probably another demon."

"God can use anyone, good or evil, for His purposes. Can He not?"

I scoffed. "Look at ye! Are ye giving *me* a sermon?"

Aodan closed his eyes, appearing almost human. My heart softened. What did I know of demons and angels? Demons knew of God's existence better than any gachen, regardless of the gachen's faith. Demons tapped into the spiritual world in a way anyone formed from dirt couldn't understand. Did Aodan have greater insight into the things of God now? As a demon? He was right. God had used those who didn't serve Him to serve His purposes. It was written in His holy word. He used the Devil himself. And He was God, after all. He could do anything.

Was it possible He might use my undead mate in His plans?

And I had gotten the sense I needed to be courageous.

Perhaps this was God's plan. Those He used didn't always like what they were called to do, like Jonah. It wasn't easy and always required courage—and trust.

God, help me trust Ye now and steer me in the right direction.

I disarmed my mental warfare. Enough talk for today. I motioned toward who knew what. "Lead the way."

CHAPTER THIRTY-FIVE

CATALEEN

I'd never dreaded an anniversary of our birth before. If only I could keep it from coming or fly past it. Anything but sit under that ominous cloud, forced to linger there. I couldn't celebrate without Aodan and Faolan. Where were they? Were they still gachen? Were they still alive?

Josh and the orphans could distract me only so much. I almost wanted to leave for America just to escape sad blessings from the clan and Ma's breakfast—alone. How would she feel having to do all that preparation for just me?

I placed Dolan on his bed and covered him with the blanket. He rustled a bit, then settled back to sleep. Soft puffs of air escaped in time to his stomach's rise and fall. Impossibly long lashes brushed his pink cheeks. He looked so peaceful. If only I could extract a portion of that calm.

I closed the door without making a sound. Josh waited for me on the swing outside the orphanage. I sat beside him on the bench, and he kicked us into motion. Everything attempted to soothe my spirit—Josh's calming presence, the swing's gentle sway, the rope's rhythmic sound, the red sun's brilliant glow in its descent, the peepers' chorus off in the distance. But my soul refused to be soothed.

"What's America like?"

Josh almost stopped the swing, then set it swaying again. "You're interested now?"

I shrugged. "Just curious."

He took a deep breath. "It's different. I'll say that. But, where I live, there's a lot of similarities. It's woodsy, mountainous, and borders an ocean. And has dump ducks." He laughed. "Lots of dump ducks."

"Dump duck?"

"Seagulls. We call them dump ducks because they're so—" He must've caught my blank stare. He waved it off. "Never mind."

"We have seagulls here. Have ye ever watched them eat? They find clams and mussels brought in from the tide and drop them on the rocks to break them open. Quite ingenious if ye ask me."

He scratched the back of his neck and squinted. "Yeah. They're probably nicer here where they're not fighting over french fries and pooping all over cars."

How could we see the same creatures so differently?

He tugged at his collar. "The ocean isn't as close to my home either. You can't walk there. You have to get in a car and drive. And in the summer, it's crowded."

"With seagulls?" Was that why he didn't like them? There were too many?

"No, people. There are a lot more people. Everywhere. Especially in the summer during tourist season. And most don't live together in communities like this. They don't work together and have meals together. Individual families do, but not entire villages."

"So, where do you live? How do you get food?" Perhaps it was best I not know and deal with what I found there when and if I arrived. Listening to him speak of this place increased my anxiety—no appreciation for seagulls. And worse—no community?

"We live in houses. My farmhouse is bigger than any home I've seen here. We grow some food, but we buy most of it at the farmer's market or the grocery store. That's why my dad comes here to mine. To earn money for food and anything else we need."

I didn't know what was worse—to live without *my* clan or with no clan at all. It sounded lonely. How would I ever fit into such a foreign environment? Tears slipped down my cheeks, and the swing came to a halt, jolting me sideways.

"Hey." Josh twisted toward me and bumped his knee into mine. He cupped my face in his hands, brushing away my tears with his thumbs. "Don't be afraid. I'll be with you. It will be all right. I'll make sure of it."

That hazel gaze poured into mine like warm honey. Regardless of whether he could keep his word, he meant what he said. He leaned closer. His warm lips brushed mine, and I jumped as if he bit me. I pushed him away and leaped to my feet. My cheeks warmed, and indignation at his audacity spurred me on.

"I'm sorry, Cataleen. I—"

"Ye want to protect me? Start by learning the proper way to court a girl." I darted off down the path to my home and covered my blush in my hands. Was this how people were in the human realm? Did the boys go around kissing girls without courting? Without asking permission?

My stomach performed aerobatics, and I touched my lips. The memory of his touch brought forth a fury of mixed emotions. What angered me most? That he dared kiss me, or that I dared like it?

I broke out into a run and tripped. Ripping fabric sounded as I caught my fall on—hooves? I lowered my head to find a brown underbelly partially covered in the torn fabric of my dress. I kicked myself as free as possible, then pranced about on my new feet. My large heart thumped. What was I? A horse? Deer? Elk? I'd have preferred something with wings, but this would do. *Anything* would do.

My lanky legs wobbled, and I nearly tripped over myself. Walking on four legs would take some getting used to. I went up and down the path a few times to practice. It wasn't as difficult as I'd thought.

I saw the world differently in my totem form. Some colors seemed to be missing, but I could see so much more all at once, and the smells...

A gust of wind swept through, carrying so many scents. In human form, I might distinguish one or two. But this? Hundreds of distinct scents cavorted my way. What were they all? I sniffed the air. Grasses. Trees. Bark. Leaves. Dirt. Moss. Ferns. Critters. Flowers. Lots of flowers. Some with a more soapy scent, others more sweet. How had I survived so long without noticing all these smells?

I might be a wingless ground animal, but my heart soared. After all this time, I'd reached my bian!

My elation deflated.

What good was reaching my bian when Aodan wasn't here to share my joy... or Faolan?

Should I go home and share it with Ma? Part of me wanted to return to Josh. But how could I after the way I'd left him? Nay, I needed to leave him be and share this with him when the timing was better, when I was prepared with a change of clothes. As it was, my torn undergarments hung precariously about my midsection. Better to return to Ma to assist me and save myself further embarrassment.

Something crinkled on my left. My head snapped toward the sound. A bird hopped along the ground, rustling leaves, then flitted into a tree. I snorted out relief.

I didn't want to be seen. Not yet. Not like this. I searched the trail, sniffing the air. I could see so much more in my periphery. My ears swiveled, listening for anyone nearby. No one was on the trail. I walked into the tree cover, then darted off toward home. My body glided through the brush with ease.

CHAPTER THIRTY-SIX

FAOLAN

I was tired of walking through Ariboslia. We'd passed beauty such as I'd never known existed. We descended a cliff that appeared to be the end of the world and bathed in the pool of a waterfall that fell from the heavens. But I couldn't enjoy it. Not when every step brought me closer to a future I'd rather not face. But there was no way out. If only God would reach down and pluck me from this world.

My steps slowed as we trekked through a wooded area. If Aodan grew weary of my lethargy, he didn't say. Nor did he accuse me of hindering our progress. Which I was—purposefully.

But why? Was I attempting to stave off the inevitable meetings with other fasgadair, especially Morrigan? Or was I trying to irritate Aodan?

Perhaps a little of both.

Why I wanted to get a rise out of Aodan, I wasn't sure. Perhaps because I couldn't tolerate walking in silence with this thing trying to keep my stride. Aodan might not be as chatty as Catty, but he had an opinion about everything and wasn't afraid to voice it. But what did he think about anything now? Or was he just fighting his urge to bite me?

I'd rather face Aodan's new nature now and ease the tension of waiting and wondering when the beast would give in to its violent urges. Sometimes the punishment was better than the waiting, knowing it was coming, and what a relief once it had passed. Either I'd survive, or Aodan would kill me. At least I'd know. And right now, I preferred the latter.

So far, I'd failed to get a rise from him. Why? I'd never seen a gachen transform into a fasgadair before. Did they all possess his self-control? Or was his unheard-of in other fasgadair?

This courageous thing wasn't for the faint of heart. It took more out of me than I'd expected, living in perpetual vigilance, sleeping lightly, waking at every sound with a knife under my bedding, ready to strike should something trigger the demon within my old friend. Always on edge...

Two fasgadair materialized in our path.

I jumped back. How hadn't I sensed them? Another downfall to Aodan's presence. His constant stink rendered my senses useless.

"What have we here?" A fasgadair with enlarged green irises sniffed, his bulbous nostrils flared. "A fasgadair traveling with a gachen?"

"Are ye delivering meals?" The other licked his fangs.

Aodan positioned himself between the fasgadair and me, placing a hand on the beast's chest. "He has my protection... and Morrigan's."

The other fasgadair widened his grotesque eyes, still revealing no whites, and stepped back. But the one Aodan held back pressed closer until his face was a mere hand width from Aodan's. "And who are ye that claims the queen's name?"

Aodan pushed the fasgadair. "Aodan."

The fasgadair laughed and mockingly repeated Aodan's name. "What kind of fasgadair name is that? Has no one given ye yer new name? And are ye being gentle, or are ye that weak?"

Before I could register what was happening, Aodan was airborne. His back crashed into a tree. He winced as he peeled himself from the trunk, twisting to inspect his side. A twig protruded from his tunic, a band of red spreading from the spot.

"Yer hurt!" I rushed to his side.

"'Tis nothing." He gritted his teeth and yanked the branch free, then pulled up his tunic to inspect the spot. The hole in his side closed as he wiped the blood away.

I sucked in my breath. If only I had such an incredible ability.

Don't even think such things, Faolan, or you'll find yerself to be one of them soon enough.

It was an unholy gift. Not something to be desired.

Aodan trained his eyes on the fasgadair who attacked him, and the creature ignited. Engulfed in fire, the beast howled, then fell to the ground. His protruding veins feathered to dust first, then fanned out until he was a fasgadair-shaped dust pile. In the ravine, the continual breeze had swept the remains away. This one stayed intact like a statue of a dead man.

The other fasgadair nudged the dusty carcass. When his foot made the slightest contact, the entire thing crumbled. He backed away, hands up, horror in his godless eyes. "Don't harm me."

Aodan neared the fasgadair. "Where can I find Morrigan?"

"Ceas Croi."

"That I know. Where is Ceas Croi?"

The fasgadair motioned the way we headed. "'Tis just around the bend. Yer almost there."

Aodan's fasgadair face was tough to read. "If it's so close, bring us."

"Um." The creature looked as if it wanted to flee Aodan's presence. "Right." He turned, keeping a distrustful eye on Aodan. "This way."

Just when had Aodan gotten so commanding over the fasgadair? He appeared to be in a weakened condition compared with the others, though the only telltale signs were his dull eyes and the way the fasgadair had overpowered him. But his ability to engulf them in flames without laying hands on them didn't appear weak.

The charged stench surrounding these unholy beings nauseated me, and I was heading into a nest of them. At what point did courage morph into stupidity?

CHAPTER THIRTY-SEVEN

CATALEEN

My bian was a ray of sunlight penetrating my gloom. But each reminder that I didn't have anyone to share it with was another storm cloud, obscuring the sun's best efforts. And there was no one.

When Cahal wasn't helping rescue babies from Gnuatthara, he was busy caring for his family. I couldn't bother him.

Ma offered to join me, but that felt juvenile. When was the last time I asked her to watch me show off a new skill? Maybe when I learned to dive off the dock. I'd show her when she wasn't busy, but it just wasn't the same.

That left Josh.

How could I bother him after the way I left him, even for something this monumental?

My entire body buzzed with excess energy. I practically vibrated as I vacillated between telling him and not.

I had to show him. If I didn't show someone soon, I'd explode.

The sun burst through the clouds, pushing them so far back it was as if they'd never existed. As I readied my bag with a change of clothes, a squeal escaped me.

"Was that you?" Ma pushed my door open and peeked inside.

"What? Oh. Yeah. Sorry, Ma. Just excited to share my totem."

"And ye should be. Ye've been waiting a long time. I'm excited for ye, child. But be careful. As fun as it is to explore in totem form, yer a deer. A prey animal. Keep watch for predatory animals. Shouldn't be any hunters this time of year, but ye can't be too careful. If danger should confront ye, change back into yer gachen form. Keep a weapon on ye. And ye haven't gotten used to four legs yet. Take care near anything that might trip ye."

"Not to worry, Ma." I shouldered my pack, showing the loose holds that should fit my animal frame. "I loosened the straps, just as ye instructed."

After a nod of approval, she planted a kiss on my forehead. "Enjoy yer gift, dear."

✯

I RACED through the trees to Sully's home, tripping on the top step in my haste. The door opened before I knocked.

Josh's smile met me in the entryway, but his brow furrowed a bit as he held the door wide for me to enter. "Everything okay?"

Sully sat at the table with Josh's da and Pepin. They placed their forks down as I stepped inside.

My stomach sucked in, and I drew back. "I've interrupted yer morning meal, forgive me."

"I've finished." Josh blocked my escape. "Did you need something?"

Only a few crumbs remained on his plate. "Aye. I have something to show ye. Can ye come outside?"

"Sure." He started out the door.

"Not to worry, son. We'll clean up for you," Josh's da called at his back.

"Thanks, Dad." Josh looked over his shoulder with a sheepish grin, then followed me until Sully's cabin disappeared from view. "What's this all about?"

"I'll show ye." I placed a hand on his chest, staying him. "Wait here."

"Uh. Okay." He raised an eyebrow.

I hid in thick brush to remove my clothes, stuffed them into my pack, and threw the pack over my shoulders. Exhilaration such as I'd never experienced surged through me as my limbs elongated at my command. My midsection broadened, and I tipped forward onto my hooves. The pack fell into place across my back.

Though I was now on all fours, my height was only a little lower. But I'd never get used to the limited colors. It was as if I wore spectacles tinted a drab green. But the smallest movement was more noticeable now. And I had a much wider range of vision. So strange.

My large deer heart thudded. I bounced in the bushes on my new feet, then lowered my head to push my way through. Once free, I bounded over to Josh.

He jumped back, startled by my bold approach. Then recognition kicked in. "Cataleen?"

I nodded my long head.

He laughed, then stroked my face. I jerked my head away. Where did this fall into the courtship rules? It must be all right. I nuzzled his hand, and his face lit up. "I've never petted a deer before. Well, I got to pet a baby deer once. But that was through a fence at the Gray Wildlife Park. Hardly the same." He held a finger up, almost too close to see. "Wait here a sec."

He took off to the spot where I'd changed. I didn't know what a sec was, but I understood the wait part.

A creature burst from the thicket. An elk? Hadn't he claimed to have an elk totem when we met? He had the most impressive antlers I'd ever seen. Majestic.

We had similar bians? I sucked in a breath. They say similar bians are a sign of compatibility. But that came from old tales. There was no truth to them.

Was there?

Josh pranced back and forth before me, then jerked his head, beckoning me to follow. We raced through the woods, leaping over obstacles and darting through the brush. My heart thumped as the landscape sped past. A new world of scents presented itself. A thrill coursed through me at this remarkable gift. And to share it with Josh? I wasn't sure how I felt about that. Would I feel better running with another deerlike animal than a mountain lion and a wolf? I still didn't understand the totem side of me. Would that have made the deer in me nervous?

Josh slowed, and I nearly collided with him. He froze. His large ears flicked, then trained on something. Probably the trickling stream. Would I be able to hear that in my human form? My ear twitched, searching for the source. I followed him through shrubs to a clearing. Water raced over and around rocks and debris, then disappeared beyond a clump of trees. He stepped into the brook and lowered his head. I did the same. The cool water encircled my hoofs. I tried not breathing through my nose as I dunked for a sip.

Something moved in the woods, and we jerked our heads up in unison. Josh charged back the way we'd come, with me close behind. He leaped into a copse, his antlers caught. As he untangled himself, I didn't hear or see anything unusual. It was probably nothing. Or long gone.

Josh had left his clothes in the shrubs, so he changed first. Once I'd changed, I bounced from my hiding spot to where he sat on a rock. "That was incredible! I keep forgetting yer gachen." Laughing, I lowered myself beside him. "You look, speak, and act differently from anyone I've ever met. Yer clearly not from around here."

"Is that why you ran away from me last night?"

I held my breath. Why hadn't I prepared for this inevitable conversation? "I didn't run away—"

"You did. I'm sorry I kissed you. Both my parents are gachen, but I was raised in America. Our cultures are *very* different." The way he snickered and drew out "very" stirred my gut. "My parents don't talk about Ariboslia. My mother wants to pretend it doesn't exist, and my dad doesn't want to upset her. So, I grew up knowing nothing about it. I'm surprised they let me come."

"Do you kiss girls in America often? Is it common there?" Of all he'd just shared, why did I choose to focus on that one bit, twisting his words? Something ugly rose within me. Perhaps this was a mistake. He was gachen, but barely. What kind of man was he? Just what was acceptable in America? The more I learned, the less I wanted to know and the less I cared for even a brief visit.

He turned away and threw an indignant look over his shoulder at me. "Of course not."

I wanted to trust him. But could I?

He plucked a leaf from the ground and ripped it apart. "I talked to Sully last night."

"Oh? What about?"

"You took off last night spouting something about learning how to court a girl."

"So ye asked Sully?" I covered my mouth, stifling a laugh.

"What's so funny?"

"I can't imagine having such a conversation with Sully. I wish I could've seen that. How'd it go?" Silent laughter quaked my shoulders.

He sat taller and raised his eyebrows. "He's quite good at giving advice."

"I'm sure he is. Ye know, at his age and still unwed." I'd never considered Sully's marital position. Why hadn't he ever married?

"He talked to me about that, too. Said he was meant to remain single for God's service. Anyway..." He narrowed his eyes. "He advised me that it's not okay to kiss a girl without first getting her permission to ask her father if he'll approve the courtship. I didn't know. I'm sorry."

His sincerity made my palms sweat. Grasshoppers pinged around in my stomach. How should I respond? I straightened my spine and raised my nose in the air as if I were royalty. "Ye are forgiven."

"So, since your father has passed," he spoke low as if afraid to mention the fact, "Sully advised that your mother must approve."

"Aye."

"So, will you permit me to ask your mother if I can date you?"

"Date? What does that mean? You want to make me older?" Why was I deflecting the conversation? My heart rolled, sending my mouth racing like a bounding deer. I didn't know what I was saying or why. Yet my mouth carried on.

"Court." He leaned in closer. Any hint of shyness gone. "Can I ask your mom?"

I sucked in a breath as my heart sputtered. My brain ceased functioning. As if I were still in deer form facing a predator, I leaped to my feet. "Um. I—"

"Cataleen?" Josh stood, the boldness in his eyes waned. He reached out, wavering as I backed away.

"Aye. Ye can ask my ma." My heart slammed my rib cage as I sped through the woods away from him.

CHAPTER THIRTY-EIGHT

FAOLAN

I couldn't sleep in the company of fasgadair, even in their totem forms. If my confidence in Aodan dangled by a fraying thread, no way could I trust our guide. His assurances that fasgadair can't sense that I'm gachen in my animal form did nothing to soothe my fears. *He* knew I was a gachen, as did our guide. Would Aodan's threats stop him from waking and feeding on me? Just how much temptation could these demons withstand?

I nestled among the trees and propped my head on my paws, scanning the woods beyond our guide, then back to him, never letting him out of my sight. When my eyelids drooped, I found a stick to chew on to keep from falling asleep.

The sun dipped below the trees. Aodan kicked my foot, waking me.

I cursed myself for falling asleep.

We collected our things and continued on our way. I kept to my wolf form. If being a wolf brought less unwanted attention, then a wolf I would remain. And I could see better at night as a wolf.

But I was so tired. Even my canine form didn't want to carry on much further. Ceas Croi probably seemed closer to the fasgadair when a sleep-deprived gachen wasn't slowing them down. Our guide kept looking back as if wondering what was taking so long. But he never hurried us. Instead, he kept a wary eye on Aodan, probably afraid one misstep might ignite him in flames.

Was Aodan going slow for my benefit, or was he as exhausted as I was? Could a fasgadair die from lack of gachen blood?

If I were Aodan, I'd rather die.

The woods cleared, and a mountain wall rose before us, blocking out the moon, plunging us into darkness so complete, even my canine eyes struggled to see.

"Ceas Croi is in this mountain. But the entrance is this way." Our guide glanced at the sky. "We should make it before sunrise."

When we rounded the mountain, moonlight lit our way once more, and I breathed easier knowing where my enemies stood. We followed a worn path cut into the hill. As predicted, we reached the entrance before dawn.

Guards covered in chain mail and armed with axes posted at the doors stopped us. Their armor and helmets obscured their features, but not those eyes. I shuddered. I'd never get used to the whiteless eyes in an otherwise human-looking head.

Would chain mail make it difficult for a fasgadair to bite? I'd have to get some.

A guard stepped forward, axe poised. One side of his upper lip rose as he peered around Aodan at me and sniffed. "What's that? An offering?"

I crouched low and stepped back. Had our guide lied? They weren't supposed to know I was a gachen. Or would wolf blood suffice?

Aodan thrust out his chest and stepped forward. "Nay. We're here per Morrigan's request. Anyone who dares touch my wolf will suffer the consequences."

The guard looked back at the other, who neared the commotion and scoffed.

"'Tis true." Our guide stepped forward, hands upraised. "I've seen it. He lit Da'Het aflame. Turned him to dust."

The two guards exchanged questioning looks, then laughed as if a joke had just passed between them.

"Of course, he did." The first guard bared his teeth and lunged for me. Just as I was in his grip, the offending fasgadair burst into flames. Heat blasted me as I writhed from his hold, snapping my teeth. Horror bulged my attacker's eyes, and he screamed. Then, like the others, he fell dead and crumbled to ash. But no dust statue remained, other than his legs. Ash billowed from the tiny holes in his heavy chain mail. His helmet teetered on the uneven path, churning the remains of his head into a pile of cinder.

The surviving guard picked up the helmet, spilling the dust.

Aodan patted out a flame in my coat, then puffed himself out at the second guard. "Ye want to test me too?"

The guard held up his hands as if he could hold back Aodan's fire. "I don't want any trouble. But if ye have any ideas of executing Morrigan—"

Aodan placed a condescending hand on his shoulder and threw him a look that seemed to question whether a brain existed in his skull. "Ye honestly think I could?" He paused, giving the dim-witted creature time to process. "Morrigan plans to make me her second-in-command."

The guard dropped to his knees. His axe clanged on the rocky path. "Then please accept me as yer humble servant."

"What is yer name?"

"Be'Norr."

"Rise, Be'Norr. As of today, you are my personal guard."

Aodan was taking to his role rather quickly considering Morrigan hadn't officially bequeathed his post yet. And I wasn't eager to stand in her presence again. Once she had what she wanted, what would keep her from killing me?

Our guide was gone. He must've sneaked away. Not that it mattered. It might be helpful for him to spread the word about Aodan.

Be'Norr led us through a maze of dim tunnels. Torches in sconces lined the walls. We came to double doors with a guard posted outside. Sword raised, he rushed us, holding us back.

The armed guard sneered at Be'Norr. "Are ye off yer head? Why have ye left yer post? And who is this?" He sniffed at me. "Why bring a wolf into our lair?"

"He's my pet," Aodan said.

Pet? If I weren't already teetering on the edge of sanity merely being in the presence of such evil, I might've had words with Aodan about that one.

"If ye value yer life, don't harm them." Be'Norr nodded toward Aodan. "He lit up Be'Drun just by looking at him."

The guard shrank. "What do ye mean, 'lit him up'?"

"I set him on fire." Aodan smiled. "He's dead."

Who was this person? He seemed happy to have ended a life.

Aodan pressed the guard's blade downward. "Let us pass. Morrigan is expecting me."

The guard's eye twitched, and he nodded to Morrigan's door. "If yer wrong, we're all dead."

"And if we're not, which we aren't, I can ensure ye receive an increase in yer station." Aodan moved toward Morrigan's door.

The guard made his eyes into slits. "Who are ye to do such a thing?"

"Second-in-command."

The guard materialized between Aodan and the door. "If ye speak the truth, give me a moment." He faced Be'Norr. "If I don't return soon, kill them." He knocked on Morrigan's door.

"Who dares disturb me?" Faint, yet low and threatening, the words soured my soul. Something in her voice made my ears want to reject the sound. Even if Morrigan didn't kill us today, how long could we survive in her presence?

The guard disappeared behind the door. Be'Norr backed away.

The overwhelming stench I was becoming desensitized to sickened me anew, and a wave of nausea coursed through me. Perhaps it was the sheer volume of undead holed up in the mountain with little to no airflow. I choked on it, struggling to breathe.

The guard reemerged with the door wide and beckoned us. "Morrigan will see you."

I stayed behind Aodan, who marched into Morrigan's territory with too much confidence. His newfound arrogance was worsening.

As we entered, a spicy musk assaulted me. Many scents converged into one ungodly brew. Herbs mostly, but something else too…. Blood. Bile caught in my throat. I hadn't escaped the presence of evil since Aodan turned into an undead, but this was an entirely new level of wickedness. My soul cringed, desiring nothing more than to desert my body and flee this unholy place.

Morrigan stood behind a counter, fingers pinched, hovering over a wooden bowl. She released a grainy substance, then reached into a container for another ingredient. Whatever ghastly concoction she was making, it mattered more than our presence. She continued her work without a glance our way.

Morrigan's lair, assuming it was her lair, looked more like an apothecary. Herbs dangled from the ceiling. Shelves and drawers of varying shapes and sizes lined every wall. Glass bottles—each unique and containing strange substances—and other stone, clay, and wooden containers cluttered the shelves, counters, and floor. A cauldron hung over an unlit fire in the corner.

Her nose wrinkled. "Ye didn't feed."

He cringed. "Ye expected me to?"

She seemed to materialize before him. He stiffened under her touch as if she'd turned him to stone.

I backed away.

She gripped his chin and moved so close she might kiss him. "New fasgadair are weak. I don't care how you show such restraint, but my leaders will not be weak."

"I'm not weak."

"Oh?" She gripped his neck and lifted him off the floor. His face reddened as he gulped air. "If you're so strong, stop me."

Her head erupted in flames. She screamed and dropped him. He straightened, staring at her on fire, a sick smile slicked to his face. Could this be it? *Could* we kill Morrigan?

She patted the flames, dousing them. The crisp strands of hair fell out. Her charred face morphed back to a healthy fasgadair pale while her black hair regenerated, growing back to its original length.

I felt like I swallowed a brick. Aodan's stricken face sought mine. He seemed to think the same thoughts—we were dead.

We were dead.

"Keep my minions in line and away from me. Anyone other than you who dares appear before me uninvited will die." She arrived at her counter without visibly crossing the distance and returned to her concoction. "Ye may go."

Aodan and I exchanged bewildered looks. Or as bewildered as we could look as a fasgadair and a wolf.

"That's it?"

She closed her eyes as if willing herself to remain calm. "What else do ye need?"

Aodan nodded toward me. "Is he safe here?"

"If ye keep him safe."

"So I can kill anyone who nears him?"

Morrigan laughed, sending the icy chill of a thousand ghosts passing through me. "Do whatever ye like. My kingdom is yours to do with what ye will."

His eyes narrowed. "Why would ye do that? Ye don't know me."

She stirred the contents in the bowl with a warped wooden spoon. "None will control my minions better than ye. How ye accomplish this task matters not to me."

"Will ye make such an announcement?"

She trained her icy black eyes on him.

His Adam's apple bobbed. "How will they know if ye don't tell them?"

"That doesn't concern me." She flicked her fingers, waving us off.

We left Morrigan's presence. With the door closed behind us, I breathed easier... as if an elephant standing on my chest were replaced by a bear.

Be'Norr and the guard gaped at us.

"Morrigan is not to be disturbed under penalty of death." Aodan glowered at the guard. "What is yer name?"

The guard stepped forward like a child facing punishment. "De'Scon."

"I promised to raise yer stations. As of today, yer my right hand."

De'Scon gripped his weapon with renewed vigor. "Aye, sir."

Aodan turned to Be'Norr. "Yer my personal guard. Choose one more to join ye in the task."

Be'Norr bowed, not looking as thrilled with the new position as De'Scon.

"Is there a place where I might gather the fasgadair to announce the new regime?"

"Aye." De'Scon dropped to his knees and bowed. "Might I ask my commander's name?"

"Aodan."

De'Scon twitched and looked up as if looking into the sun. "Haven't ye a fasgadair name?"

"How does one come about a fasgadair name?"

"'Tis given by the one who turned ye."

"Morrigan did not give me one, nor do I want one."

They sucked in their breath.

"Morrigan changed ye?" De'Scon's voice came out thin. "She hasn't changed a fasgadair since her early days, centuries ago."

"Perhaps yer not as keen on Morrigan's doings as ye like to think."

De'Scon flinched at the rebuke.

"'Tis irrelevant. De'Scon, prepare for a gathering tomorrow night. Ensure all fasgadair within Ceas Croi and its immediate perimeter are in attendance. Tell them my wolf is not to be harmed. Anyone who dares look at him sideways or disturb Morrigan does so at their peril."

"Right away, sir." De'Scon bowed and disappeared.

"Be'Norr, show us about Ceas Croi. Is there a dwelling we might claim for our own?"

"Aye. This way."

We followed Be'Norr through the dark tunnels, pulling me further and further from fresh air and deeper and deeper into the devil's lair.

CHAPTER THIRTY-NINE

CATALEEN

No one better walk by as I hid below my home's only window, listening. Josh hadn't been with Ma for long. So far, she'd offered him a drink.

"Let's sit by the window, shall we?" The rocker creaked as Ma sat.

I crouched lower.

"I think I know why ye've requested a meeting, Joshua, but please tell me." Ma slurped her drink.

"Uh. Um."

I cringed. This must be difficult for an Ariboslian male. What of an outsider? A stranger to our customs? What must he be thinking right now? That he was willing to do this warmed my heart. But even so, how would a relationship work between people from two different worlds? And what would my ma think of it?

And did I even want it?

"Sake, lad. Yer a bit peely-wally. Do ye feel ill?"

A nervous laugh jittered from him. "I'm okay."

"Out with it. Ye'll feel better. Confession is good for the bones."

"I, uh—I'm not familiar with your customs, but I'd like to date—I mean, court your daughter."

The rocking chair groaned. I could only imagine my ma's face. Satisfied? Pensive? I felt as though I sat on a ledge and the ground was breaking apart beneath me.

"Sully believes Cataleen will seek safety in yer realm. I've no doubt of his conviction. But knowing my daughter, I struggle to imagine what could make her leave her home. What if Sully is wrong and Cataleen stays? Or what if she decides to return home?"

"I—I don't know." Josh coughed. "I mean, it's not like I'm asking to marry her."

"What is the point of courting if yer intentions aren't to wed should ye find yer a good match?"

"Uh—I mean, I guess that could happen someday. I'm still in high school."

Ma laughed, and I nearly jumped out of my skin.

"From what I understand, ye know nothing of yer motherland. How do ye intend to care for Cataleen when ye can't understand her?"

"I don't know." Long pause.

"What are yer long-term plans?"

I was so nervous for him, my body buzzed as if I were a full of bees.

"I don't have any. I just want to get to know Cataleen." Another long pause. Was Ma giving him the stare down? "No disrespect, Mrs. —"

"Call me Mirna."

"Mirna." His voice rattled. "If you knew your husband would leave you alone with two children, would you still have married him? Would you have even date—courted?"

I sucked in a slow breath and held it.

Cahal tromped down the path. He spotted me and waved.

I waved back, frantic to get him to understand that I was shooing him away, not returning the welcoming gesture.

His eyes widened, and he stepped back, glancing between me and the window above me. He gave an almost imperceptible nod, then sauntered past as if he didn't see me.

Something shuffled inside. Had they seen? Or were they still sharing their awkward moment?

"Look, Mrs.—Mirna," Josh spoke, and I released my trapped breath. "I don't know what will happen. All I know is I like your daughter. I want to get to know her better."

My legs shook, and I shifted my weight.

Something scraped the floor. What was Ma doing? Staring? Consulting the heavens? The poor guy must be squirming.

He coughed again. "My family intends to bring her into our home, to protect her. I will do my part to protect her as well. And to help her adjust."

"That's all well and good, but all the more reason ye two should not have affections for one another. If Sully's prophecy proves true and Cataleen seeks shelter in yer home, those who are courting shouldn't reside under the same roof prior to their wedding day."

More uncomfortable silence. "What if I stayed with a friend?"

"I'm pleased to see yer a resourceful lad... a problem solver. That is good."

I buried my face in my hands. This was most embarrassing. Josh would have nothing to do with me after this. And I wouldn't blame him.

"Is kissing okay?"

I coughed, then smacked my hand over my mouth. *Brilliant, Cataleen. Why don't ye wave a flag in the window to announce yer presence?*

Ma laughed. "Aye. That is acceptable. But nothing more."

Ma's stern voice conjured an image of her lecture face. And a wagging finger.

I died inside. Poor Josh.

"And keep it short."

He loosed a nervous laugh. A high, tinny thing. I blushed for him.

Neither spoke. My shaking legs ached. I repositioned myself again and nearly fell.

"I believe yer intentions are honorable, Joshua. But what is the foundation that connects ye?"

More coughing. "In what way?"

"Where do ye stand with God?"

"I, uh, I believe in God. If that's what you're asking."

"That means different things to different people. What does it mean to ye?"

"It means... I don't know. I go to church and read the Bible and stuff."

"Do ye pray?"

"Uh." Cough. "Yeah. Not as much as I should."

Chatter came from up the path. A group of children crested the hill. I pushed my hand around the tufts of grass lining the path as if searching for something I'd lost. I crawled forward, still searching, until I was far enough away from the window to rise.

"Cataleen!" One kid spotted me.

I glanced back at the window. Good, I was far enough away now no one would suspect me of eavesdropping. I fell in with the kids. Josh stared as I passed by. The poor soul looked in need of rescue, like a foal desperate to escape the stable.

If only I could hear the rest of the conversation... or rescue him. Why had I agreed to this? Wouldn't it be better to get to know one another as friends? Would it make things awkward? What would happen when he wanted to return home, and I didn't want to go with him?

I'd rather go to Gnuatthara.

CHAPTER FORTY

FAOLAN

Aodan's personal guards, Be'Norr and his chosen partner, De'Rahn remained outside our rooms—cavernous spaces, each with a lofty bed, ornate chests, and dressers adjoined another, larger room sectioned off into dining and lounging areas. Nice dwellings for such grotesque creatures. I'd expected something more... more... grave like?

This resembled something I'd imagine in a king's palace. Someone with an incredible gift for stonework constructed these rooms complete with built-in fireplaces and shelves, reminding me of our temporary residence in the ravine, only on a grand scale. Tapestries depicting battles lined the walls, and fine carpeting covered the stone floor, softening the place.

"Have you any need of me at the moment, my lord?" De'Scon reminded me of Cahal. Nay, that wasn't fair to Cahal. The only thing these two had in common was their massive size—and perhaps their preference for few words, though that had yet to be seen.

"Nothing for now. We could use some rest. See that we aren't disturbed." Aodan's arrogance had gone from annoying to downright vexing.

After his new lackey retreated, Aodan threw me a change of clothes.

I wasn't sure I wanted to transition into my human form in this place. Would the others sense me despite the stone walls and heavy doors? But I wouldn't be able to talk again if I didn't. Although that might be better. I had nothing nice to say.

"Aren't ye going to change?"

I huffed out a breath, transitioned to my human form, dressed, then continued to study our new cage. Cushy seats of gold made of a material the likes of which I wasn't familiar ringed part of the lounging area. I inspected one fireplace, trying to peer up into the flue, but the flames were too hot. How did they have fire in a mountain like this?

"Do fasgadair get cold?" I asked.

"Unless something is wrong with me, fasgadair are always cold."

I studied him. He gave no indication of being cold. "You don't shiver or do anything to warm yourself."

"The cold doesn't bother me, but the warmth feels nice." He held his hands to the fire, then retreated to a bed, sank into the lofty mattress, and pulled the blood-red curtains closed.

"I suppose that's your bed," I said to the curtains now forming a wall between us. "And our conversation is over for the night. Day. Whatever it is."

I moved to the other room that must be mine, slowing as I neared the curtains enclosing my bed. What was the purpose of such curtains? There was no sun to block. Would it make me more secure? Or more vulnerable? One of the bloodthirsty demons probably lay in wait.

My hand shook as I neared the curtain, then yanked it away. Nothing but bedding. I blew out a breath, then gave my room another look to ensure I was alone.

Satisfied, I ran my fingers over the luxurious white covering. Another material I'd never encountered. So incredibly soft. I flipped the covers back as if expecting to find a brood of vipers. But no. More luxuriousness. I sat on the edge and wasn't poked as I was on my straw and feather mattress at home. Whatever filled this mattress felt amazing.

If only I could enjoy it.

I was so tired. Under normal circumstances, I'd wrap myself in the plush blankets and fall right to sleep. But how could anything pure, free from demon blood, sleep in what was essentially hell? I'd never sleep again.

After opening all the curtains wide, I tied them to the bedposts so I could see any attackers before they were upon me. Then I laid down. I must've gotten used to the fasgadair scent. The musty odor from the mountain room now overpowered the rank electric smell.

I tossed and turned for an eternity. How was I to know when night had fallen and when to wake? I was used to sleeping in a dark room with no windows, but this was different. Very different. Aside from the fasgadair stench that now took up permanent residence in my sinuses, giving me a perpetual headache, I couldn't walk into another room and look out a window. The morning birds' songs didn't filter through the miles of rock here. Nor did the frog's evening croaks. How long could I keep my head if I never knew the difference between night and day?

I glanced toward Aodan's bed. Was he asleep?

The cushiest jail in existence. My prison.

How had we gotten here?

I'd gone too far. No way would I escape with my life now.

God, did I make a huge mistake coming here? If this is part of Yer plan, please tell me what to do. Whatever happens, please get me out of here alive.

✡

"Are ye planning to lie in that scratcher all night? Come on." Aodan flicked my ear. "Get up."

I jerked, scrambling away from him, my heart thudding off tempo.

Memories flooded back, and the dread of our predicament nearly drowned me anew.

Aodan's face crumpled. "Are ye afraid of me now? I didn't mean to startle ye." He nudged my arm. "Come on, mate. 'Tis my first day as leader. Sake! I need ye."

"What? Am I yer advisor now? Ye expect me, the cattle, to help lead the hungry farmers?"

"I need ye by my side."

"I can't stay here, Aodan. I need to leave."

His mouth hung open as his horrid eyes stared.

"Won't I make things more challenging for ye? What with all the demons wanting a taste of my blood?"

His eerie skin darkened. "They need to see the face of the gachen that will cost their life if they dare touch ye."

"Isn't my blood a temptation to ye, too?"

He jumped away as if I'd snapped a whip at him. His shocked expression morphed into a sadness so profound it was obvious, despite his demonic eyes. "No matter what I become, yer still like a brother to me. I'd never hurt ye."

"Why do ye insist on keeping me by yer side? I'm a tragedy waiting to happen. Every moment I stay in this godforsaken place, my life is at risk."

He clenched his jaw, and all the candles in the chamber lit at once. "Not if I have any say in the matter." He softened. "I mean it, Faolan. Ye understand how powerful I am. I'll protect ye. Even in my weakened state with no gachen blood, I can overpower any fasgadair."

"Except Morrigan."

He closed his demon eyes, appearing like my old friend once more. Then he trained the creepy things on me with renewed intensity, chilling me. "I can't do anything to Morrigan. But as long as she trusts me, I can do whatever I want. Aside from her, I'm in control."

Do Ye hear this, God? Aodan believes he's in control. What am I supposed to do with this?

This was worse than I could have imagined. He was much too

comfortable, confident... *eager*. Worse yet, he seemed happy in an undead sort of way. Even in his current state. Especially in his current state. I didn't want my friend to spend an eternity in misery, but I definitely didn't want him reveling in his undead state either. I scarce knew which was worse.

But I had to stop worrying about him. He'd made his choice. And now, I had to find a way out, even if I died trying to escape. I'd rather die than remain here.

CHAPTER FORTY-ONE

CATALEEN

I sat at the table with Ma using my finger to scrape the last of my buttery neeps into a giant forkful. I always saved the best for last.

"Use yer knife." She sighed.

After all these years, did she think her attempts to civilize me would work? I shoved the fork into my mouth. It had gotten a bit cold, but the turnips had absorbed the butter and salt, which tasted good at any temperature.

"So, how much of my conversation with Joshua did ye hear?"

I choked on my mouthful. "Wha—?"

"Sake, Cataleen." She scraped her tatties onto her fork, using her knife, slower than usual, as if showing how it was done. "Don't play innocent. Ye know what I mean. I know ye. When have ye passed up an opportunity to indulge yer curiosity?"

My mouth hung open. Words escaped me.

Ma snickered behind a fist. "Plus, I saw Cahal waving at ye."

I smacked myself and dragged my hand down my face.

"That's a very unbecoming look." She took another dainty bite, continuing her demonstration of proper etiquette.

"Did Josh see me?" No way would he still want to court me if he had.

She swallowed her bite. "I don't think so."

"So, what did ye say? Did ye give yer permission?" A myriad of emotions swirled about like an overloaded soup—a dash of curiosity, a pinch of trepidation, soaked in a broth of pure mortification. I wrung my hands together.

She placed a firm hand on mine, flattening them, ceasing their senseless movement. Then she rose and poked the logs in the fire. "Ye didn't stick around long enough to hear?"

I twisted in my chair. "Nay. The kids came up the path."

"Well then." She held her back as she straightened with a groan. "Ye know how this works. Yer to wait until he approaches ye."

I stared at my ma as if I could read her mind if I looked hard enough. "Then ye said yes?"

Ma breathed out a series of silent laughs, shaking her head all the while. She snatched my plate and brought it to the counter. While I emptied the water from the pitcher into the washing tub, she added hot water from the cauldron on the stove.

I grabbed a dishcloth and set to work cleaning the dishes. "Ma? What if I don't want to go?"

"Cataleen, dear." She wrapped an arm around me and squeezed me into her hip. "Whoever said you had to?"

"Sully."

"Bah!" Ma snapped a towel and took a dish from me. "Never mind Sully."

"But—he's a seer. A prophet. He speaks for God."

"Sully knows more than I do, but Sully is not God. And we all have choices to make. If ye want to stay here. Stay. No one is forcing ye to go." She freed a plate from my grip. "Is something else bothering ye?"

Wringing out my cloth, I sighed. "I don't want to run away. I want to do something good."

"Such as?" She returned the clean plate to the hutch.

How could I suggest what I was thinking after staying home to help Ma? "I don't know. Something meaningful, like Achaius and Cahal saving babies from Gnuatthara."

"Not to worry. Everyone has a purpose. God will show ye His plan for ye when it's time."

Was my purpose just to help care for babies someone else rescued? Or fleeing to some unknown future in the human realm? Would God give me the desire to go to Gnuatthara if it wasn't part of His plan?

I couldn't bring myself to mention this. Not yet. Not now that I was the only family she had left.

Then there was Josh. Regardless of Ma's answer, he wanted a relationship with me. A romantic relationship. If I went to Gnuatthara, what would happen to us?

If going to Gnuatthara was God's plan, He wasn't making it easy. Somehow, I'd have to tell Ma *and* Josh.

Did I even want to go?

I swirled the murky dishwater. 'Twas as cloudy as my future. I'd lost my brother and best mate. Now I waited, wondering if Aodan would do something horrendous to me as Sully suggested. Wasn't that bad enough? Now I also had to try to sleep, wondering if Josh would approach me on the morrow.

If he did, what would I say?

CHAPTER FORTY-TWO

FAOLAN

De'Scon led us through a maze of tunnels. Though there was plenty of room for us, he had to stoop. Be'Norr and De'Rahn held back the river of blood drinkers in brown cloaks filling the hall behind us. We entered a room that opened to a cavern. A balcony. Many other balconies lined its sides. I stood behind Aodan as the fasgadair streamed in like a brown wave, closing us in, flooding the cave floor and each opening. A sea of peely-wally faces with what appeared to be hollowed-out eyes from this distance bobbed in the brown waters. The electric smell burned my nose. I became light-headed and lay at Aodan's feet.

Why had he insisted I accompany him?

At least he'd relented and allowed me to stay in wolf form.

An assembly of fasgadair stood on an elevated ground-level platform. They played flutes and drums, much like our music back home, but darker, sadder, and more aggressive. Something in the haunting melody and primal beats punched a hole in my heart, filling it with a despair so consuming I longed to fall to my knees and tear my clothes.

Or perhaps it was being in the presence of so many demons. Probably both.

A rustle sounded beside us, and the demon sea parted. Morrigan, the mother of these abominations, walked through. By Aodan's face, her presence surprised him, too.

"Morrigan. Ye honor me with yer presence." He bowed.

If I wasn't tempted to vomit before, I was now.

She eyed us, then moved to the opening. A wave of silence spread from those with the best view outward until the entire assembly had seen Morrigan and quieted.

"My children"—her dead voice echoed off the cave walls—"victors of death, today I bestow ye with a gift—a new leader." She motioned for Aodan to step beside her. "Aodan of Notirr. I have given him full authority. You will do unto him as you would unto me or suff—"

A fasgadair materialized beside her. His red eyes appeared full of blood.

Her fingers wrapped around his neck. "What is the meaning of this interruption, Gi'Wrann?"

His face reddened, almost matching his bulging eyes. Gasping, he clawed at her hands.

She loosened her grip.

He caught his breath as the color left his face. "I–I've come to warn you. This fasgadair you've given to lead us"—he aimed a bony finger at Aodan—"his twin's child, his niece, will end his rule. She will be our undoing."

Aodan sputtered. "What nonsense. My sister is not with child."

I shuddered as if shaking water from my coat.

"Not now, not a year from now, but soon." No expression intruded on his unnatural face. "You must stop her, keep her from having the child."

Morrigan squeezed once more. "Kill him."

Gi'Wrann gurgled and fought for release.

Aodan didn't move.

Morrigan swooped up Gi'Wrann, throwing him over the balcony

railing and letting him dangle above the scattering crowd. "Prove yourself to your new people. Prove ye are worthy to be their leader."

For the first time, Aodan didn't seem eager to kill. His Adam's apple dipped.

"Do it." She snarled.

Gi'Wrann burst into flames. She released him, and he fell to the ground in an ashy heap.

Morrigan leaned in to Aodan and spoke in a low voice. "After ye introduce yourself, return to Notirr and kill your sister, or I will."

She vanished. The only evidence of her departure was the flowing cloaks from the still-parted fasgadair.

I locked eyes with Aodan. No way would he kill Cataleen, not if I had any say in the matter.

He waffled, then stepped closer to the rail. "Morrigan has made it clear that she is not to be disturbed. Anyone who appears within her chambers uninvited will die. All questions or concerns for her will come through me. And nothing will happen that I don't approve." He waved me forward. "Starting with this wolf. Anyone who dares lay a hand on him will die like Gi'Wrann."

Not a cloak swished in the place. I could hear no breath.

"Good. The first rule." He held up a finger. "No one disturbs Morrigan. Second, anyone who touches my wolf will die. And third, no one will touch my home village of Notirr."

Aodan surveyed his captive audience. Was he unsure what to say or increasing his power with his silence? "More rules will follow as I acclimate myself to this new position. Until then, go about your business as usual. Bring your problems to De'Scon. He is next in command. That is all."

De'Scon bowed to Aodan. "Have you any need of me at the moment, my lord?"

"Make yourself available to our subjects as they depart. Ensure everyone understands my role and rules."

"Very well, my lord." De'Scon bowed again and joined the retreating cloak sea.

My ears twitched. Okay, every bit of me, from my ears to my tail, twitched, unsure who this new creature, my old friend, was. His countenance had changed. Even from his initial change as a fasgadair. He'd changed once again into something more. Had Aodan always been so hungry for power?

I'd made a mistake coming to this unholy place.

And now Morrigan wanted Catty dead. Her first command was for Aodan to kill her. What would he do? He couldn't kill his sister. Could he?

"Ye coming?" Aodan sounded more like his old self.

But I hesitated to follow. Other than Be'Norr and De'Rahn, the place had cleared out, and I didn't feel so sick. My mind cleared some, but now I panicked for Catty.

I forced my unwilling body to meet Aodan. Be'Norr and De'Rahn followed. As we emerged through the entryway, something snatched me, yanking my hackles, lifting me. The monster caught flame and released. My feet slid on the stone in my hasty retreat.

Aodan whirled on his guards. "From now on, one of ye is to remain stationed with him at all times. And one of ye needs to be in front, ensuring the way is clear. Understood?"

Both guards' pale complexions took on a green tinge.

Be'Norr cleared his throat. "How experienced with fasgadair are you?"

Aodan ignited the hem of Be'Norr's cloak.

Be'Norr smacked at the flames until they dissipated. "I mean no disrespect, my lord. Clearly, you have incredible self-control. But many —I'd argue most—fasgadair become crazed with thirst for blood, especially when they first change." He nodded to me. "Keeping him nearby is like teasing them. They can't resist. Especially with the food shortage. The threat against their lives will stop some, but not all. Some might prefer to die."

A moment ago, I wouldn't have thought it possible for the doom and gloom soaking my soul to darken further, yet it had. Even in my wolf form, I wasn't safe. What would happen if they found out I was a gachen?

But that wasn't the pressing issue—Catty was. I needed to know what Aodan was going to do. He'd already gone too far to appease Morrigan. She'd promised to keep our village and everyone in it safe. She was a liar. We knew it and went along with it. How could we be such fools?

One thing was certain—I'd kill Aodan before I allowed him to touch Catty.

CHAPTER FORTY-THREE

CATALEEN

Part of me wanted to go about my business as usual. Eat breakfast, then help with the orphans before joining Ma with the mending. She had a stack of clothes from the villagers in addition to our own. Ma would tell me she didn't need the help, but I needed the distraction. Anything other than the chores I used to do with Aodan and Faolan. And if I could avoid Josh, all the better.

Should I tell him what I wanted to do? Courting didn't make sense right now. I'd have plenty of time for that later. Sake! I wasn't even sixteen yet.

But I would be soon.

If I needed something to distract me and bring me back to reality, the reminder of our looming birthday was it.

When I arrived at the orphanage, I met up with Kasey to get the kids breakfast. I got busy serving, feeding, and cleaning up after the kids. Next thing I knew breakfast was over.

Josh never showed.

Maybe he had something to do this morn. I'd return home to do the mending with Ma. He'd look for me there.

As I rocked in the window darning stockings, the sun taunted me with its steady ascent, trying to alert me of the passing time until the midday meal.

Still no Josh.

I returned to the orphans, then stayed to assist with dinner. All day long, I flipped between excited, disappointed, concerned, frustrated, confused, and outright enraged. I gave in to negative emotions, consoled myself, then fell back into whatever raging emotion dominated. And repeat. Was I losing my mind? Why was I so... unbalanced?

Where was he? Why act so eager... go as far as to meet with Ma only to avoid me? Had Ma denied him? Had something scared him into changing his mind?

After dinner, I stepped outside and walked in the general direction of Sully's house without realizing it until I came to the turnoff. Should I check on Josh?

Nay. I couldn't bring myself to go there. Not after he had the talk with Ma. I'd appear desperate. If he changed his mind and I showed up there, he'd be forced to explain himself. I'd embarrass us both. It was unbecoming and not how things were done. If he wanted to pursue a courtship, he'd have followed through and come to me.

He didn't.

Wasn't that better? It took the pressure off me saying nay.

I turned back to clean up after dinner.

Kasey paused sweeping, resting her chin on the tip of the broomstick. "Ye don't have to do this, ye know. 'Tis my responsibility."

"Ye could use the help, right?" I snatched my apron from the hook and tied it around my waist.

"Wouldn't ye rather spend time with the babies and the other helpers instead of cleaning up this mess?"

"I'd rather clean." I'd love to play with the babies. But not today. I was in no mood to chat with the other helpers or pretend to be in good spirits. And I'd much rather take my aggression out by scrubbing. So, I filled the washbasin with warm water and set to clean the dishes. "Why don't you go take a break? I can finish sweeping after I do the dishes."

"Are you sure?" She leaned the broom against the wall and began removing her apron. "I wouldn't mind checking in on my mum."

"Of course. Go." I dipped my fingers in the water and flicked it at her.

"Okay, okay." She laughed, shielding herself with her apron, and dove for the door. "I'll be an hour at most."

"No need to rush."

The door closed. Alone at last.

I'd barely cleaned a few dishes when a knock sounded.

My heart jumped into my throat as I ran to pull the door open. "Josh?"

"Nay." Achaius stepped into the entry with Cahal.

My hopes both plummeted and rose. Would I have an opportunity to talk to them about going to Gnuatthara? But how could I, when I hadn't talked to Ma yet?

"Ye were expecting someone else?" He wrinkled his nose. "Sorry to disappoint. I hoped to see how my wee ones are doing?"

At Achaius's voice, several babies crawled and toddled toward him with their caretakers following. He crouched down, attempting to hug them all at once, and fell over until he was a laughing heap on the floor with babies crawling all over him. He took a moment to right himself. Then they followed him onto the carpet and listened as he told them a story.

As Achaius entertained the children, Cahal picked up a towel and a dish and set to work.

"Where's Kasey?" He accepted a dish from me and dried it.

"I told her to go rest. She does this nearly every night." It may seem like a burden, but she loved it. She had a purpose. I needed a purpose. I needed to accomplish something instead of sitting around waiting for some boy who hadn't even completed his education. Achaius, Cahal—everyone around me had a purpose. Everyone but me.

If I went to America, I'd never return. But Gnuatthara? It was just a trip. I'd return. Probably.

"When are you and Achaius going on another rescue?"

Cahal waited a beat. "In the morn."

The sixteenth anniversary of my birth. Could this be my opportunity to avoid it?

He placed a weighty hand on my shoulder. "I know it's yer special day." Something akin to panic crackled his deep voice as he bent over his task, the roof a bit low for him. "Achaius says a storm is brewing. He wants to stay ahead of it."

"Ye think I want to be here for that?" I asked.

His head jerked up, nearly striking the ceiling. "The storm?"

I dropped the dish in my hand back into the dishwater. It clanked on the other dishes and sent up a splash. "I want to come with ye."

He sucked in a breath. "Yer ma—"

"I'm not leaving forever."

"'Tis dangerous."

"That doesn't stop ye. Besides, if the prophecy is true, I won't die."

"What's that?" He leaned in as if he'd misheard me.

"Just trust me. If Sully is right, I'll make it back alive." And perhaps, in our travels, I'd run into Aodan and Faolan.

CHAPTER FORTY-FOUR

FAOLAN

I paced about my extravagant quarters. My jail cell. My punishment for following Aodan. I had to get out of this godforsaken mountain. Why didn't Aodan bring me with him? I wanted to hear what Morrigan had to say when he confronted her about Catty. I wanted to hear what *he* had to say. Better yet, I wanted to see him kill her. I would never be at ease again until she was dead.

But Aodan had his chance. He wouldn't kill her now.

Would he?

I should escape while he was away. But how would I get past Be'Norr and De'Rahn? One was always standing outside my door. Then I'd have to get through the fasgadair-infested tunnels, past the guards outside, and across miles and miles of woods.

If, by some miracle, I managed all that, what would happen if I came across a fasgadair far from Aodan's threat?

God, help me. Please get me out of here with my life.

How often had I prayed a similar prayer? My pleas for escape were going unanswered. Was I praying the wrong prayer? Was this my punishment for making the wrong choice?

The door burst open, and I hid behind the partition.

"Where are ye?" Aodan called.

I stepped into view and rushed him. "What happened? Surely, she doesn't believe this prediction."

"She doesn't know if it's true or not, but she wants me to kill Cataleen either way. As a precaution."

"Ye can't be considering it."

"Of course not!" He slumped into a high-back chair and fisted his hair. "But I've got to do something. If I don't, Morrigan will. I've got to get Catty someplace safe. Somewhere Morrigan can't touch her."

"Does such a place exist?" I asked.

"I don't know, but I'm sending ye back to figure it out."

"Back where?" I searched his face, but his fasgadair eyes were unreadable. "Home?"

"Ye weren't banished. Ye can return. Convince Cataleen to flee." Aodan knelt before me, his freakish eyes probably pleading, but who could tell? "Get her out of here, Faolan. It's her only chance."

He dropped his head. "The longer I remain in this state, the less human my thoughts become. I fear what I will do if she remains." He gripped my shirt, sending me rocking. "Please, Faolan, if ye ever loved me—do this for me. Get her out of Ariboslia, where Morrigan won't find her. Where my thoughts can't reach her. Even now, from this distance, I get glimpses of some lad she can't stop thinking about. Please. Get her away from me. Save her."

I swallowed the emotions welling within, threatening to make me cry as I'd laughed moments before. The threat against Cataleen. My friend behind the fasgadair mask pleading for her life. And some lad invading her mind. Was he responsible for the predicted child? Whoever the dobber was, he better not have touched her. I clenched my fists.

Aodan released me and stepped away. "I'm pleading for yer help, mate. Why do ye look like ye want to murder me?"

"It's not ye," I growled.

I shook off that last thought. The dobber didn't matter. Not yet. Catty and Aodan did. Both evoked warring emotions within my unstable being. Aodan was releasing me, offering the freedom I so desired. And not just for myself, for Cataleen. A dormant power within me woke and brought me to my feet. "When do ye want me to leave?"

CHAPTER FORTY-FIVE

CATALEEN

I rose early and sat at the end of my bed. My body felt heavy and didn't want to move. My sour stomach couldn't handle the thought of breakfast.

How could I leave today of all days? I hadn't even had the courage to tell Ma yet. This would break her heart. Had she made preparations for our traditional breakfast? Had the clan made plans for dinner? They'd want to bless me.

But could I handle being here for that?

And what of Josh? Should I seek him out before I left?

Where was he? What if something happened to him?

Then again, how could I stay here, courting some lad, enjoying my life when my brothers were out there trying to survive without a clan... when innocent babies were being sacrificed to fasgadair?

A fire at the thought burned within, and I jumped to my feet, fueled, ready to scale mountains, fight demons, whatever it took to save even one life.

A bright light filled the room.

My bedpost caught fire!

My breath caught. The flames grew. Heart thudding, I scrambled for my blanket and beat the fire to death. A flickering flame emitted light behind me, and I spun around, armed with my blanket. But it was only my lantern.

When had I lit that?

Assured no more rogue fires threatened my home, I collapsed back onto my bed to catch my breath.

How had that happened? In all the time since finding out I could start fires, I was never even tempted to use my ability. And I *never* set a fire unintentionally. So why now? Was I losing control?

My door creaked open, and my ma shuffled in, bringing light from a lantern with her. "Do I smell smoke?"

"Uh... yes?" I lifted my lantern to inspect the damage. There was none. How could that be? I hadn't imagined it. Even Ma could smell it.

"What are ye looking for, child?"

"N–nothing." I took a deep breath. I'd have to worry about this incident another time. But I still needed to talk to Ma about Gnuatthara. "Ma, I have something to tell ye."

"You wish to accompany Achaius and Cahal to Gnuatthara?"

I sucked in a breath. "How—"

"They came to see me whilst ye were still with the orphans." She set her lantern on my nightstand, sat on my bed, and patted the mattress beside her.

I set my lantern down and snuggled into her.

She smoothed my hair. "I don't know yer reasonings for wanting to join them, but I understand enough. I stayed up all night talking to God. He gave me peace about ye going."

"Oh, Ma." My decision to go hadn't felt real until now, receiving her blessing. Tears I hadn't felt coming slipped down my cheeks as I squeezed her tighter. "I don't want to leave ye."

She held me as if I might break apart if she let go. "My dear, dear child. Leanabh. 'Tis yer responsibility to set off and do what God wills of ye. I'm no prophet, but I believe this is part of His plan for ye. How will ye ever learn how He'll use ye, what He'll do in and through ye, if ye don't get out of this house and live yer life? He didn't put us here to collect dust."

Something sounded from the other room.

"What was that?" I swiped at my tears.

We grabbed our lanterns and walked into the living room. Rain splattered the window. If the sun was rising, rain clouds choked it out. Someone knocked on the front door. Ma and I both jumped.

I placed my lantern on the kitchen table and motioned for Ma to wait where she was. Then I walked through the dark living room to the window to see who was outside. I squinted through the darkness, discerned a shadowy figure, then squealed when recognition set in. I ran to the door and pulled it open. "Josh?"

He stepped onto the mat, sopping wet. His hair, still spiky in places, dripped, sending rivulets down his face. Somehow, he looked more beautiful than ever.

My emotions waffled within me. "Y–you're soaked!"

Ma appeared beside us with a towel.

"Thank you." He mopped his face, then scrubbed at his hair. Was that how he got his tousled look?

Ma steered him toward Aodan's room. "Get out of those wet clothes and put on something of Aodan's. Yer about the same size."

Josh opened his mouth like he was going to say something when she shoved him inside and shut the door.

"Help me put on a pot of cider before he catches a cold." She poured the cider into a pot and lit the stove.

I scrambled about the cupboards for cinnamon and ginger. Ma helped me prep the contents, then add them to the cider. Josh emerged from Aodan's room wearing his tunic and trousers. Could he be more adorable with his wet hair and familiar clothes?

"What should I do with these?" He held up his wet clothes.

Ma draped them on the backs of the chairs as we sat.

"What are ye doing here?" I asked.

"I want to go with you. To New Tara, or whatever it's called."

"That's it. You said it right." Then I frowned. "Why do you want to go?"

"I–I don't—" He took a deep breath. "Sully told me you were leaving."

"You don't go on a dangerous quest to be with some girl," I said.

Ma stirred the cider, and the spiced-apple scent teased my queasy stomach. Her shoulders quaked ever so slightly. Apparently, I amused her.

"It's not that. I—" He blew out a breath. "Sorry I didn't come see you yesterday. When my dad found out I talked to your mom, he made me go mining with him."

What should I say to that? That I wasn't looking out for him all day, wondering? I'd make myself out to seem either desperate or angry. I wasn't either.

Still, his damp features, all crumpled up and sorry, tugged at me. Pitiful even, he spread both hands. "What do you want?"

"What do *I* want?" I wanted to turn him away. But then I also fought the urge to kiss him. What was that about? Agitated by my body's betrayal of my emotions, I sighed. "I don't know what my ma said... if she gave ye permission or not."

He reached for my hand.

I snapped mine away, placing them in my lap. "But I don't want to know."

Ma threw me a curious look over her shoulder as she stirred the cider.

"Why?" His voice cracked.

The hurt on his beautiful face tore my heart in two. I hated myself for refusing him. But my resolve deepened. Maybe we'd have a relationship someday, but it was too soon. I had more important things to do right now. "'Tis not appropriate to go on a dangerous quest spanning several nights with an intended."

"Intended?" A light sparked in his eyes. "Does that mean you'll let me come with you?"

"'Tisn't up to me," I said. "'Tis up to yer ma and da."

Ma set a steaming cup of cider before us.

I sipped my cup, grateful the heat diminished the alcohol some. But its warmth soothed.

His eyes dimmed. "No. It's up to my dad, and he's already given his permission. Sully approved, and that was good enough for him. But I don't want to go if you don't want me there."

I leaned back, cradled my warm cup, and drank in the look of him. The spicy apple couldn't tease my senses like he could. "Why do ye want to go?"

He groaned. "The honorable thing to say is that I want to rescue babies, like you. But if I'm honest, I just want to make sure you're safe."

My mind reeled. "I thought you had to return home for something... a senior year?"

"I've been told the trip only takes eighteen to twenty days. It will be tight, but that will give me about a week before school starts in September." He took a sip of his drink and gasped. "I thought this was cider?"

"It is." I cocked my head, baffled. "We ferment it from crab apples."

The crinkles smoothed from around his nose. "Oh, hard cider. The cider I drink at home doesn't have alcohol. In America, you can't drink alcohol if you're under twenty-one."

"Under twenty-one what?" He was confusing me again.

"Years. If you're younger than twenty-one years old."

So, I wouldn't be allowed to drink cider? "Why? What are you supposed to drink? Water and milk? How do you make healing tonics?"

"We have medicine. And lots of other drinks. So much more than here. There's coffee, tea, soda, juice... And our cider is sweet. It doesn't burn. You should try it."

Sweet drinks that didn't burn? Would they not make me gag? This was the only promising thing I'd heard of his land so far. I shook my head and stood. "That's well and good, but if I'm to go to Gnuatthara this morning, I should get ready."

Standing, Josh waffled there, one hand on the back of his chair, the other tugging at his spiky hair as his gaze flipped from me to Ma. "Are you okay with me coming too?"

Ma sat and sipped her warm drink and smiled at Josh. "Of course, it's okay. And if yer da and Sully approve, I'd say the matter is settled. But ye best be ready to go when Achaius and Cahal come to fetch ye."

CHAPTER FORTY-SIX

FAOLAN

I followed Aodan past the guards at the main entrance, around the mountain, into the woods. Traveling through the woods in the dark was much easier as a wolf. I was growing used to it. Perhaps even preferred it.

The one drawback to being a wolf was not being able to talk. And I needed to know what Aodan planned to do. Was he going to come all the way back to Notirr with me? What would he do when he got there? Go home? Might he harm Cataleen? If he didn't kill her, would Morrigan know? So many questions. Yet I couldn't risk one. Not yet.

I'd deal with him later. For now, I needed his protection, at least until I was closer to home.

Catty's face came to my mind, urging me to quicken my pace.

How much time had I spent in Ceas Croi? I glanced at the sky through the trees. Too bad I couldn't read the stars like Aodan. How far from Notirr was I? Was this area warmer than Notirr? It felt like summer hadn't ended yet and showed no signs of fall. The air was still muggy, even at night.

Perhaps I hadn't missed our anniversary.

How had our lives come to this? Inseparable, yet separated. Each alone fighting our own demons. What must Catty be going through without us? And when would Aodan become the villain Morrigan hoped him to be?

I'd fallen behind and rushed to keep up. The urgency fueling me could only carry me for so long.

I couldn't worry about Aodan now. If he got too close to Notirr, I'd deal with it then. I needed to keep him away from Catty. Even if he didn't harm her, Morrigan wouldn't hesitate. And she could cross this distance in the blink of an eye—couldn't she?

I had to hurry.

�✶

BEFORE THE SUN WAS VISIBLE, gray light heralded its impending arrival. That meant... we headed east? We'd been in dark woods all night, so it was impossible to tell if anything was familiar. Aodan stopped near a copse of bushes. "We'll sleep here for the day."

I shifted into human form. The fresh air felt wonderful on my skin, in my lungs, despite the humidity and his fasgadair stink. Anything was better than that stifling mountain. "I thought we were going north? Why are we headed east?"

"This is the way we came."

The trees surrounded me as I covered myself with my cloak. This wood could be any other.

"Remember the waterfall?" He loosened the cord on his tunic.

"Aye."

"After we climb it, rather than continue north through the ravine, we'll go east. I can't accompany you all the way home, so I'm delivering you to those who can."

I tugged my waterskin from my pack. "Who is east?"

Aodan sat, waiting to finish undressing. "The Treasach. Gnuatthara."

"I thought traveling from Gnuatthara to Notirr wasn't safe?" I took a long drink.

"It wasn't. Still, people managed it. It will be safer now that I'm in charge."

"Don't you need to get back to your kingly duties?" Where had that biting tone come from? Being trapped in a prison lousy with fasgadair must've taken a toll on me.

Aodan scoffed, shaking his head. "Things haven't turned out the way we planned, but—"

"Bah! That's an understatement."

"I'm trying to help." His voice crumpled, hurt little-boy tones echoing from the past.

I didn't care if he was hurt. Sake, I wanted him to hurt. I wheeled around on him. "Stop helping! Just stop."

He stood, puffing up his chest, and moved in on me, his demon stench hitting me. "I need to make sure ye make it back to Cataleen alive. I can't guarantee yer safety whilst yer out of my sight." He prodded my chest, pushing me backward, his eerie eyes flashing. "So, I'll accompany ye as far as I can go, whether or not ye like it. That understood, mate?"

I pressed into his finger, still poking me though it hurt more than a finger to the chest should. "Perfectly."

Aodan backed away. Nay, he was right there one second, then there were feet between us without him seeming to have moved. Come to think of it, he looked healthier—for a fasgadair—more energized. His eyes shone as they hadn't before. Had he drank gachen blood whilst in Ceas Croi?

I shuddered. I would not ask. Nay. I didn't want to know. I'd just put my head down and get out of here and back to Cataleen as fast as possible.

"Get some sleep." He finished undressing, shifted into animal form, and curled up beside his things.

I sat nearby. The fasgadair scent dissipated with him in animal form. As I absorbed the sun's slow reawakening, I breathed in the damp air and allowed it to cleanse my body, mind, and soul. *God, please help us.*

CHAPTER FORTY-SEVEN

CATALEEN

My body ached from seemingly endless days riding in the carriage. I'd never ridden in one before, and it wasn't nearly as pleasant as I'd expected. Without a proper road, we followed the ruts where Achaius tried to create one. I clung to the rail as we bounced along, jostling like pebbles in a crashing wave. The cushions no longer softened my seat. I might as well have sat on the hard bench. I should've brought a pillow.

Achaius had set up some stops along the way to switch out the horses, which gave me a brief, but sorely lacking reprieve.

Josh woke with a gasp, eyes flaring wide.

How could he be so adorable, even confused? "Bad dream?"

He rubbed his eyes and yawned. "Hardly. It's not possible to sleep in this thing."

"Ye looked like ye were sleeping." I pulled the curtain back, revealing the same endless parade of trees. "Not to alarm ye, but I've heard tell there are giants in these parts."

His eye twitched. "There are giants in Ariboslia?"

"I've never seen one. Nor have I met anyone who has. But there are rumors. I'm told there's a tower to the west of us. We might drive close enough to see it in the distance. It's massive."

He straightened, pressing himself against the backboard. "Why would we drive so close? Wouldn't it be best to avoid it?"

The horses whinnied, and we lurched to a stop. Achaius and Cahal shouted, shaking the carriage as they dismounted. The view offered nothing but trees. Josh peered out his window, then pushed me back, away from the entrance.

"Don't move." He held a finger to his lips as he sneaked from the carriage.

What was out there? It couldn't be giants. Could it?

I slid across the bench to the other window and edged the curtain aside as far as I dared. Two men approached from the woods carrying spears.

Wait. Oh no. My stomach plummeted into my feet. If my eyes weren't toying with me, this was worse—much worse—than giants. Tevin and Lorcan.

I replaced the curtain and slid back into my seat. My heart squirmed as if infested with worms as I pressed myself against the headboard. *Please don't let them see me.*

Or should I go out there? Nay, I'd agitate them. Achaius and Cahal knew them. They could handle this.

The door opened, and I squished myself as far into the corner as possible. Incomprehensible voices filtered through the window, then footsteps approached.

Achaius ducked inside. "Cataleen, would you step outside?"

The worms strangling my heart squeezed tighter. "Whatever for?"

"Lorcan and—"

"I know who's out there. Why should I want to see them?"

He twisted his lips to one side. "Please just hear them out."

I took a deep breath, trying to still the blood rushing through me, warming my face, making my fingers twitch, but it was no use. As I climbed free of the carriage and gazed upon my enemies—those who tore my family apart for mere play, pure enjoyment—my heart hammered faster, threatening to break through my chest. I couldn't hear past the heartbeat thundering in my ears. Didn't matter that they looked war-torn, ragged, hungry. It didn't make me feel better.

Were Aodan and Faolan in a similar condition? Or worse? All because of these two vile men?

Achaius motioned to my sworn enemies. "Lorcan and his son seek a ride to Gnuatthara."

My mind spun, and I faltered. Josh ran to my side to steady me.

Achaius widened his stance and cocked his head my way, a softness in his eyes. "What say ye? We won't consider their request if ye don't approve."

Rage swept through me like a hurricane. "Why even consider it? Our clan banished them. Shouldn't that mean we've nothing to do with them? Let them survive on their own, like my brothers."

Tevin's face wasn't as pale as it used to be. His freckles seemed to have multiplied. But now, he blanched. As he closed in on me, I tore myself from Josh's grip and backed into the carriage.

Tevin grappled for my hand and squeezed tight, his wide eyes desperate... horrified? "Please, Cataleen. I beg your forgiveness. Please have mercy on us."

Lorcan scoffed behind him, but didn't move to stop his son.

I ripped my hand from his and pushed him away. "Ye seek my forgiveness after what you've done?"

Tevin tumbled back, appearing on the verge of tears.

"How many years have ye tormented us? Plotted and schemed to have us banished?"

He dropped to his knees, clutching his fists, his eyes imploring. "Please, Cataleen. You don't know what 'tis like out here. Would be bad enough without a clan—food, shelter, comforts. But ye know of the creatures, Cataleen." He gazed about as if to ensure there weren't any surrounding us now. "Bloodsucking creatures. They come out at night. We've narrowly escaped." Tears spilled down his cheeks. "We can't continue to live like this. We must get to Gnuatthara."

Lorcan yanked his son to his feet. "Oh come now, get up. You're embarrassing yourself."

With a jerk, Tevin tore himself from his father's hold. "I *am* saving us. I'll do whatever I can to save us."

I crossed my arms. "Why haven't ye made it to Gnuatthara by now? You've had ample time."

Lorcan moved toward me, holding out his cane. "Now ye look here—"

Tevin splayed a hand across his father's chest, stopping him. "No, Da. Ye look. Yer actions"—he took a deep, shuddering breath—"and mine, have gotten us here. Let's end this now."

His face blotching red, Lorcan raised his cane. Then, as if remembering where he was and noticing the onlookers, he wrenched his jaw and lowered his cane. "We've said enough. Either they'll give us a ride to Gnuatthara, or they won't."

Everyone looked at me.

Tevin slid to his knees once more. "To answer yer question, we've stayed in these parts because the fasgadair seem to fear the tower-giants. But there's no shelter here. Nor do we wish to happen upon giants."

I studied him—trying to see the soul behind the mask that made my skin writhe. Something stirred within me—sympathy? For this scunner?

God, what would Ye have me do?

I didn't need to await a response. The answer was obvious. God would never turn His back on a soul pleading for His help, so how could I? A plank protruded from the back of the carriage. I pointed to it. "They can ride on that. But they'll not ride inside with me."

I stormed back to my seat and counted the knots on the uinnseann wood headboard across from me. The carriage jostled as the passengers arranged themselves and we set off once more.

God, what are Ye doing? I'd prayed to see Aodan and Faolan, not these idiots. Forgive me. I know Ye created them, too. But what are Ye doing to me? Are Ye trying to destroy me?

CHAPTER FORTY-EIGHT

FAOLAN

We made our way back to the waterfall. The sight of it both encouraged and depressed me. We were making progress —*slow* progress. We climbed to the top and skirted the lake, now searching for a safe place to cross the river.

Keeping up with Aodan's pace was more challenging than the terrain, particularly given my sorry state. Dirt seeped through the holes in my ratty shoes. I fought the urge to stop and free them from the debris. There was no use. They would fill up again moments later. I might as well give in to the gritty feeling. My stomach had given up hopes of receiving a decent meal. The holes in my stained shirt offered the only comfort, allowing the wind to cool my sweaty skin.

Why had I insisted on continuing in human form?

In case I wanted to talk. But we weren't talking. And now it was too late to change. Aodan would keep going without me. I knew why *I* hurried. But what was *his* rush? He had no plan. Where could we go beyond Morrigan's reach? Other than heaven.

I sucked in a breath.

Would Aodan kill her? Would his twisted mind justify it somehow, thinking he was being merciful by getting her away from Morrigan and sending her to heaven?

Nay. He wasn't so far gone. Yet. He was bringing me to Gnuatthara, not home. Far from Catty. She had nothing to fear from Aodan from such a distance.

Unless...

Might Aodan's plan be to drop me off at Gnuatthara so he could get to Notirr before me?

That thought leadened my limbs, and I stopped, swallowing the bile burning my throat.

Aodan noticed me. He waved an impatient hand, and his face contorted as he closed in on me. "Why've ye stopped? We don't have time for this."

I couldn't swallow the slimy, sick taste coating my mouth. It clung to me. "Why are ye bringing me to Gnuatthara?"

He loosed a groan. "I already told ye. So ye won't be alone. Someone will help ye get back home."

"How do ye know that?"

Aodan threw up his arms. "Thanks to Cahal's family, there's a system set up to rescue abandoned babies. That includes carriages. It will be faster for ye. But they'll not allow a creature like me in their midst."

I stared at him, hoping something about him would give away any lies. "What are ye plans... after we part ways?"

"I'm going to return to Ceas Croi to keep an eye on Morrigan."

A wave of nausea swept over me. "How? Even if ye saw her leave, ye couldn't stop her."

"I—"

I closed in on him. "Yer lying. Morrigan told ye to go to Notirr and kill Catty. What do ye think she'll do to ye when ye've returned early without doing what she asked?"

A low growl rumbled deep in his throat, and he bared his fangs at me.

I backed away.

"Just do yer part to protect Catty while I do mine." He continued searching for a way across the raging river.

No point in pressing him further. Not now. But one thing was certain—I didn't trust him. Not anymore.

CHAPTER FORTY-NINE

CATALEEN

Four agonizing days passed. Each time we stopped to switch horses, to eat, or to rest, I avoided Tevin and Lorcan. Lorcan didn't seem to mind one bit. He kept away from the others. But Tevin seemed eager to connect with us. Not that I'd seen much. Though I longed to escape my carriage, it had become my hideout. I rarely left.

We stopped at another outpost. Josh charged out of the carriage in a hurry. He probably needed to heed nature's call, like me. But no matter how urgent my need, I wouldn't rush out. Tevin might be lurking about.

I stuck my head out the door and checked both ways. Josh was gone. Someone came to greet Achaius. They engaged in conversation while Cahal stood by. With Lorcan and Tevin nowhere to be seen, it seemed safe. I blew out a breath and exited.

"Cataleen?" Tevin's distressing voice whined from behind.

I jumped, leaving my stomach behind, then rushed off toward the rickety building, kicking up dirt. "Get away from me!"

He grasped my wrist and whirled me around to face him. His arm erupted in fire. With a yelp, he flung my hand away and flailed his arm, fanning the flames.

Did I just—

Achaius rushed at us, tearing off his shirt. He threw Tevin to the ground and smacked his arm until the flames retreated. Then he tossed his shirt aside to inspect Tevin's arm. His sleeve was still intact. Tattered and dirty as it had been, but not burned. Achaius's shaky hands hovered over the sleeve, then tore it upward, revealing healthy flesh beneath.

But how was that possible? I'd seen the flames. No material, substance, or body could withstand that and not take any damage.

"What's this?" He jerked Tevin's arm to inspect every angle, then did the same with his shirt sleeve. "Ye were on fire."

Tevin pushed Achaius off him. His gaze met mine as he stood and tugged his worn sleeve back in place. "I don't know what happened. But I'm fine, as ye can see."

Cahal came up beside me.

"Did ye see that?" Achaius pointed to Tevin.

"See what?" Cahal retrieved Achaius's shirt from the ground.

"I... He..." Achaius inspected his shirt. It, too, looked no worse than it had. He cringed and gripped the back of his head. "Sakes, I don't know."

Cahal wrapped a protective hand around my shoulder. "Did Tevin do anything to her?"

"Nay." I skewered Tevin with a warning glance.

"Good." Cahal steered me in a different direction. "Outhouses are this way."

"Thanks." I allowed him to guide me away from Tevin and Achaius gawking after us.

Had I done that? I must have. Aodan wasn't near. And Aodan's fires caught. It had consumed Tevin's shirt and spread throughout the barn. But mine? The bedpost. It hadn't showed signs of being burned either. Was it possible my fire was safe?

Even if it was, no one would understand. I couldn't let anyone find out, or I'd be banished, too.

But why hadn't Tevin said anything? The old him would have taken any opportunity to cause trouble for me. Why not now?

Had he changed?

Either way, I didn't want him near me.

What if I couldn't control my fire-starting ability in front of the wrong person next time?

Nay, there couldn't be a next time.

I touched Cahal's hand on my shoulder. "Can someone make Tevin stay away from me?"

"We're try—"

"What is he trying to do? Has he forgotten? He used to lie in wait to torment us. And now he's doing the same thing? For what?"

"I think he wants—"

"I don't care what he wants. He's creepy, and I don't want him anywhere near me."

Cahal blew out a breath. "I'll do what I can."

I took a deep breath and slowed. Tevin hadn't exposed me. Was *I* being unreasonable?

Nay, how many people would have allowed him to ride with them? I owed him nothing. He was fortunate I'd given in that much. He should take what he could get and leave me alone.

As soon as I could, I climbed into the carriage. My legs complained at being returned to their confinement, but what choice did I have? I dared not risk encountering Tevin.

The sun had dropped below the horizon for the night, dragging its red and orange blanket to bed as crickets sang the sun to sleep. Light from the campfire rose beyond the cramped building. If only I could be out there, laughing and chatting with those who'd made it their mission to help rescue babies. I should be out there. Instead, I was trapped in here.

Tevin was ruining everything.

I shouldn't have allowed them to join us. Each moment I spent in their presence was a betrayal to Aodan and Faolan. Josh rocked the carriage as he entered and handed me something wrapped in linen. "Supplies are low here, so we're using our own rations. There's some porridge left."

"Thank ye." I unwrapped my piece and took a bite. It was getting harder and losing flavor as the days went by. I much preferred fresh porridge dipped in cream, but it wasn't bad.

"We'll be able to restock when we get to Gnuatthara."

"When will we be off?"

"They're just finishing tying up the horses. We'll head out any minute. Achaius says we should reach Gnuatthara before the sun sets tomorrow." He bit into his piece and made a face.

I stifled a laugh. "Clearly you've no taste for porridge."

"After it's been sitting around, hardening in a drawer, then wrapped and traveling for days?" He rapped a knuckle against his piece. "It's like a brick."

"What do you eat in America?"

"Pizza, burgers, fries, and ramen. Lots of ramen. And coffee. I miss fresh-brewed coffee."

"I've never heard of those." What if I hated their food, as he didn't seem to care for ours? "But you've mentioned coffee before. Isn't that a drink?"

"Yes, I lived on it back home."

Lived on a drink? That sounded unhealthy.

Achaius shouted something outside, then prompted the horses to move. We lurched forward, then rocked as we left the outpost and returned to the so-called road.

"There are lots of foods you eat here, too. My mom makes meals every night for dinner. Usually, shepherd's pie, stew, or some kind of soup. And we have salad with most meals."

"Salad? Oh, good." That was reassuring.

"I like mine with ranch."

"Ranch?" Why'd he have to top off something familiar with something foreign, yet again?

"Yeah, it's a..."

An image of a road sprang to my mind along with the sound of crickets, but it wasn't from me. I'd never glimpsed the road from that angle before. And so clear, though it was night.

Did Aodan send that? But why? It was so arbitrary.

I pulled the curtain aside and peered out the window as if expecting to find him outside. Even with the moon bright, I couldn't possibly see anything out there.

But I could still hear crickets. Had Aodan sent that, too? Or was I already hearing them?

Hope rose within me like a paper lantern. We'd found Tevin and Lorcan. Was it possible we'd find Aodan and Faolan, too?

CHAPTER FIFTY

FAOLAN

A song of crickets woke me. I enjoyed it until reality struck me and I jumped up.

Where was Aodan?

The matted grass offered the only evidence he'd been here.

Sake, Faolan! Why'd ye allow yerself to fall asleep? Now he's ditched ye.

I shifted back to my human form and dressed. I'd have a better chance tracking Aodan in my wolf form, but I needed to be in my human form. I felt more in control that way.

Something rustled in the bushes, and I ducked behind a tree.

"Faolan?" Aodan called.

Releasing a pent-up breath, I stepped out from hiding. "Where were you?"

"I found a road. Gnuatthara isn't far."

"Ye couldn't have waited for me?"

"Ye were finally sleeping. I didn't want to wake ye. And I found these." He held out his closed hand. "Take them."

I reached out, and he dumped a pile of something. "Berries?"

"Aye."

With it darker than usual, we started our evening trek. "You should've woken me. We've lost time."

"Not if we don't stop to eat. I've more berries." He patted his pouch. "Eat those. They'll keep ye till ye can get a proper meal in Gnuatthara."

We walked through the trees with a chorus of crickets serenading us. How peaceful this would be if my traveling companion didn't steal my friend and crave my blood. I kept expecting the worst from him, and it never came. Could it be I was wrong about him?

We made our way to a clearing.

"'Tis the road!" Aodan practically skipped ahead.

I studied the ruts cutting through the grass. "Not much of one, if it is."

Could it be a road? Finding evidence of other gachen and getting out from under the cover of trees sure felt good. I couldn't see as well at night in human form, but the moon cast a calming glow. And seeing Aodan seem happy, if only for a moment, soothed me.

I spotted something off the road. "Is that a—"

"Carriage." He sped off at an inhuman speed.

My heart leaped into my throat and remained lodged there. Would he give in to his craving for gachen blood? I didn't want to see that, but I couldn't allow it either. And what if that was Achaius? I hurried to catch up, but by the time I reached Aodan, he was already storming off, spouting something.

God, please keep him out of trouble.

Aodan disappeared in front of the carriage. The horses whinnied as the cart jerked to a stop. Then he reappeared and yanked someone off the back rail. They raised something... a cane?

Was that...? Dread seeped into my blood and thickened it, slowing my movements.

Lorcan.

Aodan yanked Lorcan into his chest and gripped his neck as if he held a knife to it. But he had no weapon. Other than his inhuman strength and his teeth. And his fire.

Another person scrambled to hide on the other side of the carriage. Must be Tevin.

The drivers dismounted and approached Aodan and Lorcan.

"Achaius? Cahal?" I called.

They looked my way, then returned their attention to Aodan.

"Yer consorting with banished clansmen?" Aodan shook Lorcan in his grip as if he was made of straw.

"Aodan?" Catty's voice emerged from the carriage.

My head snapped toward it. She leaped from the carriage and closed in on her brother.

"Sister?" Aodan stepped away from her as if she'd attempted to ignite him on fire. "What are ye doing away from Ma? And what are ye doing runnin' aboot with these dobbers?"

She stopped short. Her mouth hung open. Even in this dim light, I could see the color leave her face. "'Tis true. Yer a–a—"

Lorcan writhed in Aodan's grip. Aodan faltered but recovered. "Aye. I'm a fasgadair."

Tears streamed down her face. She held a hand to her mouth as if to keep from saying the wrong thing.

His eerie eyes narrowed at the odd-looking lad beside her. "And who in Ariboslia is this dobber? I leave ye for two moons—"

I hadn't noticed the lad standing by the carriage door. I'd never seen him before. Had they both been in there—alone? Was this the lad she couldn't get off her mind? The father of the predicted child? Fury swirled within me like a tempest, blowing away my fears.

Catty wiped her eyes and set her jaw. "Sixty-six days."

Aodan snarled. "Not long. And already yer gallivanting with some dunderhead. Alone in a carriage? Really, Cataleen. Have ye taken leave of yer senses? But what's worse? Yer traipsing about arm in arm with traitors!"

She flinched. Then she took her stance with hands on hips. "First off, I'm avoiding them like the red sickness. And second, yer a fasgadair! Who are ye to say one word to me?"

Now those eerie eyes widened, revealing no white, and a collective shudder rippled through everyone watching.

He roared. "I sacrificed myself for my clan. I gave up my life, my very soul, so ye could live. And for what? Seeing ye now—alone with some numpty and hobnobbing with these galoots? I'm not sure yer worthy of saving."

She winced, and her hand flew to her chest. "Ye think *I* need saving?"

He snarled at her. "I know ye do."

My heart shattered as if it had been frozen and then smashed with a sledgehammer. Whatever had rooted me to my spot released its grip. I ran to stand between them. "Control yerself, mate."

"Faolan?" Catty's gaze searched me as if uncertain she could trust her eyes, yet full of hope. "Yer not a fasgadair?"

I waved it off. Now was not the time. I jerked my head toward Aodan. "Thanks, mate. I'm safely delivered. Off with ye."

"Ye think I'm going to leave her with Tevin and Lorcan?"

"Leave them be." Catty peered over my shoulder. "They seek safe passage to Gnuatthara. That's all."

"Well, they won't get it." Aodan tightened his grip on Lorcan's neck.

Catty pushed me aside. "I said, leave them be."

I'd never seen such fire in her eyes. I feared she might set her brother ablaze.

Aodan pushed Lorcan onto the ground. "Or what? What are ye going to do to me, Catty?"

Lorcan recovered his cane and moved to strike Aodan.

Aodan turned on him so fast I couldn't register the change. The cane erupted in flames.

Horror blazed in Lorcan's eyes as he flung it away. He recoiled, tripping in his haste to flee.

Like a flash of lightning, Aodan appeared behind Lorcan, wrapping his arms around him.

"Naaaaaaay!" Catty wailed.

Tevin came running from behind the carriage. "Daaaaa!"

Lorcan screamed. Aodan drove his fangs into Lorcan's neck with a sickening sound.

Catty ran to stop Aodan, as if she could. I intercepted. While she fought to escape me, the nameless lad came to my aid. Together, we spun her around and pulled her away from the unstoppable tragedy unfolding. As we dragged her into the carriage, Achaius and Cahal returned to their seats up front. Tevin pushed his way inside and slammed the carriage door. Before I'd sat, we took off, bouncing as we raced along the pitiful road.

I stuck my head out the window and took one last look at my long-lost friend, bent over Lorcan's fallen body, giving himself over to the monster within.

CHAPTER FIFTY-ONE

CATALEEN

Grateful for the darkness, I sobbed throughout the night, barely aware of Faolan, Josh, and Tevin riding in the carriage with me. I should have been grateful to have Faolan returned to me with his soul intact. But my grief at losing them before couldn't compare with *this*. Aodan might as well have died. Nay. He was worse than dead. If he'd merely died, I'd see him again in heaven. But what had happened to his soul? Would he live forever in that undead state? If he could die, where would he go?

A fresh wave of sobs racked me. Faolan pulled me into him. Although he was a bit ripe, his familiar scent smoothed the edge of the bitter sting that tore my soul into shreds.

The rising sun filtered through the curtains. Had I slept at all? I'd soaked Faolan's tunic with my tears. After giving the wet spot a useless wipe, I peeled myself from him, feeling dried-up—hollow.

The carriage slowed to a stop. Achaius and Cahal dismounted. I peeked behind the curtain. A monstrous man who made Cahal look short greeted them. His mere size would have sent my heart racing and urged me to hide, but I'd spent my emotions. Instead, I watched—almost as if I was in someone else's foreign body and had little control or care.

The carriage door opened, and Achaius poked his head inside. "We've arrived. This is the outpost outside Gnuatthara. They have another baby."

Though I thought my well had dried up, a fresh pool of tears dripped down my face. Just hearing of another child made me cry? Why was everything making me so weepy?

Faolan rubbed my back. Josh sat across from me. What was that look on his face? He looked so... helpless. And nauseated. Tevin sat beside him. My fury toward him paled now compared with my grief. And regardless of the type of man his father was, he was still his father. And he'd watched him die in a heinous way at my brother's hands.

Tevin's filthy clothes hung from his bony frame. His hair had grown and tangled in clumps over his haunted eyes. Was he about to vomit? A green tinge tinted his hollow cheeks. He moved his mouth, gaping like a fish out of water. Then he slumped, giving up on words, but his sorrowful gaze returned to me.

I could feel his sorrow. An all-consuming sorrow, like mine, left no room for anger or hate. I, too, wanted to say something. But had no words. Not at a time like this.

Great. More tears. Grinding my teeth against them, I returned my gaze to the window.

Cataleen!

My back snapped straight. *Aodan?*

Faolan nudged me. "Cataleen? Are ye well?"

I'd never felt him use the mind-link with such force. *What do ye want from me?*

Images of Morrigan, hordes of fasgadair, and Lorcan's lifeless body invaded my mind. *Leave this place! Go home!*

Why?

"Cataleen?" Faolan shook my shoulder.

Josh snatched my hands.

If ye wish to live, leave now!

A stream of horrifying images flashed through my mind. I gripped my head as if I could force the images out, but they wouldn't stop. An endless loop kept playing and playing over and over. I squeezed my head and screamed. The images stopped. Then white flashed across my vision, and I slumped into Faolan.

✶

I woke with a groan. Every muscle in my body ached. My head felt like I'd caught it in a winepress, but for its lolling from the rocking carriage.

"She's coming to!" Josh's face filled my view.

"What's happening?" Was I lying down in the carriage? My pack was shoved under my head, and my legs were bent to allow me to fit. I swiveled to straighten them. The movement intensified the ache.

Josh and Faolan rose from their seats across from me as they tried in their awkward, unhelpful way to assist me. They trained worried gazes on me. Beyond them, Tevin held a bundle in his hands. A baby?

"We rescued a baby?" I sat at an angle to stretch my sore legs.

"Careful." Faolan tugged my pack out of the way.

"Are we on our way home?" My dress caught underneath me.

"Aye." Faolan helped me tug my dress free and sat beside me.

"How long was I out?"

"Nearly a day." He handed me a waterskin. "Here, you need to drink."

I took a long pull. My throat was so dry.

He snagged the waterskin and shoved a cloth in my hand. Dried fish and cheese. "Do ye know what's happening to ye, Catty?"

"Aodan." I chewed a bite of flavorless cheese. "He keeps showing me things. Horrible things."

Across from me, Tevin and Josh shared grave looks. Beyond the dark windows, trees rushed by. "We're not stopping to rest?"

"We'll stop at the next outpost."

Hello, sister.

A fresh wave of images bombarded me. The same ones as before, but with a few new ones of another lifeless gachen body. Where had this one come from? I'd no time to consider it as another wave washed over me and knocked me out.

I came in and out of consciousness, surviving brief moments of clarity. Each time, someone was ready to make me drink and eat. As if Aodan was following me, he knew the moment I woke. Not long after, more images bombarded me. Each time, new images entered the loop of more gachen falling at his hands.

✲

Aodan upped the severity of his images of gachen afraid for their lives and fasgadair feeding on them. Their screams echoed in my mind, intermingling with my own.

The images made way to a constant state of being, as if he'd somehow trapped me in his head. Where was my real body? I walked with Aodan throughout a mountainous palace as he gave orders to his new underlings. Rounded up gachen, saving some to be farmed. Fed on the remaining gachen, bleeding them dry.

I couldn't break free.

"Catty?"

Was that Faolan's voice? But where was he? I couldn't turn to look for him. Aodan had captured my mind. I had to walk where Aodan walked, see what Aodan saw, along a dark corridor to a guarded door.

Something held my hand. But nay. I couldn't look. The hands I could see, Aodan's hands, swung freely by his side, covered in a drab brown cloak. Was I feeling my actual body somewhere else? Was someone squeezing my hand somewhere? Wherever my body lay? Trying to reassure me?

I passed the guards stationed outside Morrigan's door. They bowed low. Inside, Morrigan stood before a bowl, mashing ingredients with a pestle.

"Is it done?" Morrigan didn't look up at me.

I bowed. "It will be soon."

Aodan? Aodan's voice came from my mouth.

Was this a dream? Why did it feel so real?

She materialized before me and wrapped impossibly strong fingers around my neck. "How dare ye return to my presence without killing her?"

I gasped for air. My throat and lungs burned as she squeezed. My face blazed as I gurgled, desperate for air.

"Cataleen!"

Josh? Where was he? Why didn't he rescue me?

"I—" Aodan tried to speak.

The hand around our throat loosened its grip, but held us dangling above the ground.

"W–we're connected." Aodan strained to speak. "I can kill her through the connection."

The brutal hand released. We fell to the ground. Our hands flew to our throat, expecting to find Morrigan's hands still there, choking us, as we gulped air and coughed.

"Catty!" Faolan's voice again.

My body felt as though it was shaking, but it wasn't. We peeled ourself off the ground in Morrigan's lair and stood.

"I see you've fed." Morrigan disappeared and reemerged by her current creation. "Tell me about this *connection*."

We rubbed our throat. "We have a mind-link. It's stronger now, in my fasgadair form. I can ensure she dies. Ensure Gi'Wrann's prediction doesn't come true."

She picked up a pestle and wagged it at us. "Do not forsake the prophecy. The end to your rule is only the start. It threatens me as well."

"It won't happen."

"It better not. I'll hold ye responsible." She wriggled something squirmy from a nearby canister, tossed it in the bowl, and smashed it with the pestle. "And if she doesn't die soon, I will kill her myself."

CHAPTER FIFTY-TWO

FAOLAN

Watching over Cataleen night and day was taking its toll. It had been days of her drifting in and out of consciousness. I had to be ready to make her drink and eat and get her home as quickly as possible. We needed to put some distance between her and Aodan. If only I could spur these horses to move faster. But the terrain was terrible in spots, and the horses needed to be switched out.

God, give me patience.

I could kill Aodan. Never in twenty lifetimes would I imagine myself capable of such a thing, but watching Cataleen fight to hold on to moments of consciousness? If she ate and drank enough while she was coherent, she might survive this. But would she keep her head? Best not to think about it. I pushed the thought from me with a sharp exhale.

And what was happening to her in her unconscious state? What was she experiencing when her body flew into fits of convulsing? When she looked like she was choking... *Had* she been choking?

This was Aodan's doing. Could he physically harm her through their connection? But why would he want to hurt her? She was going home, away from him. What threat could she be to him?

But then, Aodan wasn't human anymore. Just what had he become? Was he capable of reason?

He had to be stopped. But how? He was the most powerful being in existence, aside from Morrigan.

And God. Don't forget God. Nothing was more powerful than He was.

God, help Cataleen. Tell me what to do to help her.

Her helpless form rocked with the horses. If only we could make her more comfortable. She'd be sore when she woke, cramped with her legs tucked to fit on the bench.

Curses, Aodan! You best not cross my path if ye value yer life.

"You should sleep."

The voice in the darkness startled me. Though he sat beside me, I kept forgetting Josh was there. I shook the waterskin. "I have to make sure she gets enough water."

Josh held a hand out. "I can do it."

I jerked the waterskin away. "Who are ye? What were ye doing with Catty?"

He massaged his knees. "I'm Nathaniel and Fiona's son."

"I don't know any Nathaniel or Fiona." I squeezed the waterskin. The water squishing back and forth was oddly soothing.

"Ever heard of Shea MacClune?"

Tevin gasped. I'd forgotten *he* was there, too.

"Everyone has heard of Shea. He's the lad the fasgadair killed before getting caught in our village. What have ye to do with him?"

"He was my uncle."

I squinted, searching for what that meant. "Hang on. Fiona, your ma, she's Shea's older sister?"

Josh's hands moved up to rub his upper legs as he stretched them as far as they could go before hitting the bench. "Yes."

I tried to remember what happened to the MacClunes. "She disappeared not long after Shea died. No one ever said where she went."

Josh scratched his chin as if thinking about how to respond, then took a deep breath. "She left with my dad—to another realm."

Tevin let out another gasp.

I eyed Josh's strange clothes and hair. What were those blue trousers? The material looked like nothing fromAriboslia. Something was off about him. "What business have ye here?"

"Sully prophesied that Cataleen will come to our realm to protect her from her brother."

I laughed. "Catty would never leave her home."

Then I watched her lying there, unconscious. I never would have believed Aodan would kill a man. Never in his entire lifetime could I imagine him attacking his sister. Both had happened. In one day. Maybe Catty *would* leave. No matter how much distance we put between her and Aodan, it didn't seem to matter. He must be getting stronger. Maybe sending Catty to another realm was the only way to save her. My chest clogged up unshed tears. I tried and failed to swallow the lump forming in my throat as I gazed upon her fragile form.

"What's this 'other realm' ye speak of? Is it safe?"

Josh ran his fingers through his hair, making no difference to his strange haircut. "Is anyplace safe? There are no vampires, if that's what you mean. And Aodan won't be able to reach her."

Thinking about all this hurt my head. I'd have to speak with Sully as well as Catty's ma when we returned before she went off anywhere with some stranger. And if venturing to another realm was the only option, I would go with her.

Cataleen squirmed in her sleep. Was she coming to?

"Catty?" I searched her face for signs of waking, but saw none. I reached out and grasped her hand, pulling it onto my knee.

Josh put a hand on my arm. "You should rest. I'll wake you if she regains consciousness."

I shook my head. "Nay. I have to be here for her."

He took the waterskin from my lap. "There's still four days left of our trip. Are you going to stay up the entire time? What kind of help will you be to her?"

After a long pause, he heaved a heavy sigh. "I know you don't know me. You don't trust me. But there are two of us."

"Three." Tevin raised a finger in the air.

"Bah! As if I'd ever leave ye alone with Catty." I leaned forward to look past Josh to Tevin. "Ye keep sittin' there in silence if ye don't want to be thrown out with the bloodsuckers."

Tevin rammed his back against the backboard, hiding from my sight. Part of me felt guilty. He'd just lost his father. But a bigger part of me didn't care. He caused this. All of it. He could suffer the consequences.

I gripped a fistful of my hair. "Why won't she wake up?"

Josh was right. I needed rest. But would I be able to even if I tried?

✺

WE DELIVERED Catty home and settled her into bed. She looked so small. Sweaty hair matted her face. I moved the hair from her clammy forehead.

Her entire body jerked. "Nay. Nay, nay, nay."

Catty's ma filled the doorway, blocking the light. "Is she dreaming?"

"I don't know." I laid Catty down, then lifted her feet onto the bed. "She's had a few moments when she seemed to have heard me. But those are getting fewer and further between."

Mirna sat at the end of the bed. The light from the doorway spilled onto her sad gaze fixed upon her daughter. "Did she have any visions?"

"Before she fell into this... this *trance*... she said Aodan was sending her visions." I dragged a tired hand down my face. "I don't know what he's doing to her. He sent me back to rescue her, to get her out of Morrigan's reach. Though we don't know how. I don't *think* he's trying to kill her." I wasn't so sure anymore, but I couldn't say that to her.

She sucked in a breath. "Sully's been trying to convince her to go to America with Nathaniel and Joshua."

So her ma supported their crazy plan? She'd throw Catty from one fire into another? "So Josh said. America? What do you know of it?"

"America is in the human realm."

"Humans. Hmph." The silly beings who thought gachen to be gods, getting us sent here. They did us a favor. But now Catty would have to find a way to survive among them? I didn't like it. Not a wee bit.

But I'd seen firsthand what the fasgadair were capable of. And for Aodan to torture her like this? Was he serious about pushing her away for her protection? Or had he given himself over to the demon within? Either way, Cataleen needed to escape. "Why didn't she go?"

Mirna let out a series of scoffing breaths. "Have ye met my daughter? Stubborn as a mule, that one."

I smiled and touched Catty's face. She felt warm. Too warm. "I'll admit I don't care for this plot to send her to America. But we need to save her somehow. If Sully thinks this is the way, we need to send her."

"I don't want to do anything against her wishes." Mirna released a long, tortured breath.

I tried to summon a reassuring smile. "I'll be with her."

She cupped a hand to my cheek, then nodded. "Let's call for Sully. Perhaps 'tis time to make her go."

※

I'D ONLY GOTTEN a few hours of sleep during our travels and exhaustion seeped into my bones, weighing me down. Though I sat at an immobile table, I felt as if I were still rocking in the carriage. I wanted nothing more than to crawl into my bed and sleep for an entire moon. But I couldn't peel myself away. I fought through my hazy mind to be present as Da, Sully, and Josh's da crowded the table.

Josh looked as bedraggled as I felt. Yet he remained. Perhaps he was a decent sort.

Though my worry for Catty hadn't eased, having others share the burden strengthened me. Others with more wisdom than I had.

Catty's ma poured water and delivered mugs to Josh and me. "Ye must be famished." She hurried to the porridge drawer, cut off two slices, then plated them. The stoneware clinked on the table.

"Thank ye." My stomach rumbled for a bite.

She dissolved into her chair, and her mouth set in a grim line. "We need to make plans to take Cataleen to the human realm. If we have to deliver her in an unconscious state, so be it."

"Agreed." Sully laced his spindly fingers together and placed them on the table. "Why don't these lads finish their food and get some sleep? We can leave in the morn."

I shook my head. "I'm not leaving her."

"She's home now." Catty's ma patted my shoulder.

Sully aimed his blind eyes at me. "I'll stay to watch over her as well."

"That's all well and good." I swallowed a lump of porridge. "But I'll sleep on the floor if I must. I'll not leave her."

CHAPTER FIFTY-THREE

CATALEEN

I woke in my room. Was this a dream? How did I get here? I racked my brain for the last thing I remembered—Aodan. He'd found us. He... killed...

Nay. Nay, nay, nay. I couldn't believe it. I wouldn't.

Had I dreamed the whole thing? How else could I be home in bed without remembering how I got here, though I'd been days away?

Something was off. My lantern was lit, and my door was open. I never left my door open whilst I slept. Hushed voices wafted my way, but I couldn't make out the words. Who was out there?

"Catty?"

The voice sounded like mine. It sounded as if *I* had spoken. Had my lips even moved? I didn't move them. I tried to search the room to see who had spoken. But my head refused to obey. My arms, legs... nothing moved. Panic sent my heart racing like a runaway horse. Why couldn't I move?

"Catty—'tis me. Aodan."

I had spoken. But I hadn't. The words came from me, but they weren't mine. How and why was I speaking to myself as if I was my brother? Was I off my head? Maybe I was still dreaming.

"Yer not dreaming, Catty. Ye must leave Notirr. Morrigan is plotting to kill ye."

I tried to ask what was happening, but I couldn't speak. Had Aodan somehow taken control of my body? I wanted to run away—run to our ma. I couldn't dislodge the scream trapped in my lungs. My heart thumped. I couldn't even breathe to control the rising fear. A black haze filled my mind as everything within me fought for release.

"Settle yerself, Catty. Do ye want yer heart to burst? Just go to sleep and let me do what needs to be done."

Go to sleep? Go to sleep! What did he plan to do?

My body sat up as if of its own accord and crossed through to the kitchen—wishing to scream all the while.

"Cataleen?" Ma's concerned voice came from the table, but I couldn't turn to look at her.

In my periphery, I made out those gathered by the table with Ma—Sully, Faolan and his da, and Josh and his da. In my mind, I cried, begging for help. But nothing came out as I passed their confused faces without meeting their eyes.

My body continued past them, pulled out a drawer, seized a knife, and aimed it at me.

Naaaaaaay! Nay, nay, nay!

Please, God! Please release me from this!

CHAPTER FIFTY-FOUR

FAOLAN

I leaped from my chair. Josh reached her first, clutching the hand with the knife and working it loose as I grasped her and pinned her other arm down should she try anything. My heart pounded and twisted, tightening with each thump. Josh freed the knife and threw his arms around her.

What was happening to her? How could she even consider doing that to herself? And right in our presence, as if she wanted her suicide attempt to be witnessed and stopped.

Nay. That wasn't Catty. She would never do something like that. There had to be another explanation.

I backed away, watching her in Josh's fierce embrace. Who was this lad, and what were his intentions? There seemed to be something between them. Unless it was one-sided. But something was definitely happening from his side.

Catty slumped. Josh gathered her into his arms and carried her to the armchair.

She blinked at all the faces surrounding her, trying to make sense of things. "What happened?"

I knelt before her.

"Faolan!" She jumped up and threw her arms around me.

"Whoa. Easy." I embraced her, then helped her back to her seat.

"What are ye doing home?" She looked around as if just noticing her surroundings. "How did I get here?"

"'Tis a long story."

"But ye—yer not a fasgadair. How is that so? Aodan…" Her eyes darkened and glistened. She straightened, the brightness returning to her eyes. "Or am I mistaken?"

Grimacing, I shook my head. "Yer not mistaken."

"But ye—"

"Enough of me for now. We'll get to that later. What of ye? What happened? Why'd ye try to stab yerself?"

"She didn't." Sully's gravelly voice came from the kitchen table. The only one who hadn't moved from his seat. "'Twas Aodan. Am I right, child?"

"It must—I think so." Catty bobbed her head as if attempting to see Sully past Josh and me. "I'm feeling a bit confined. Would ye all please —" Palms down, she flicked her fingers outward, ushering us away.

We obliged, but Josh pulled up a chair to remain close beside her. I kept a watchful eye on him. How much had happened between them in my absence? Guilt raged in my gut like an angry bull. Catty didn't have a da to watch out for her. Rather than watching Aodan's descent, I should've been here, protecting her.

I would never leave her again. Not if I had a choice in the matter.

Sully made his way from the kitchen to his favored seat in the Tuamas' gathering space—the rocker. "So, lass… Are ye ready to leave for the human realm?"

"Nay. This is my home."

He turned to Mirna. How did he always know where everyone sat? "Now that Aodan can take complete control of Cataleen, it is imperative that she leave."

I scrubbed a hand over my face as I tried to wrap my head around it all. "If Aodan is controlling ye, if he raised the knife, I don't believe he was trying to kill ye. He sent me to save ye. To urge ye to flee. Morrigan wants ye dead. Not Aodan."

"Doesn't matter." Sully rocked as he rubbed his beard. "After I share with the others what took place here today, they'll agree. They'll want to see ye safe. And no one will want someone under Aodan's control in their midst."

My heart broke at the fear and utter astonishment crumpling Catty's face. I crouched before her, reaching for her hands, but stopping from touching her for fear she'd pull away. "Ye must go. 'Tis the only way to keep ye safe. Morrigan has made Aodan leader of the fasgadair, but no one controls her. She might come here to kill ye herself. I know ye. Yer the most unselfish person I know. Ye don't want to leave yer mum, yer village. But as long as yer here, they're not safe. Even if Aodan commanded Notirr to remain untouched, he has no power over Morrigan. None."

Sully stilled the chair and leaned forward, his sightless eyes staring into hers with ferocious intent. "If ye don't leave willingly, we'll banish ye."

Catty's face broke. She buried her face in her hands as she rocked in silent sobs. Josh wrapped an arm around her shoulders and raised his head. His eyes pleaded for someone to do something. Anything.

Mirna fell to Catty's side, opposite Josh, and hugged her. Over Catty's head, she nodded to Josh's da. "When are ye leaving for the human realm?"

The man scratched the stubble darkening his chin. "We were supposed to leave two weeks ago. I've extended our stay for Josh, but school starts in a few days. We need to get back."

"Good." Mirna snugged Catty to her side, jostling her like a wee one. "You'll leave in the morn."

CHAPTER FIFTY-FIVE

CATALEEN

We stepped into the gray dawn. Dew glistened on the grass, and a cool breeze swept through. I inhaled the sweet scent of the wildflowers scattered over the hill homes. I'd spent my entire life here. Until the recent trip to Gnuatthara, I hadn't even traveled anywhere else, and I didn't remember most of that venture. I was more of a burden than a help.

This was not how I saw things happening. And now, I was being forced to leave my home. Banished. Not officially. But being banished couldn't feel much different.

Had I burned this place into my heart? Or would my memory fade over time?

I tried to memorize everything I saw so I could walk this path again in my mind—the flagstones embedded in the mossy earth, the grassy slopes over the houses, the rounded windows and curved doors in the one wooden wall, the wildflowers spreading colors among the grass. Especially the aotrom blossoms. The color Josh said didn't exist in his world. Would I ever see it again?

Large birds squawked as smaller ones twittered, awakening the morning with song. Did any of these birds exist in America? Would I hear their calls again?

Just how much would I miss?

I blinked back tears and lifted my chin as I followed Ma to the main gate. Faolan gripped my arm as if I were an elderly woman and might collapse. His da hovered close.

Arms crossed, Cahal leaned against a fence post. He, Josh, Josh's da, and Quin focused on Achaius as he animated his speech with his hands. Josh stood with one leg kicked up behind him, bracing himself against the fence. When he saw me, he pushed off and approached. I couldn't decipher the look in his eye.

"What of the rest of the village? Won't I have a chance to say goodbye?" They were all my family.

With a teary smile, Ma squeezed my shoulder. "There isn't time. And Quin thought it best to keep your leaving quiet."

Like Josh's parents? Sure, his da came back from time to time, but I still didn't know him or his wife. Would my clan forget me, too?

Though Faolan still held me steady, Josh splayed his arms as if expecting me to fall, ready to catch me. "Cataleen, are you okay? How are you feeling?"

Tears welled in my eyes. I swiped at them and forced a smile. "I'll be all right." If only I believed me.

"Cataleen." Ma pressed in between Josh and me, pulling me into a tight embrace. She grasped my shoulders and pushed me far enough away to look me in the eye and stroke my temple with her thumb, as she did when I was young. My heart broke at the tears slipping down her cheeks. "My wee bairn. Leanabh."

The pain stabbing my heart raced throughout my soul at Ma's old terms of endearment. My childhood flashed before my eyes—falling into the creek, toppling off Faolan's pony, crying from Tevin's taunting. She was always there to bandage me, kiss my wounds, give me a nourishing meal.... And now, what would happen to me? Would I marry? Have children? Without her? My chest constricted, all the pain knotting up so tight I'd never be able to evict it. Just when I didn't think I could possibly hurt more.

"It pains me to send ye away, leanabh. I wish I could go with ye."

"W–why c–can't ye?" I clung to her so tight, with both my arms and my heart.

"My place is here—*yer* place is to follow where God guides ye. My leanabh is all grown up now, and I'm too old to survive in a foreign realm." She swept my hair from my face. "Yer young yet. Ye will survive. And Faolan and Joshua will be with ye."

Sully came down the path with Pepin. The sun at their backs shadowed their unmistakable forms—small and stocky Pepin beside tall and slender Sully with a stick in search of anything that might trip him up. "Come now, Mirna. You can at least accompany your daughter to the megalith."

Ma shielded her eyes. "Isn't it far?"

Sully motioned to Pepin. "How far is it?"

"For those not going through the megalith?" Pepin shuffled toward the north, surveying the trees to the west, then shrugged. "Half a day at most."

"Half a day?" Josh's da pinched his eyebrows in disbelief. "It took me and my dad a whole day."

"Pepin will build another megalith. Aye?" Sully tapped his stick against a seilcheag, sidestepping it.

I picked up the snail and moved it to where it was less likely to be trampled.

Pepin gave a sharp nod. "It will take longer to travel to your home once you're in the human realm. But, if Morrigan finds a way through, Cataleen will be harder to find."

Ma gasped. "Might Morrigan find her there?"

"'Tis only a precaution, dear Mirna." Sully tugged his beard.

Ma quirked her lips. "So, there's time to get home before nightfall?"

Pepin harrumphed, his squat but solid body looking as immovable as stone. "As long as you don't dally."

"I'll see you safely home." Cahal gave Ma a rare and reassuring smile.

"As will I." Faolan's da removed his cap and bowed to Ma.

"Then I shall join you." Smiling, she put an arm around me. "I'll take as many more breaths with me bairn as I can."

I wrapped my arm around her and squished her soft middle, holding on tight. How could I say goodbye to her? My clan? My home? At least Ma had them to care for her whilst I was away.

"Load up." Achaius trundled along a small wagon with packs on it.

Pepin added his to the pile.

Ma tugged my satchel from my shoulder.

"Why do we need a cart? Can't we carry our packs?" I asked.

The others shared awkward glances, avoiding my gaze.

Then in struck me. "This is for me. In case I…"

Patting my arm, Sully flashed a smile. "Just another precaution."

We set off past the guards. The gates to my village closed behind me. Would it be forever? Would I ever see my home again? I tried not to think about it, tried not to look back. Instead, I stared at my feet, leading us into the wood.

Josh sidled up to Pepin ahead of us. "How many megaliths are there?"

"Too many. Some were built illegally, then forgotten. But when law-abiding pech come across them, they tear them down."

"Are ye not law-abiding?" Faolan hollered from beside me.

Pepin threw Faolan a look over his shoulder as if just realizing he was there. "The pechish council has their laws for a reason. I respect them. I, too, will abolish illegal or forgotten megaliths. But the pechish court would never grant me approval to build a megalith anywhere for any reason. No matter. I have God's approval. His approval is all I require. When God instructs me to raise, demolish, or leave a megalith, I obey."

"What will happen to the megalith you build for me?" I called to Pepin's back.

His red braid swinging as if to continue without him, he stopped and waited for us. "I will destroy it."

I gasped, and Ma tightened her grip on my arm.

"Cataleen won't be able to get back through?" Though Ma spoke to Pepin, she kept her alarmed gaze on me.

"Not that way." The wee fellow slashed at a branch in his path.

"'Tis only a precaution, Mirna." Sully strode onward while his stick continued guiding him through the brush.

Faolan heaved a heavy breath. "This is what Aodan wants—to get Catty beyond his reach. Beyond Morrigan's reach. But Sully is right to have precautions in place. I hate to tell ye, but ye must know. Whilst there's still something good in Aodan, it grows harder to see by the day. He's giving way to the darkness within him. He may change his mind and wish Catty harm, too."

"But how will Nathaniel return to mine?" Ma frowned at Josh's da's back.

"I'm not tearing down the megalith he uses," Pepin said. "I don't even know where it is."

"Doesn't matter." Josh's da walked sideways ahead of Ma. "I've gathered enough gold and jewels to care for my family long past my death. I don't need to make these trips anymore."

"That would be safer." Sully nodded.

Ma breathed deep. "I'm sure that will be a relief to Fiona."

"And good for Cataleen. I'll watch over her, Mirna, as if she were my own." Josh's da winked at me.

He put me at ease. There was something in his easy way. But his wife concerned me. And everything else Josh told me about the realm. My insides shriveled like dried meat.

"Not to worry, Mirna. 'Tis all in God's hands," Sully said.

While there was no better place to be, I shook, and not from the cool morning air. Leaving home was hard enough. But under these circumstances? And I wasn't traveling to another village. I was going to another realm! And the portal there would close behind me forever.

"Are ye sure I need to leave?" I scooted up to Sully, dared grab at his sleeve. "Aodan seems to be leaving me alone now. Maybe I'm out of his reach."

Several sad gazes flicked my way.

"Cataleen, this is—"

A stream of fallen gachen bodies flooded my mind, and I tripped. Someone caught me. Mumbling voices rushed my ears, but I couldn't make out any words. They sounded fuzzy... far away. They faded out, replaced by screams and pleas, begging someone to stop as the images of lifeless gachen bombarded me.

CHAPTER FIFTY-SIX

FAOLAN

"Catty!" I held her in my arms, keeping her from falling, but barely.

Gasps and shouts erupted as others realized what was happening. Catty's dead weight was slipping from my grip when Josh snagged her arm and pulled her up. Together, we dragged her to the cart. Josh's da and Cahal moved the packs to one side to make room.

"I hoped we wouldn't need this." Achaius dropped the gate on the back of the wagon so we could get Catty inside without hefting her over the rail.

We sat her down at the edge while Mirna laid out a blanket. Then we eased Catty back and dragged her up into the wagon by the blanket. Achaius bent her legs to get them to fit and closed the gate, sealing her inside.

Once we had her settled, Cahal and Achaius grasped the handle to pull the wagon together.

Mirna gripped the cart's rail and walked beside it. I kept watch to make sure Catty didn't slide, as the others probably were, too. We hardly dared take our eyes off her for most of the journey.

For Catty's sake, there was one thing I had to ask Catty's mom while I had the chance. I sidled up to her and spoke in a hushed tone, should Catty be awake enough to understand. "Ye told Sully yer staying behind because yer too old to travel to a foreign world. But yer not old. Not really. Don't ye want to be with yer daughter?"

Her shoulders slumped. "Of course, I do."

"Then what is it?"

Her gaze flicked to Catty. "I'm not well."

I sucked in a breath and searched her for signs of sickness, but found none.

Mirna seemed to know what I was doing. She waved me off. "It's nothing terrible. But I have spells. My heart won't withstand the travel, and I must remain here for treatment. They might not have a means to help me in America."

"You need to tell Catty."

She whirled on me, seeming to grow a few inches. "No one is to tell Catty!" Her gaze roamed to the others as she shrank back to normal size and lowered her voice. "Catty is such a stubborn lass. Ye saw her with that knife. Will ye risk her refusing to go?"

I noticed my jaw hanging open and snapped it shut.

She huffed a sad laugh. "I'll be fine as long as I get my treatments."

Why had I even broached the subject? I never wanted to carry another secret from Catty—a lie she'd loathe me for keeping should she find out. But I could do nothing now. Mirna was right. I couldn't tell her.

As we followed Pepin through the wood to the megalith, the sun rose higher in the sky, and my body felt my lack of sleep. My bones were weary, and my head grew fuzzy. I steadied myself on the wagon. Josh too. He wobbled, as unstable as I felt.

We came to a clearing in the woods. An open field encircled by trees.

"Beò feur." The momentary excitement gave way to sadness as I remembered playing in beò feur with Aodan and Catty as kids.

"What's that?" Josh asked.

"Beh-oh fee-ahd." Enunciating as if to a child learning to speak, I pointed to the ground. "It's an animal that looks like grass."

Josh watched the ground. "It sinks into the ground as we approach."

"Look behind ye." I nodded toward the back of the wagon.

Josh looked back, then under the cart. Then at everyone else's feet. "They reappear as soon as we pass."

"They're impossible to step on. We've tried." Remembering Aodan flying, determined to crush the uncrushable creatures, I stifled a laugh.

"Ye wee rascals." Catty's ma clicked her tongue and shook her head. "Ye were always coming home filthy with torn clothes. Just couldn't leave them alone."

"We never got to play with them long, though. They left too quickly."

"I'm sure yer antics made them move on faster than usual." A hint of humor glinted in her sad eyes.

"Move on?" Josh tilted his head.

"Aye," I said. "The beò feur don't stay in one place long. They feed on the grass that was there. Once they've exhausted the supply, they move to another field."

"That's terrible. Don't they kill your crops?"

"Nay. Farmers love them. They only eat grass. After they've fed, the excrement they leave behind causes new growth fuller and thicker than before, and they aerate the ground as they travel. When our livestock feed on the renewed field, they seem healthier, and plants that grow where they've traveled are more bountiful."

"Sounds helpful." Josh studied the beò feur as if plotting how to catch some and introduce them to his world. "We don't have anything like that at home."

Just how different would his world be? But no reason to ask. I'd be there soon enough.

Pepin stepped in front of the wagon and held out a hand. "Stop here."

Everyone stopped in the middle of a field of beò feur.

"Here?" I cocked my head at the blankness, then crossed my arms.

But Pepin ignored me. He was walking back to the wood line where he muscled a large rock from the dirt.

"Can I help with that?" Josh's da made no move to help.

Pepin lifted the massive rock over his head and returned to us. The grassy creatures parted the way. Everyone gathered as Pepin slammed the rock down. The ground shook. He released his grip, and the rock stayed on end.

Josh gawked. "It's not tipping over?"

Pepin had embedded the stone into the ground, but only a small portion. A finger length at most. It should fall.

He brushed his hands and continued back to the wooded area. "Pech have abilities with stone gachen don't have."

"Clearly." Josh's da whistled.

The beò feur forgotten, we gaped as Pepin carried two more boulders across the field. He dropped one parallel to the first, then the last over the tops of the other two, forming two walls and a roof.

"Is that it?" While it was interesting to behold, it seemed a little—uninspiring—considering it was a portal to another world.

A groan came from the wagon, and we hurried to Catty as she tried to sit up.

I hopped into the wagon to help her.

Josh leaned over the rail. "Are you okay?"

"Of course she's not okay," I snapped, pulling her away from him.

Catty blinked, then focused on the megalith. "Is that the portal? Is it time to go?"

Sully rifled through the packs, searching for something. "Let's eat first."

I helped Catty down from the wagon with Josh hovering, ready to swoop in.

"Beò feur." She gave a sad smile. "We used to have so much fun trying to stomp them, remember?"

I returned her smile. If only we could go back to those trouble-free times. "I remember."

We gathered together on the ground, trapping the beò feur for a spell. Sully handed out slices of hard cheese wrapped in cloth.

"Pepin?" Catty fidgeted with her amulet.

"Hmm?" He stopped chewing.

"Why is my amulet so different from Josh's?"

He swallowed his food. From the rough gulp, his mouthful could've used a bit more chewing. "His is a typical inter-realm travel amulet. The engraving of mirrored mountains symbolizes the line between two worlds in the same plane of existence. They're not uncommon. Like the megaliths, the pechish council monitors their construction and use, so I'm curious how he came about his?"

When Pepin threw him a suspicious glance, Josh shrugged.

Josh's da sniffed and gave his nose a couple of swipes with a handkerchief. "A pech traveled through Notirr seeking wares for trade. I can't recall his name." He squinted and searched the treetops as if they might hold the answer. "Lyosha?"

"Never heard of him." Pepin wiped the sweat from his brow with the back of his sleeve.

Josh's da squinched up his brow as if all pech should know each other. "How many pech are there?"

Pepin was about to take another bite, then rewrapped his cheese in the cloth, and placed it in his lap. "Too many to count. We were the first race in Ariboslia before God banished the gachen to our realm. We rarely come up from underground anymore, but we're everywhere."

Josh's da lifted his eyebrows and pulled down the corners of his mouth. "It's a wonder I've only met two in my life, especially since I come back to mine."

"The pech are good at hiding." Pepin unwrapped his cheese and took a large bite.

"That explains Josh's amulet." Catty folded up her empty napkin neatly and placed it beside her. "What of mine?"

Pepin swallowed his large bite, then pounded his chest as if that helped it go down. Then he smiled as one recalling a beautiful memory. "I made yours. The only one I ever made. Successfully, that is. An angel instructed me. It's one of a kind."

"Wha—" Catty's head jutted out in Pepin's direction.

Josh's da's mouth hung open. "An angel visited you? What was he like? Or she? It?"

"I believe it was a he, but who can know?" Pepin scratched his chin. "He was bright. And frightening."

"Bright and frightening." Catty shook her head. "You met an *angel*, and that's all ye can say? Anyway, how is my amulet different?"

"I wouldn't call Drochaid *yours*. But I used different materials and engraved it as the angel instructed. It acts as a language translator and should allow for inter-realm travel, like Josh's. We'll find out for sure in a moment. But, other than the engraving and materials, I don't know how it's different. I only know God brought me here. It's for you to use now."

I studied the rock structure. "What made you build it here?"

Pepin chuckled. "There is much I don't know. I was never much good at divining." He snorted at our blank faces. "That's when you seek out ideal places for a portal, depending upon its purpose. It's like divining water underground to dig a well."

We nodded. *That* we understood.

"The megaliths are the only constant between the realms. While the planet on which it rests is the same, the geography is not. In one realm, a megalith might be on land. In another, it might be in a lake. I was a terrible student. In my divining class, my megaliths led to briars, streams, and other less-than-ideal locations, not even close to the positions assigned to me."

That didn't bode well. "So what makes you think this one will lead to the right place?"

Pepin grunted. "It will."

Mere words didn't make me more confident. We didn't need Catty traveling into the bottom of a lake. "I'll go through first."

Sully wiped his mouth on his empty napkin and stood. "Pepin will go first. Faolan, you will be last."

Why did the order in which we left matter? I studied the prophet as if I might glean some of his secrets by staring.

"Ready?" Pepin motioned toward the portal.

Catty gawked at the stone structure. "How do you use it?"

"Use it?" He cocked his head like a dog seeking to understand.

"Once our amulets are within range, the portal opens, and we crawl through." Josh raised a brow to his da who confirmed with a nod.

"And we just end up in your world?" She paled further.

"Where will we end up, Pepin?" Josh's da asked. "I've only ever used the other one. What if we end up in the woods somewhere and get lost? There are lots of woods in Maine."

Pepin quirked his lips. "Not to worry. This is the right spot. I will guide you."

"How do you know?" Josh's da's suspicious gaze roamed over the structure.

"I saw it in a dream."

"Angel visits. Prophetic dreams. Ye sure yer just a pech?" Catty asked.

"Yep." Hands clasped behind his back, Pepin rocked on his heels. "Just a pech."

We exchanged awkward glances. Then he dropped to his knees and poked his head through the rocks. His front half disappeared. It was one thing to talk about. Another thing entirely to witness.

He backed up, and his top half reappeared. "It's safe. When you're ready, follow me. Hand me my pack."

Josh threw Pepin's pack at him, which Pepin then shoved through the opening. Once the pack was gone, Pepin disappeared after it.

"Cataleen." Sully placed a hand at her back. "You're next."

She looked like she'd just seen whatever haunted the shack in the cornfield. "Are you certain I have to leave?"

"Catty!" Was she so daft? "Don't even *suggest* not going. Aodan will attack again. Are ye tryin' to provoke him?"

Sully gave a solemn nod. "Regardless of whatever Aodan is attempting to do, 'tis God's will. Ye must go."

CHAPTER FIFTY-SEVEN

CATALEEN

Josh wagged a first in the air, whatever that meant. His face, set in what he must think was an encouraging expression, gave the impression he was ready to fight. "We'll be right behind you."

Tromping feet approached, and we turned.

"Tevin?" He was the last person I wanted to see right now.

Ma jumped to her feet. "What are ye doing here?"

Quin moved to intercept him. "Ye can't be here, lad. We banished ye."

Tevin wavered, wobbling like he was about to collapse, then lunged forward. "But I've repented."

"I'm sorry for all ye've been through." Quin placed a splayed hand on Tevin's chest, staying him. "We still require a meeting with the elders before—"

"It doesn't matter. I don't want to stay in Notirr. Not where I'm hated." He pushed past Quin and knelt before me, hands clutched, eyes pleading. "Please, Cataleen. Have mercy on me and allow me to accompany ye."

I sucked in a breath. Was this really happening right now? His pitiful posture somehow hardened and softened me toward him at the same time. "Didn't we leave ye in Gnuatthara?"

His brows pinched tight and rose as he swept a glance over the others. Then he gave a nod, and his posture relaxed. "Ye were unconscious most of the trip home. Nay, I returned with ye." He rubbed his hands together. "I've nothing here. No clan. No home. No father. Nothing. Please, Cataleen. I won't bother ye. Just let me find another realm, free of fasgadair, where I don't have to be alone."

Fury burned within me, and I stood. "Why should I help ye? This is all yer fault. Everything! If not for ye, Aodan wouldn't have been banished. Morrigan would never have found him. He wouldn't be a fasgadair. He wouldn't have killed yer da. And I wouldn't be leaving my home, my ma, my clan to some unknown world."

Tevin threw himself at my feet, clutching them, crying.

I backed away. Tevin had always bullied us. I would never trust him. But my heart gave way to the slightest pity. Wasn't he a victim in this too? A victim of Lorcan's upbringing with no mother to soften his rough edges? I groaned. "Is there a place he can go when we arrive? *Not* with me?"

Josh's da nodded. "I've friends who run a bed-and-breakfast. I can arrange for him to stay there until we find something for him."

"Fine." I steeled my eyes and my heart against his pathetic face. "Come with us then. But keep yer distance."

Pepin's head appeared in the portal.

"Give her a moment, Pepin." Sully waved him off.

Pepin closed his eyes, huffed out a breath, and disappeared.

I gave Ma another, less teary hug. Somehow, Tevin's appearance made me less sad. Then I said my farewells to the others.

Sully crossed the distance to me. He lifted my chin, forcing me to look into his face—his sad smile. He cupped my cheek as I imagined my father might've. "You're not alone. You have friends with you. God is with you. You are loved."

Fresh tears spilled down my face, splashing his thumb. Those words pierced my soul. Sully must be more than a mere prophet. His understanding ran too deep. How did he always cut straight to the heart?

He wiped my tears. "God has always provided for you and will continue to do so. You must believe. Trust."

Was that the heart of my troubles? All this time? Ever since my brothers left? I failed to turn to God and know I wasn't alone. Did I trust people more than the Almighty Himself? Shame filled me for wallowing in self-pity rather than trusting God.

Sully's gray eyes couldn't convey what others could. Something in the iris seemed like an opening to a person's soul. Sully's were closed off. Yet, whether it was his eyes or his touch, something empowering emanated from him, more than his words. Or, perhaps, his mere words had renewed my strength and my heart's conviction. Whatever the miraculous thing was, hope returned to me. Nothing had changed. I was leaving my family and my home. But I could sacrifice myself for them, for all of Ariboslia, for God—if that was His plan. I would allow Him to use me.

I trust Ye, God. Help me trust Ye more.

I stood and wiped my face. Sully smiled anew, with no trace of sadness. He pulled me into a hug. One by one, the others moved in, wrapping their arms around me until I felt like a caterpillar in a cocoon. When I emerged, would I be a new creation?

Ma was the last to let go. She cupped my face. "Ye will always be my wee bairn. Me leanabh. No matter where ye are."

My throat tickled as I blinked back the well of fresh tears. I inhaled her lavender scent, hopefully not for the last time. "And ye will be with me."

I gave them all a last wave, then crawled over the retreating beò feur, through the portal, over roots and leaves, to my new world. Another forest appeared around me. I gasped, then stood, and brushed my long skirt. The world surrounding me didn't seem as bright, but a pressure in my head was now gone. Was that Aodan's presence? Had he affected me more than I realized? Was the mind-link a constant, physical thing that only another realm could sever?

Tevin crawled through next. As I watched him, a thought washed over me—"Forgive him."

That didn't come from me.

My body trembled, rejecting the thought, urging me not to follow through. But I had to. Not because he deserved it, but because God wanted me to. I had just told Him I trusted Him. Now I had to prove it and follow his prompting.

Tevin rose, dusting the dirt from his knees as he gawked as his new surroundings. His gaze stopped on me and flickered. Did he see the resolve in my heart? Did he hear it hammer as I forced down everything within me screaming to reject this decision to trust God?

God, help me.

I straightened my spine with new resolve as I faced my enemy. "I forgive you."

He flinched as if I'd hit him. His eyebrows twitched, then smoothed. He pressed his lips into a thin line as his eyes shone with welling tears. He blinked them back, wiping a stray from the corner as his lips vacillated between a smile and a frown. "Thank you."

Free of the mind-link and the unforgiveness hardening my heart, I felt as if I might float away.

Josh crawled through and brushed the dirt from his knees. His da appeared behind him.

"Do you recognize these woods, Dad?"

His da frowned and shook his head. "No."

Pepin squinted and surveyed the area. "It's further south than the old one. Never fear. I'll get you home."

"How?" I asked.

"Pech have a good sense of direction. Your kind rely on the suns and stars to guide you. The pech don't have those things when tunneling underground."

I stared at the megalith. "What's taking Faolan so long?"

"I'm sorry, Cataleen." Grim-faced, Pepin walked to the megalith and toppled the stones.

CHAPTER FIFTY-EIGHT

FAOLAN

Still on my knees, heart pounding, I gawped at the pile of stones. The ground continued to shake from their collapse. Nay. It had stopped. It was me. I was shaking. I gripped my hands to still them, then stood, taking in the shocked expressions surrounding me.

My mind reeled. So this wasn't some accident or a trick of my eyes? The others saw this, too? The portal was—?

Nay. Nay, nay, nay. That wasn't possible. My heart accelerated and plummeted like a diving falcon. I grabbed the rock on top, strained to pick it up, and screamed. "Catty! Cataleen!"

Arms encircled my waist and pulled. I let the stone go to peel them off me.

"Son, ye must let her go."

The sadness in my da's voice incited my panic. I pushed him away and latched onto the stone. She couldn't be gone. She couldn't.

"Cataleen!"

My scream frightened the beò feur. The green carpeting receded to dirt as far as the eye could see in the wake of their retreat. My chest heaved as I gasped for air.

My da grabbed me again. "This is God's will, son. Let her go."

More arms joined his, grabbing at me, yanking me away.

I crumbled and let them pull me away, staring at the rocks. "I could've been crushed."

Why did those words come out over all the other thoughts fighting for importance in my mind?

"God wouldn't have allowed that," Sully said.

I spun on him. Gripping his collar in my fists, I stared into his gray eyes. "God did this on purpose? Why? To keep me out?" I shook him. "Did ye not see this coming? How could ye let this happen?"

Cahal ripped me off him.

I squirmed in his giant arms. "She's all alone. In a foreign world. I must get to her!"

Cahal deposited me a safe distance from Sully who seemed unrattled.

He fixed his collar. "You're not meant to go. Not yet."

"When?" A spark of hope lit. I motioned to the pile of rocks. "Can ye rebuild the megalith?"

"Only a pech can rebuild it. For now, ye must wait."

"Was it an accident? Will Pepin rebuild it from the other side?" I crouched to the rocks. What would it look like on the other side? Right now, it wasn't a portal. Would it just appear to be a pile of rocks, then return to a portal? Did the rocks even exist in the other realm?

Sully laid a heavy hand on my shoulder. "Our wait will be longer than mere moments. It will be years before ye see Cataleen again."

"Years?" That wasn't possible. Rage coursed through me, fueling me, making me shake. I tore myself from his grip and glared as if he were in control of all of this.

The boiling energy roiling through me slowed to a simmer. Anger steamed away, evaporating into despair beneath his sad eyes.

"Years?" I'd have to wait years to see Catty again? My body

screamed to do anything but that. Sorrow sluiced through my soul, weighing me down as I collapsed by the closed gateway.

EPILOGUE

CATALEEN - NINE YEARS LATER

I walked with Fallon and her friend, Stacy, through the woods to the megalith. Fallon's black hair flew behind her small body. Stacy's red curls bounced. Their little flip-flops flapped as they ran. They reached the megalith and climbed aboard. I held back, keeping my distance as the girls played, clutching the amulet in my grip. I couldn't risk the portal opening and the girls finding themselves in Ariboslia.

The familiar stone structure had been here for years now. Nearly a decade. Yet my visits were just now becoming more frequent. Why? Because Fallon and Stacy loved it so? They also loved the park and the tree house we'd just built. So what was my excuse?

Home lay just beyond that megalith.

I ran my thumb over the amulet—the key.

Why was home invading my thoughts so much these days? God had blessed me with a wonderful life. Cornish was nice. Everywhere I needed to go was within walking distance. But this world had taken some getting used to. I didn't dare venture too far outside the rural town. Josh had given up on bringing me to Portland or any crowded places with tall buildings squeezed together and cars racing around.

Ugh. Cars. Hateful things. Why did people seem meaner the moment they sat behind a steering wheel? Did some witchery about the vehicle change their personality? I'd never find out. Despite Josh's efforts to teach me to drive, I refused. I avoided being a passenger as much as possible, reserving such terrible experiences for worthwhile trips, like visits to the ocean.

How I missed the ocean. I rarely saw it these days. And only in the off-season when fewer people visited.

More than the ocean, I missed home. My ma. My village.

I wished Tevin would come home soon. He was the closest thing I had to Notirr now. I laughed at the irony. My younger self would never have imagined Tevin becoming like a brother.

"What's so funny, Mama?" Fallon came running, sandals flap, flap, flapping.

"Oh, just thinking about Uncle Tevin."

"Is he coming home?" Her eyes flared wide with hope.

"Not for some time, leanabh."

She slumped and protruded her lower lip. So dramatic. I laughed again, and she screwed up her face at me.

"Would you like to go see Aunt Shannon and Uncle Kent?"

Her face brightened as she wiggled. "Can we go now?"

"In a little while. After we bring Stacy home. Why don't you go play with her while you can?"

She turned with dramatic flair and ran to Stacy, who had moved from the megalith and was riding the low branch of a tree like a horse.

If only I could bring Fallon home. Ma would adore her.

Was it safe to bring her there now?

I should ask Faolan when he visited next. But I never knew when he would. He preferred to wander Ariboslia, keeping tabs on Aodan to ensure he kept his promise. So far, he had. The fasgadair hadn't moved north. Notirr was safe. But Aodan ruled by Morrigan's side. Would he do that for an eternity? Was there a way to rescue him, or was he too far gone?

I swallowed back a rising sob and breathed deep, imagining I was in the woods just outside my village—still a kid with Aodan and Faolan when all was right with the world.

It would be good to visit the inn. My first home in America before marrying Josh, the place where I found a new family. Tevin became like a brother, and Shannon and Kent became like second parents.

Tevin understood what it was like to move to America from Ariboslia and be adopted into a foreign family. It united us. We were a village unto ourselves.

God, only You could have made Tevin like a brother to me. And only You could have seen how much I'd need him. Thank You. Keep him safe.

I hated that Tevin had joined the military. We rarely saw him now.

I sighed.

What was my problem? God had provided for me. I had plenty here to occupy me. I tended the gardens and cared for my family. I was loved. So, why were my visits to the gateway home becoming more and more frequent?

I loved my life with Josh. Fallon was a happy three-year-old. This was the only world she knew.

But wasn't that a problem, too? She thought she was human. She knew nothing of her own kind. We couldn't tell her the truth. Not yet. We didn't want to upset Fiona, and Fallon was too young to be trusted not to say something.

But why should we continue to placate a fully grown woman rather than prepare a child? What would become of Fallon when she reached her bian? What if her first transition happened in front of humans? Would she be angry with us for keeping her gachen heritage a secret?

We had to prepare her.

She was gachen. She needed to know her family. My ma. Her grandma. Her roots. How could I let her grow up without knowing who she was? And how could I tell her in a way she'd understand?

I had to show her—to bring her home. If only for a brief visit. Josh would never agree. He'd tell me it was too dangerous. I'd just have to go alone.

SHAMELESS REQUEST FOR REVIEWS

Authors need reviews! They help books get noticed, and I love to know what readers think of my stories. So, if you enjoyed this book, please consider leaving a review where you purchased this book, Goodreads, BookBub... anywhere you think a review might be helpful. I'm forever grateful!

You are loved,

JF Rogers

ASTRAY PREVIEW

Prologue

In the foothills of rural Maine

Under the cover of night, hidden in the rickety tree house in the backyard, De'Mere waited, watching. The fort offered all he needed, privacy and the perfect vantage point. He peered into the upper right-hand window of the old farmhouse across the lawn. The alarm clock's glow illuminated Fallon's room in an alien-like green. Only her feet at the edge of the bed lay within view. Their stirring told him she was having a nightmare—again.

He slumped against the rough, far wall and peeked at the sky through wide gaps in the roof. The sun would soon rise. He'd retreat to the wood to rest until it was time to return. Then his real work would begin.

"De'Mere," a thunderous, yet oddly melodic voice called.

De'Mere bristled as chills coursed down his spine. He jumped to his feet, bumped his head on the low ceiling, and dropped to his knees to peer out the windows.

"De'Mere." The voice seemed to float in midair right in front of his face. He fell back, away from the window, and reached out, groping air with his right hand for something solid, perturbed that his otherwise keen eyesight failed him at this crucial time. This must be how a blind man might feel, sneaked up on, spoken to without warning.

"Your time has nearly come." The voice stimulated a fresh course of chills surging throughout his being. It commanded attention, and for a creature such as himself, invoked fear. Its very presence filled the confined space. "Do you remember what to do?"

De'Mere continued his search for clues as to its whereabouts. It seemed to be everywhere. An internal struggle raged between his desperate desire to find the owner of the voice and his equal need to shy away. He craved a glimpse, if only to determine where to draw near or in which direction to run.

"Do you know what to do?"

"Yes," he answered in a hurried, hushed tone, afraid to elicit an unwelcome audience, which didn't appear to concern the disembodied voice. But then, perhaps it wasn't audible to anyone but him. "But how do I make sure she's there?"

"Just do your part. Tonight."

The air no longer squeezed De'Mere like an invisible vise. The unearthly being was gone. He took a deep breath, savoring his solitude. But the hollow cavity within him widened. If only he could fill the void.

He returned his attention to Fallon's bedroom. The sheet lay flat. She must have risen while he'd been distracted. Had she overheard their voices and come outside? He peered down the hole in the floor. The ladder was bare. Careful to avoid the squeaky planks, he crossed to the window closest to the house. He dared stick his head out enough to search the darkness below, hoping it wasn't a mistake. He'd come too far to risk exposure now.

The night was still. As if all living things had been frightened away. The breeze dared not even rustle a leaf. He ducked back inside and searched the path to the house. Still nothing. Crickets chirping in the distance offered the only sign of life.

He glanced back at the house. Light filled the bathroom window. A shadow moved beyond the drawn shade. Releasing the air he'd been holding, he laughed softly at his paranoia. He was much too far away for a mere human to hear.

"Tonight," De'Mere whispered, the word lingering in the air.

After all these years, the time had come. His watching and waiting would soon be over. He'd play his part. The trick would be getting Fallon to play hers.

He descended from the tree house by dropping out the trapdoor. After landing with a soft thud on the unkempt lawn, he ran on all fours for the cover of the tree line.

✫

Chapter One

The sun's unnatural glow blinded me. Tears coursed down my face as I struggled to take in my surroundings. With each blink, a woman with long, blonde hair dappled in gold sparkles grew clearer. She sat motionless on the sand, watching the ocean waves. I couldn't see her face, but imagined she awaited her long-lost love from beneath the watery depths. A breeze swept across the shore, swirling the white dress around her delicate frame as tresses danced about her face.

The wind carried my name, long and silvery sweet, "Fallon…Faaaaallon."

A shiver ran through me. Was she calling me? Did I know her? A dream. This had to be a dream.

Something about her was familiar. Overcome with an unsettling compulsion to be near her, I walked in her direction. But the woman remained the same distance away. I paused, blinking to ensure I wasn't seeing things, and then quickened my pace. Still, I made no ground. I ran. Again, no progress. Frustrated, I stopped.

The woman slowly turned to face me.

Shadows overtook the landscape as storm clouds choked the sun. Neither of us moved, yet the woman was closer. The entire scene was now mere feet before me, as if I'd somehow crossed a considerable distance. In one fluid motion, her hair transformed from blonde to black. As the serene face mutated, curiosity morphed into disquiet in the pit of my stomach. I gasped. I recognized deep purple eyes unobscured by thick lenses. The pasty, oblong face minus the acne. Me—only beautiful. With an eerie lack of emotion, the doppelganger's face tilted sideways. My stomach tightened with each passing second that those dead eyes watched me until I nearly doubled over in pain.

Without warning, its mouth widened. Baring sharp, menacing fangs, it lunged at me.

Just before it reached me, my body spasms jerked me awake, as if I'd fallen from the ceiling onto the bed. Entangled in my sheets, I fought to free myself. As reality set in, my thudding heart descended to its natural rhythm. I let out a slow, even breath and glanced at the alarm clock's glowing digits, squinting to make sense of them—3:56 a.m.

Something was off. The air sizzled, as though an unseen electrical current ran through it. I felt a presence. Within reach, yet so far away. The more I grasped for what it might be, the more it evaded me. Something lurked in the shadows. I was certain of it.

I put on my glasses and fumbled with the bedside lamp, knocking it to the floor. I stilled, holding my breath, waiting for whatever remained hidden in the darkness to jump me.

Nothing moved.

Rather than drape my feet over the bed and give any monster lurking there a chance to grab my ankles, I stood and jumped far out of reach. I landed on the creaky oak floorboards and hurried to the bathroom to flip on the light switch before something could sneak up behind me in the dark. I shook my head at myself. If Stacy could see me now, avoiding the boogeyman under my bed, she'd tease me mercilessly.

After splashing cold water on my face, hoping to wash away the dream, I put on my glasses and eyed my reflection. My face, littered with acne no astringent could clear up, scowled back. My purple eyes, magnified in the thick frames, glared. If only I were truly as beautiful as in the dream, for the brief moment before it changed. The fanged creature came to mind. I shuddered, grabbed a towel, and dried off.

I lumbered back to my room and picked up the lamp. The light erased all but a few shadows, which I took time to investigate personally.

I eyed everything with extreme scrutiny, even the flowery, yellowed wallpaper, peeling in places, certain a chameleonlike creature could hide itself there. But nothing bulged. I flung back the once beautiful pink bedding that now looked like something from a hamster cage. Ratty. But the sheet lay flat.

Other than the wear and tear, my room hadn't changed in ten years. Not since Bumpah died. After that, Fiona stopped taking care of... well...everything. She threw money at me every once in a while so Stacy's mom could take me clothes shopping or to doctor appointments. Other than that, she never gave me anything, not even on my birthday.

My birthday. Today. My seventeenth birthday. The first day of summer. I flopped on my bed, grateful school was over until fall, but I couldn't face another birthday without Bumpah. No, I wouldn't allow myself to think about it.

I glanced at the book overhanging my bedside table and snatched it up, eager to escape to the world within its pages. My bookmark fell out, and I grumbled as I found my spot.

Reading about other worlds usually calmed me, but the words refused to sink in. Instead, Bumpah kept popping into my mind. The hollow within me widened. I needed him to pull me out of my funk. I could almost hear him joking, comparing my moods to the New England weather. "If you don't like it, wait a minute," he'd say. Then he'd sing and dance around like a goof. Inevitably, a smile returned to my face.

I needed Bumpah to calm the storm, to make my birthday special. All I had was Fiona, and she couldn't care less. Instead of loving me as her granddaughter, she treated me like an annoying customer lingering past closing. Or worse.

The whirlwind of darkness engulfed me. Tears slipped down my cheeks. I pulled my knees up and wrapped my arms around myself. My hands ran over the scars, reminding me I could, once more, deal with the pain. But no, I'd promised Stacy, the only one who knew my secret and still cared about me, for whatever reason. Perhaps I should try talking to her God.

"God, if you're really there, I don't know why you'd listen to me, but Stacy keeps asking me to, so here goes. God, I don't know what to do. I'm so angry. All the time. I can't help it. My grandmother hates me. I don't have any family. I'm all al—" My voice cracked and tears poured. "I don't want to be this way." I slammed my fist against the pillow. "Why'd you take my family away? You never even gave me a chance. Are you even there? Do you even care?"

Nothing. No response. I wiped my eyes and returned to my book with renewed focus, determined to escape reality. At least I could tell Stacy I'd tried. If her God was real, He must hate me.

✡

When the sun's rays streamed into the room, overheating me, I found the book open with the pages bent under my face. I folded them back in place, checked for drool, and returned it to my bedside, hoping the librarian wouldn't notice or care. Then I threw on a crumpled pair of jeans and a black T-shirt before heading to the kitchen.

I paused at the top of the stairs and took a deep breath. As I stared at the worn treads, I prepped myself for the off chance that I might come in contact with Fiona. "It's just another day like any other. Don't expect anything from her. It doesn't matter that it's your birthday." No matter what, this year, I would not get my hopes up.

I shuffled downstairs then through the dining room to the kitchen. Fiona's immense plate collection in the hutch rattled in my wake.

Fiona sat at the kitchen table, eating a late breakfast. She dropped her head, shaggy gray hair falling around her face as she wiped her eyes, and shoved a postcard into the pocket of the drab brown sweater she always wore—even in this summer heat.

I almost turned and left, but I needed coffee. Sighing, I plodded to the coffee maker, eyeing the cracked black-and-white checkered tile as I went. My tangled mass of black hair dangled in my face, shielding me from view.

Fiona slurped her coffee. "Look who decided to grace us with her presence."

I wanted to ask if "us" included her many personalities. I bit my tongue. Instead, I grunted something resembling "morning."

I hoped she'd leave it at that. Nothing good came from conversation with Fiona. The more I allowed the woman to voice her opinion, the greater the chance I'd run away in tears. She was a guilt-trip ninja, striking when I least expected.

"I have something for you."

A warning thumped in my chest. I continued to stir the cream and sugar in my coffee, too much of each. I turned to face her. "What is it?"

"Oh, for Pete's sake, stop gawking and come here, Fallon."

I peered with extreme caution into her outstretched palm.

"Well, take it." She shook the object clasped in her meaty fingers.

Like a game of Operation, I snatched it and removed my hand as fast as possible as if to avoid the buzzing sound. I then backed to a more comfortable distance.

A necklace. I sucked in my breath. The pendent seemed ancient. A heavy circle made from some type of gray stone attached to a leather cord. Seven cone shapes pointed from a circular indent in the center, giving it the shape of a star or a sun. Strange marks, like hieroglyphics, each unique, etched deep between the points.

It had been so long since I'd received a gift I didn't know how to respond. "What is it?"

"Not quite sure. It belonged to your mother."

"My mother?" The amulet fell, the cord caught around my finger. I pulled it to safety and let out a heavy breath. My mother. I couldn't remember the last time she was mentioned in this house.

Fiona's steel-blue eyes lost their sharpness for a nanosecond. "Yes." Then with a quick shake of her head, adding more volume to her frizzy hair, she stood and brought her dishes to the sink. "Well, enough of that."

"No." My mother's ghost had been summoned. I couldn't let it float away.

Fiona stuck out her jaw and glared at me with dead, unblinking eyes. My stomach jumped into my throat. I had ventured into dangerous territory, but I might never have another chance to find out about my mother. I'd searched this house from top to bottom for pictures—any insight into my parents—only to be denied. I tried softening my tone. "I mean...did my mother give this to you?"

Fiona dropped her gaze and returned to the sink. "No. She didn't."

"Well, who then? You've been holding on to it all these years? Why'd you give it to me now?"

Fiona placed her hands on her disproportionately large hips, lowered her head, and sighed. She remained like that, as though worn out from fighting down whatever humanity remained entombed within her otherwise heartless carcass.

After a few eons, she faced me. "Fallon, I really didn't know your mother well. This was given to Nathaniel after her..." She paused as if searching for the appropriate word. "...disappearance. He was instructed to hold onto it until your seventeenth birthday then give it to you. He's not here, so I'm doing it."

"Someone gave it to Bumpah *after* my mother...? Who?"

"I don't know. I wasn't there. He never said."

"But *why*? Why give this to me now? What for?"

Fiona folded her arms across her chest. She leaned toward me. Her pear-shaped frame extended as her face scrunched in a scowl, forcing the peach fuzz to stick out on her upper lip.

"I was tempted to throw the stupid thing away. I'm only doing this for Nathaniel. I promised."

Was she for real? I knew she hated me, but this was a whole new level of heartlessness. To want to toss the one thing connecting me to my mother...that was cold. My eyebrow twitched as I tried to think how to respond. I opened my mouth, but words escaped me. Her unblinking eyes bulged in my direction. Words I'd been dying to say for years flew from my mouth. "You're not the only one who lost your family, ya know. I miss Bumpah too. It's not fair. I can't even remember my parents. And I'm...I'm..." I knew what I wanted to say but couldn't bring myself to do it.

"You're *what*?"

Her nasty tone loosed my tongue. "I'm stuck with *you*!"

"Don't try to bait me. Nathaniel would still be here if it weren't for you. He was too old to be chasing after a rambunctious kid. As for my son—let me just say—no parent should outlive her child. *You* miss people you never knew. I lost the only people I ever loved. And where's your mother? I don't know. Her casket is empty next to my son's. Is *that* fair?" She paused as though I might actually reply. "For all I know, she killed him."

Fiona's chest heaved as she gulped for air, her face red. Blotchy. I stood frozen. Though her words stung, they didn't send me crying as they once had. Instead, they fueled my anger. I wanted nothing more than to smack her across the face. I fought to keep my clenched fists by my side. "What about me? I'm your granddaughter, remember? You didn't lose *everyone*."

Fiona shoved her hands into her pockets. "Oh for Pete's sake, I don't have time for this nonsense. I have more important things to attend to. Not all of us sleep until noon." She trudged out of the kitchen, leaving dirty dishes in the sink.

Blown off again. Fiona didn't have anything to do but send herself postcards from her dead husband, add to her ridiculous plate collection, and resent being stuck with me.

I dropped my cup into the sink, chipping it, and adding to the pile.

Several fantasies flashed across my mind. Most involved Fiona spinning and falling after a swift blow from a frying pan. Hurtful words I wished I'd said resonated in my mind. I cursed myself for allowing her to suck me in. I should know better by now.

My mind returned to the amulet. My first tangible connection to my mother. I placed it around my neck. It fell heavy against by breastbone. Warmth radiated from the spot, comforting me as if a missing piece of my heart had returned. I held it up to study the markings once more. As my fingers traced the cone shapes, feeling the rough surface, it sparked, like static electricity in the dark. I jumped. The necklace slipped from my fingers and thudded against my chest. My heart skittered. I yanked the stone off and dropped it on the counter.

Want to read more?
Pick up Astray at jfrogers.com/books/astray/

FREE BOOK

Pepin's Tale

Don't judge a pech by his size...

Pepin's Tale brings us to Ariboslia before Aodan's rise to power and before Fallon's birth. A runt by his people's standards, dwarflike Pepin can't get anything right. Even his family rejects him. And the one person who takes pity on him is ready to cast him out.

Then an angel appears, turning all Pepin thinks he knows upside down.

But he has a choice to make—deny what he believes to be true or become the two-headed uilebheist's next meal...

Download Pepin's Tale today to find out how one small pech can make an eternal difference.

Get your FREE copy at jfrogers.com

ALSO BY J F ROGERS

Continue the Ariboslia saga with Cataleen's daughter, Fallon.

Astray - Ariboslia Book 1

A mysterious amulet leads Fallon to everything she's ever wanted... and possibly her death.

Adrift - Ariboslia book II

Fallon returns to Ariboslia... but the creatures she wants save want her dead.

Aloft - Ariboslia book II

Fallon and Morrigan face off for the ultimate battle... in their minds.

The Smeraldo Flower

Beauty and the Beast meets the Phantom of the Opera in the Secret Garden in this standalone novelette. A retelling of the Italian folktale, La Citta di Smeraldo, inspired by BTS's song *The Truth Untold*.

Be among the first to know when new books are released.

Join J F Rogers's clan today! jfrogers.com/join/

J. F. Rogers lives in Southern Maine with her husband, daughter, pets... and an imaginary friend or two. She has a degree in Behavioral Science and teaches a 5th and 6th grade Sunday School class. When she's not entertaining Tuki the Mega Mutt, her constant companion and greatest distraction, she's likely tap, tap, tapping away at her keyboard, praying the words will miraculously align just so. Above all, she's a believer in the One True God and can say with certainty—you are loved.

Connect with J F Rogers

amazon.com/J-F-Rogers/e/B01G7N0KSK
bookbub.com/authors/j-f-rogers
facebook.com/jfrogerswrites
goodreads.com/jfrogers
instagram.com/jfrogers925
pinterest.com/jfrogers925

ACKNOWLEDGEMENTS

As always, I must thank God first. He is my Creator, my inspiration, my All. Next, my loving husband, Rick, and beautiful daughter, Emily.

Special thanks to:

- My talented critique group, Damascus Blades—C W Briar, Amanda Cartwright, Gina Detwiler, Katherine Massengill, L G McCary, A K Preston, and Tracy Sassaman. It was so great to meet most of you in person finally!
- The amazing Deirdre Lockhart with Brilliant Cut Editing.
- 100Covers, the incredible cover artist, Rica, and the infinitely patient Phyllis Ngo.
- My local writer friends who support me in so many ways—Sharon Gamble, Amanda Ovington, Marlene McKenna, Julie Bernier, Danielle Blankenship, Paulina Shadowens, and Annalie Lewis. I'd be lost without you all.
- My Beta readers—Jenny Cardinal, Claire Gagne, Vickie Grider, Angela R. Grimes, Debbie Harris, Birgit Lehmann, William Long, Debra Shaw and Monique Summers.
- My Kickstarter backers—Mindy Aumann, Ron and Jeannine Descoteaux, Anne Alix, Sharon Gamble, Amber Lee M Miller, Sunny Side Up, CJ Milacci, Melissa B., Lily Kennison, Patty Rau, James R McGinnis Jr, Marlene McKenna, Kimberly Von Wald, Angela Grimes, Sarah Daniels, Ray and Dianne Rogers, William Long, Kathy

Brasby, Jenny Widner, Melissa Price, Mark Griffith, Gina Detwiler, Danielle Blankenship, Steven A. Guglich, John and Georgianna Pilkington, Amanda Cartwright, Nicole Olstad, Bas, Lanetta Buskirk, Julie Bernier, Vickie Grider, Abigail, Lena Tesla, pdmac, Sarah Garth, Rachael Ritchey, Richard Novak, Joshua C. Chadd, Julie Balzum, Sanders, and Chiu Lee.

- My ARC readers, clan members, family, and friends.
- I have to give a special shout out to my youngest clan member and ARC reader who wants to be a writer one day. She has been such an incredible support to me. She remembers every detail of all my books and she's full of ideas! Thank you, Claire Gagne. I'm so glad God brought you into my life. I have no doubt you will publish great books in His timing.

So many people showed up to encourage me along the way in God's perfect timing. I am beyond blessed. Thank you! I love you all!

You are loved,
J F Rogers